Praise for:

'Bursting with magic, heart and
humour – bound to delight'
Abi Elphinstone, author of *Sky Song*

'A wild feat of extraordinary imagination, fizzing with mystery,
magic and humour. It's impossible not to fall in love with the
story's brilliant characters and unforgettable world. Readers
are sure to be daydreaming about flying cities
and fate tattoos for years to come'
Aisling Fowler, author of *Fireborn*

'A twisty Gothic adventure full of magic, mystery, secrets and
soaring cities! Had me hooked from the start'
Rashmi Sirdeshpande, author of *Never Show a T-Rex a Book*

'It's impossible not to get swept away by the spectacular world of
New London and I can't wait to watch, and cheer on,
the meteoric rise of Meticulous Jones'
Siobhan McDermott, author of *Paper Dragons*

'This brilliant adventure sparkles with charm and imagination.
My fate is to be bewitched, enchanted and obsessed with *Inkbound*'
Megan Hopkins, author of *Starminster*

INKB☠UND

METICULOUS JONES
AND THE
SKULL TATTOO

INKB🕱UND

METICULOUS JONES
AND THE
SKULL TATTOO

PHILIPPA LEATHLEY

HC CB

HARPERCOLLINS
CHILDREN'S BOOKS

First published in the United Kingdom by
HarperCollins *Children's Books* in 2025
HarperCollins *Children's Books* is a division of HarperCollins*Publishers* Ltd
1 London Bridge Street
London SE1 9GF

www.harpercollins.co.uk

HarperCollins*Publishers*
Macken House, 39/40 Mayor Street Upper
Dublin 1, D01 C9W8, Ireland

1

ISBN 978–0–00–866092–5
EXPORT TPB ISBN 978–0–00–866101–4
PB ISBN 978–0–00–866095–6

Philippa Leathley asserts the moral right to be
identified as the author of the work.

A CIP catalogue record for this title is available from the British Library.

Typeset in Weiss Std 11pt/18pt

Printed and bound in the UK using
100% renewable electricity at CPI Group (UK) Ltd

Conditions of Sale

For my magnificent mum,
and my marvellous goddaughters,
Iris and Nancy

NEW LONDON

The Ink Museum

ASTRONOMY QT

Winter's Knock

Starlight Cafe

Goldenfate House

HIGHFATE

Green Ink Station

Nobel Bridge

DOCKS

Edison Bridge

Post Office

Wind Tunnel

Stamp Square

LOWFATE

Grey Ink Station

THE DARKNESS

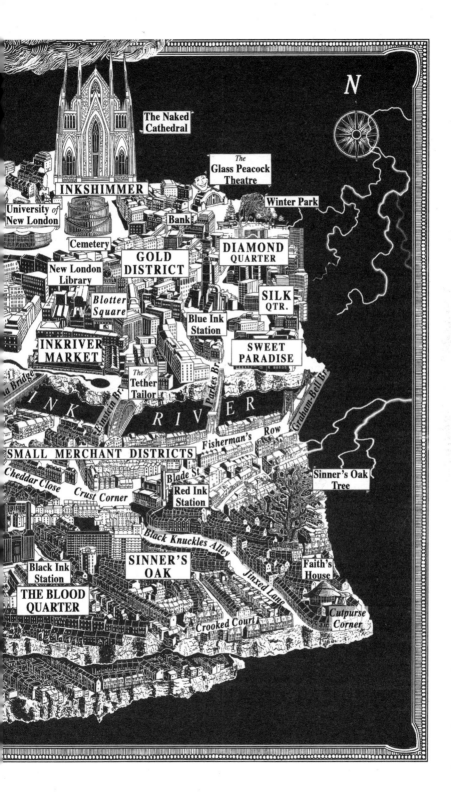

CHAPTER ONE

Darkwell

There was something wrong with Metty's ticket. She inspected it for the hundredth time while the train thrummed around her and snaked through the tunnels of the London Underground. She had to squint to read the letters at the top. *Darkwell,* they said in a dangerous purple shimmer.

But there was no such place!

Frowning, Metty turned the ticket over and checked the back. The small print was hard to decipher, not that it mattered. She'd spent hours poring over maps of the Underground, using her finger to trace all the colourful routes. She knew them by heart, and she'd never seen anywhere called Darkwell.

And now their train was racing towards the end of the line. They were fast running out of stations.

Metty jumped as the captain let out an almighty snore, drawing disapproving looks from the other passengers. She glanced at her father. He was slumped against the window, fast asleep, with his arms crossed and a trilby hat pulled low to cover his eyes.

Anyone would think he hadn't rested in days, but the captain always seemed exhausted. Their housekeeper said he'd spent too many years in the navy, being rocked to sleep by the churning ocean, and that he'd forgotten how to live on dry land.

Metty was about to prod him when a speaker crackled above her head: *'The next station is Aldgate, where this train terminates. Please take your belongings with you when you leave.'*

'Captain,' she whispered, jabbing her father. 'Captain, wake up!'

He snorted awake, sitting up so violently that he almost lost his hat. His deep brown eyes, puffy with tiredness, swept over the carriage, then found Metty beside him. 'What happened? Are we there yet?'

'We're at Aldgate,' she said as the train chugged into the station. She hitched up her eyebrows, giving him an exasperated look. 'It's the end of the line.'

'Not for us.' The captain yawned and settled back again.

'But the voice on the speaker said . . . Look, everyone's getting off.'

'Don't worry about what they're all doing. None of them are going where we are.'

'You mean Darkwell Station?' Metty said in a doubtful voice.

'That's the one.'

'But there's no such place.'

'How do you know?' said the captain, eyeing her thoughtfully.

'Because I've never seen it, and it's not on any maps.'

A smile stretched across her father's face as he sat up again and leaned forward, resting his elbows on his thighs. 'Fact is, my darling, the most interesting places never are. And I can see that upsets you terribly.' He chuckled and bumped Metty under the chin. 'Now hold on to your seat. Tightly.'

'Why?' she said with a twinge of nerves.

'Because I believe we're about to set off.'

Metty had only just grabbed the nearby pole running from the floor to the ceiling when a metallic squeal echoed outside, followed by a rumble that sent shivers through the entire train. It sounded as if something was tearing up the tracks in front of them. Metty winced and hunched her shoulders towards her ears, willing the noise to stop.

At last, the rumbling faded, and she twisted round to look through the window. She couldn't see anything apart from the platform and a set of stairs leading up to the street. All the other passengers had disappeared, leaving just her and the captain inside the train.

The speaker whirred above her head again: '*The next station is Darkwell.*'

Her father grimaced, as though bracing himself for something unpleasant. 'This bit always makes me want to throw up,' he said. Then, seeing Metty's horrified expression, he added, 'Don't worry – I'll try to avoid you.'

'But what's about to . . .?'

The question slid back down her throat as the train lurched and rolled forward on the tracks. They were suddenly tilting like a cart at the top of a rollercoaster about to plunge down a terrifying slope. There was a click-clacking sound as the wheels of the train turned faster and faster, picking up speed.

And then, before Metty could even scream, they dived into a pitch-black tunnel that must have opened in front of them.

Blood roared in Metty's ears, making her dizzy. The carriage lights flickered off, and there was nothing but blackness in the descending tunnel, thick and gloopy like an ocean of tar. Her insides felt as if they'd turned to soup, sloshing about as the train dropped through endless darkness. At last, they screeched to a stop, drawing level with a new platform.

Metty looked queasily at her hands. She was gripping the

pole so tightly that her knuckles had turned chalky white. The captain's arm was stretched across her chest, pinning her to the seat. She hadn't even noticed him reach out during the chaos of flying downhill.

'This is Darkwell,' declared the speaker in a bored voice, 'where this train terminates. Please take your belongings with you when you leave.'

'There,' said the captain, getting shakily to his feet. His face had lost its normal ruddiness and looked sickly. 'That wasn't so bad, was it?'

Metty observed him in frosty silence.

She glanced around as she followed her father off the train and out of Darkwell Station, holding the sleeve of his coat. They appeared to be in some kind of cave. The ceiling was a shelf of black rock brightened by rows of twinkling icicles. Crammed beneath it, and stretching away from the station, was a short, cluttered street.

Metty counted twenty buildings altogether: big Gothic townhouses, mysterious shops, strange little cafés and a theatre with a flashing sign. There was something old-fashioned about the place, like stumbling into a street from the 1920s. Halloween was coming up in a week, and the residents of Darkwell had decorated accordingly. Pumpkins leered in front of the tall houses. Cobwebs were draped all over the lampposts alongside huge rubber spiders, enchanted to twitch their spindly legs. Metty's eyes widened at the magical green fog swirling through the cave. It gathered round the buildings, conjuring a delightfully ghoulish atmosphere.

'Are we *underneath* the Underground?' she asked the captain in an awed voice.

'We're underneath Old London,' her father said. 'Quite a long way under, as it happens.'

'But why's this place hidden? Does everyone know about it?'

'Oh, plenty of people *know*. Getting down here's the tricky part – tickets are rather hard to come by, and horrifically expensive. Darkwell's a bit . . . exclusive, you see.'

'Illegal, you mean?' Metty said with a mixture of dread and excitement.

Her father was normally very respectable. She was surprised he'd brought her to somewhere so shady, never mind so obviously magical. Magic had been strictly controlled in England for the last few decades. There were a few exceptions, of course: harmless things like using enchantments to fix a broken leg, or hurry along awkward roadworks, or communicate with someone via mirror, but most acts of magic were against the law. According to the captain, the streets of Old London hadn't always been so bare and colourless, without a single enchantment to brighten them, although they'd been like that for as long as Metty could remember.

'Not illegal *exactly*.' Her father steered her towards the largest and most glamorous townhouse, right at the end of the street. 'Darkwell's got a bit of a reputation, that's all, like most pockets of magic left over from the old days. Don't look so horrified, Met. You know I wouldn't bring you down here for no good reason. Speaking of which . . .'

They stopped opposite the looming townhouse, and the captain rang the doorbell. A moment later, an elderly butler came to greet them. Tattooed on the man's hand, just beneath his knuckles, was a silver key. Metty stared at it in fascination, trying to remember what such a tattoo meant. Her fingers strayed towards her jacket pocket and the little book tucked inside it.

'Afternoon,' her father said, sweeping off his hat. The cheerful boom of his voice startled Metty, and she lowered her hand again.

'Good afternoon, sir,' the butler replied warily. 'How may I help you?'

'We've come to meet the famous prophetess.'

'Indeed. And is Madame LeBeau expecting you?'

'I should hope so. I made the appointment last week and paid an extortionate amount for it.' The captain paused, looking down at Metty with a proud smile, although she noticed a hint of dread in his eyes. 'Bit of a special day for us, actually. It's my daughter's birthday, you see.'

'Ah,' said the old man with a curious glance at Metty. 'In that case, you'd better come inside.'

They followed him into a hallway with a black chandelier and a polished hardwood floor. Framed posters decorated the walls, the kind you might find in a theatre advertising upcoming shows. One drew Metty's eye in particular: a portrait of a lady wearing a sequinned dress and holding a crystal ball in her long dark fingers. Words flamed across the poster.

Madame Fayola LeBeau

Celebrated, World-renowned Medium and Prophetess.

Witness the Exquisite Oracle for
ONE WEEK ONLY
at the
Shadow Trove Theatre
Doors open at 8pm

Ticket Prices Non-negotiable. No Refunds.
Satisfying Fate Not Guaranteed.

'That's not who we've come to see?' Metty whispered. 'She looks terrifying!'

The captain chuckled. 'Don't tell me you're getting cold feet.'

'I'm not!'

Metty had been dying to see a prophetess for ages, longing for her tenth birthday to hurry up and arrive. She wasn't about to miss out now the day was finally here.

Her father looked at her kindly. 'It's normal to get anxious before a fating, you know. Everyone feels a little—'

Metty groaned. 'I'm not anxious.'

The butler led them to the first door in the hallway. 'Please take a seat while I inform the lady of your arrival,' he said with a sweep of his hand.

The captain held the door for Metty, who found herself entering an old-fashioned drawing room with vintage furniture and heavy curtains. There were two long sofas and a coffee table in the middle of the room, holding a pile of magazines and newspapers.

Metty was about to sit down when something distracted her: golden glimmers of light trickling down the walls like honey. She looked up, frowning, and a gasp escaped her lips.

Floating on the high ceiling were hundreds of jellyfish. Some were tiny, others as big as watermelons, and their bodies shone light into the otherwise gloomy space. Metty

21

was entranced, unable to look away. The jellyfish were clearly painted onto the ceiling, and yet they moved like real living creatures, gliding along as if in water, their tentacles and spongy heads rippling at the touch of invisible waves.

The butler cleared his throat. 'Wonderful, aren't they? My mistress has quite an eye for enchanted decor,' he said, watching the jellyfish with a thoughtful smile. Metty hadn't sensed him creep up behind her. 'I take it this is your *tenth* birthday, child?'

'Um, yes,' she said, tearing her eyes from the ceiling.

'And that's why you've come to see Madame LeBeau?'

Metty swallowed and gave a determined nod. 'I'm here to find out my fate.'

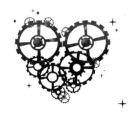

CHAPTER TWO

The Ship and the Rose

Metty had wanted to discover her fate for as long as she could remember. She'd spent years daydreaming about what it might be. A songbird predicting she'd become a famous singer; a telescope meaning she'd grow up to be an explorer; or something so unique she couldn't even imagine it.

She was always jealous when a child at school had their tenth birthday, then turned up the next day with a magical tattoo on their hand. At lunchtime, all the fated kids ever did was compare symbols and try to figure out what they meant. Tattoos like footballs and ballet shoes were obvious enough, but there was one boy in her class with a lion, and that could predict all sorts of things: strength; bravery; even growing up to have glorious hair. At least, according to the dictionary of fates Metty's aunt had sent for her birthday.

23

'It's Captain Moral Jones,' her father said to the butler, who was jotting down their names in a logbook. 'And this charming, impeccably dressed young lady is my daughter, Miss Meticulous Jones. That's spelled with one t, and don't forget the second u.'

'How unusual,' said the old man, failing to hide a smirk.

'Yes, there's a bit of a competition in my family over who has the silliest name. I reckon my brother Monotonous wins.'

'Or Great-Uncle Maniacal,' Metty suggested.

'Yes, but he isn't alive, darling.'

'So?'

'Death obviously disqualifies people.'

The butler heaved a mournful sigh. 'That it certainly does,' he said, then seemed to remember himself.

Metty's eyes drifted to one of the newspapers lying on the coffee table. **WORLD'S 80TH MAGICAL CITY: NEW CAIRO LAUNCHES IN TWO YEARS** read the headline on the front page. Underneath it was a picture of some Egyptian businesspeople standing before a model city.

'New Cairo?' Metty said, glancing at her father.

'Another New Capital. At this rate, there'll be hundreds of the daft things, one for every country.'

'I believe China already has three,' the butler pointed out.

'Why do they keep building more if there's already so many?' Metty asked.

She'd heard stories about the New Capitals her whole

life – fantastical cities spread all over the globe – but had never actually visited one, not that she could remember. Supposedly, they were the only places on earth where magic was completely legal, where enchantments glittered on every street corner and anything seemed possible.

'Showing off, I expect,' the captain said. 'I wonder where they plan to build it. Near Egypt, one assumes. They normally try and keep them close to home.'

'Over the Red Sea, apparently,' the butler said, putting away his fountain pen. He shut the logbook and smiled warmly at Metty. 'Now that's all sorted, you might as well go upstairs. There's a young man already waiting outside the seance room. I expect Madame LeBeau will see you both at the same time.'

'We'll wait a little longer, if you don't mind,' the captain said, glancing at his watch with a tight expression that could only be described as constipated. It took a lot to make Metty's father anxious, but she knew that look and what inspired it. Or who. 'We're expecting my ex-wife. She tends to run late, but I'm hoping she'll be along soon.'

Waiting for the next train seemed to take years, and Metty was soon itchy with boredom. What's more, she was getting worried about the time. If her mother was too late, then the prophetess might refuse to see them, and if Metty missed her appointment, that was it. Fatings were always on a person's tenth birthday, and there were no second chances.

'Relax,' the captain said, patting her shoulder. 'She'll be here.'

Metty hummed, unconvinced. Getting to her feet, she wobbled along one of the sofas in the drawing room. A few jellyfish on the ceiling drifted down the walls to get a better look at her. A tiny one with shivering tentacles floated right up to her face.

'Hello,' she said, putting out her hand. The jellyfish started to glide away. 'It's all right – don't be scared.'

Metty traced its bulbous head, then jumped as it flashed and zapped her finger.

'Stop terrorising the lights,' the captain said, tugging on the back of her jacket.

'I'm playing with it, that's all.' She flopped onto the sofa and blew on her stinging fingertip, then turned to her father with a mischievous grin. 'Anyway, I thought you wanted me to make more friends.'

'Funnily enough, I didn't mean hazardous light fixtures.'

Still restless, Metty reached into her pocket and took out the book her aunt had sent that morning.

THE OFFICIAL BRITISH DICTIONARY OF FATES
500 Common Fates and their Meanings
49th Edition

She ran her thumb along the red spine. The editor's note on the first page said that only five per cent of people had a rare fate. Most got one of the usual tattoos: a wrench for a child who would grow up to be a mechanic, or a stethoscope for a future doctor. Metty hoped hers wouldn't be something common.

She flicked through the dictionary, searching for a key. She glanced at the butler, who'd picked up the newspaper with New Cairo on the front page and was reading it in the corner.

'Do you know what a key fate means?' she whispered to her father.

'Shush.'

'I'll tell you. It says right here.'

'Metty, don't be rude,' the captain murmured.

She rolled her eyes. Adults had such funny rules about fates. Metty couldn't see why it was impolite to talk about them.

'Key fates are associated with locksmiths, housekeepers, or having lots of secrets.' She narrowed her eyes at the butler. 'I think he's probably secretive, don't you?'

The captain looked sternly amused. 'I'm going to steal that book off you and hide it somewhere.'

'No, you won't.'

Metty stuffed the dictionary back in her pocket just as a powerful rumble filled the house, sending vibrations up the walls. The jellyfish clustered together, as if distressed, forming blinding columns of light on the ceiling. Metty sprang up from the sofa and looked through the window.

A tube train shot like a bullet from a hole at the top of the cave and stopped along the platform outside. A second later, one of the carriage doors opened and a single passenger stepped off the train. Metty's mother paused, running a hand through her stylish brown hair, then she sashayed towards Madame LeBeau's house.

Daphne Wolff was one of those hypnotic beauties that belonged on a film screen with skin like starlight and oceanic eyes sparkling beneath two sculpted eyebrows. As always, her lipstick perfectly matched the cherry red of her dress.

'Here we go.' The captain sighed, getting to his feet.

The doorbell rang, clanging through the house, and the butler went to answer it.

'Don't panic, I'm here!' Daphne said, waltzing into the drawing room a few seconds later. She approached the captain first, planting a kiss on his nose. It left a red smear. 'Sorry I'm late. I had so far to travel.'

She turned to Metty next, kissing her on both cheeks, then rubbed off the lipstick marks with her thumb. 'I was all the way over in Rome, you know. *New* Rome, that is. Had to travel here by lightning, which absolutely destroyed my hair – it took me *so* long to fix! Gosh, isn't it freezing? I didn't think to bring a coat.'

'Good of you to finally turn up,' the captain grumbled.

Daphne ignored him. She beamed down at Metty, then grabbed her chin and turned up her face, making a thorough inspection of it. Metty supposed she must've changed quite a lot since the Christmas before last.

'My goodness, this cannot be my baby girl looking so grown up! Happy birthday, sweetheart. Did you get all the gifts I sent? Of course you did. Look, you're wearing the shoes I bought in New Paris. Aren't they fabulous?'

The white shoes were a size too small and had already left blisters on Metty's toes, but she'd worn them anyway. It seemed rude not to.

'Actually, they're a bit . . . I love them,' she lied.

Her mother lit up like a child presented with a jar of sweets.

'Do you really? I'm so—'

'Look, Daph, delightful as it is to see you, we're running late, so perhaps this could wait until after the fating,' the captain said stiffly.

Daphne turned to him with a coy smile. 'Oh, Moral, don't pretend you haven't missed me.'

'Could I get your name, ma'am?' the butler said, readying his fountain pen.

'Sure, it's Daphne Wollf – that's Wollf with two ls.'

Metty cleared her throat while the old man wrote down her mother's name. Her nerves were really kicking in now. What if her fate was boring, foretelling that she'd grow up to be a banker or something? What if she was destined to be cowardly or stupid, or – worse – fated to die in a gruesome accident? The captain said that tattoos predicting horrible deaths didn't really exist, but Metty wasn't convinced.

She looked at the fate on her mother's hand: a red rose with a thorny stalk. Metty had seen it many times before, but never taken much notice of it. She didn't think she and Daphne had ever talked about fates. In fact, her mother was gone so often, they hadn't talked much about anything.

Metty pulled out her dictionary again, trying to be as subtle as possible. There was no entry for roses specifically, which meant it wasn't a common tattoo.

FLOWERS: *associated with floristry, excessive marriages, or deadly hay fever*

Metty blinked in alarm. Her mother wasn't a florist – in

fact, as far as she knew, Daphne hadn't worked a day in her life. She'd only been married once, to the captain, and Metty didn't think she even had mild hay fever, let alone the deadly sort. She closed the book and frowned at her mother.

'Um, Daphne?'

'Yes, sugar?'

'I was just wondering: do you know what your fate means?'

Daphne's lips drew into a pleased smile. '*My* fate? Well, there's always been some debate about that. It's not one of those boring traditional ones, you see.'

'You mean like mine?' the captain said, raising his right hand, where a sail unfurled proudly over the ship tattooed there.

'It suits you, dear,' Daphne said.

'What, boring and traditional? Thanks very much.'

Daphne's smile became self-conscious as she held out her hand for Metty to take a closer look. 'My mother always said a rose meant I would blossom into a great beauty. She was obviously a little biased, but . . .'

'I suppose she wasn't entirely wrong,' the captain said begrudgingly.

'Wonder what I'll get,' Metty said, then winced. 'Does it . . . hurt? Being fated, I mean?'

'Not a bit,' said her father.

'Oh, horribly,' said her mother at the same time, then rolled her eyes at the captain's stormy expression. 'There's no point lying to her – not when she's about to find out for herself. Look, honey, the truth is it hurts like hell. But it only lasts a minute, like getting your ears pierced.'

Metty hadn't had her ears pierced and wasn't much comforted.

The captain squeezed her shoulder. 'Listen, Met, you don't have to go through with this. Not if you don't feel ready.'

Metty gave a tiny shrug, trying not to let fear get the better of her. 'But if I don't get fated today, I can't try again, can I? It's now or never.'

'Good point,' Daphne said, flashing a dark look at the captain. 'And some of us have travelled an *extremely* long way for this. Anyway, it's exciting! I bet we'll find out you're destined to be something fabulous, like a famous actress.'

'Are we ready, Miss Jones?' said the butler.

'All right.' The captain sighed. 'Let's get this done, shall we?'

'I'm sorry, sir, but the two of you will have to wait down here. Madame LeBeau likes to see the children on their own.'

A cold feeling trickled into Metty's stomach like she'd just swallowed an ice cube.

'You mean I have to go by myself?'

'Don't be silly,' Daphne said, giving the butler her most charming smile. 'Fayola's a special friend of mine. That's the only reason we chose to come here. I'm sure she won't mind if I pop along too.'

'Not on your life!' the captain said. 'I'm not waiting down here while you—'

'I'm very sorry,' the butler interrupted, 'but your daughter must go alone. That's the way it's always done. Come along, Miss Jones. I'm sure you've nothing to worry about.'

Metty followed the old man back into the hallway, nerves gathering in her stomach like a flock of sparrows. He led her to a flight of stairs so long and cloaked in shadow that it was impossible to see the top.

'Go right ahead,' the butler said to Metty.

She paused, throwing a final look at her parents. Daphne's face was bright with encouragement, the captain's much more worried.

Metty took a deep breath. Then she gripped the banister with a trembling hand and began to climb.

CHAPTER THREE

Ink and Blood

Metty was sweating by the time she reached the top of the staircase, although that might have been nerves as much as anything. She'd never felt so sick in her life.

Visiting Madame LeBeau had been Daphne's idea. Most kids went to a free prophetess from one of the New Capitals, funded by the government. But some parents paid to send their child to someone like Madame LeBeau, a person more skilled, more gifted, who could manipulate their fate and make sure they ended up with something special.

Metty wasn't even certain she approved of elite fatings. She was surprised that her father had agreed to it. Maybe the captain had been worried that her tattoo would turn out to be boring or embarrassing, and that was why he and Daphne had paid for Madame LeBeau. The thought of disappointing him made Metty even more anxious.

Her dress collar was sticky, clinging to her neck as she crept along the upstairs hallway and arrived at a door painted orange. Perhaps it was just her imagination, but a spicy fragrance seemed to rise from the wood like gingerbread and sweet cloves.

A boy with neat black hair was waiting outside, just as the butler had said. He was leaning against the wall, hands in his trouser pockets, wearing a smart navy blazer that complemented his dark brown skin. He turned towards Metty with a startled look.

'Hi,' he said and raised one hand.

'Hi,' said Metty, feeling awkward.

She went and stood in front of the brightly coloured door. The boy's eyes crawled over her with such intense curiosity that Metty nearly told him to stop staring.

'You here to see the prophetess as well?' he said at last.

'Yeah. To get my fate.'

'Me too. Feels like I've been stood here ages. I knocked but nobody answered. It doesn't even sound like anyone's in there.'

'Have you checked?' asked Metty.

'Course not.'

'Maybe we should.'

'You can if you want,' the boy said, lip curling into a sneer. 'But I'm not going in, not till I'm invited.'

Metty gave him a scornful look. 'All right, I'll do it.'

She grabbed the door handle, ignoring the dread scuttling down her spine.

The boy whistled, leaning against the wall again. 'Your funeral.'

The door wasn't locked. Metty was almost disappointed. Swallowing, she twisted the handle, and it slid silently open.

The room beyond was a dim circle with a small stage at the very back, hidden by a magenta curtain. There were no windows and shadows everywhere, silhouetting all the chairs in front of the stage. Metty wrinkled her nose as she breathed in a prickly smell. It reminded her of the spice cupboard back home.

'Hello?' she called out softly, taking a tiny step through the door. 'Um . . . Madame LeBeau?'

Nobody answered. There was no sign of the lady, just a heavy silence.

Metty moved further into the seance room, and her attention shifted to the stage curtain. She could only imagine what secrets lay behind it.

'You might as well come in,' she said to the boy, having to drag her eyes from the stage. 'You were right. There's no one here.'

'You're very bold, aren't you?' the boy said as he planted himself in the doorway, arms folded. He still didn't dare join her inside the room.

Metty shrugged. It hadn't sounded like a compliment.

'What's your name anyway?'

'Metty. What's yours?'

'Benedict,' said the boy, lifting his chin smugly. 'I'm guessing it's your birthday too. Your parents must be well off to pay for someone like Madame LeBeau. My dad says she only fates the kids of celebrities or really powerful people.'

Metty pulled a face, feeling even less like she wanted an elite fating.

'Who are they then, your parents?' Benedict asked. 'Are they waiting for you downstairs? Mine are having a meeting down the street. My mother's so important these days, she's always— Hey, what are you doing? You're not supposed to go up there!'

'Says who?' said Metty, already halfway up the steps leading to the stage. She glanced around to make sure there wasn't a sign hanging nearby. In her experience, dangerous activities were usually forbidden by large red signs. Satisfied there wasn't one, she climbed the rest of the way.

'You'll get in trouble,' Benedict whined.

'Doubt it. Anyway, that's my problem.'

'You'll get *me* in trouble!'

Metty rolled her eyes. Then she stiffened as a chill crept down her neck. It was like death itself was standing behind her, breathing on her skin, making it goosepimple. Coming from somewhere beyond the curtain was a quiet hiss.

Metty was paralysed for a heartbeat, torn between two instincts. The first was to jump off the stage and run from the seance room back to the safety of the hallway. The second, and the instinct she ultimately obeyed, was to pull back the magenta curtain and expose the monster behind it.

It turned out to be nothing frightening at all, just an armchair and a copper telephone on a table. The phone was old-fashioned, like something from a museum, with a rotary dial and a wire curling from the handset. Metty stepped closer and the hissing got louder. The sound was ghostly voices, she realised, whispering from the mouthpiece. And they weren't the only thing. Lilac mist oozed from the telephone and settled round the base.

'You should stay away from that,' Benedict said from across the room. 'Looks cursed.'

Metty pretended she hadn't heard him, reaching for the handset. Her fingers brushed the cool metal and she eased it out of the cradle, lifting it to her ear. The snakelike whispers sharpened. She could almost make out a few words.

'Hello, are you deaf? Do not touch that phone!' Benedict said with such pompousness that the stupid thing might have belonged to him. He even took a step forward, crossing the threshold of the room. 'Are you completely—'

'I'd be careful with that if I were you. You never know

who's listening on the other side,' said a melodic voice behind Metty, deep and smooth as silk.

Startled, she dropped the telephone, and it clicked back into the cradle. She spun round to see who'd spoken, although she already had a pretty good idea. Madame LeBeau had appeared from a doorway between two cabinets. Metty's eyes must have glided right past it.   .

The woman was even more striking in the flesh, wearing a feathery red-and-gold dress that brought to mind a phoenix bursting from the ashes. She had brown skin, and her glossy dark hair fell all the way to her hips. Her eyes were like jewels of amber, glowing at Metty, who blushed and stepped back from the telephone.

'Nice of you to finally arrive,' Madame LeBeau said, sweeping her way onto the stage. The skirt of her dress trailed after her like a spill of gold paint. On her left hand was a long crimson glove with a circle cut out of it to show her fate tattoo: a staring red eye.

'But I knocked,' Benedict said in a wounded voice, still hovering in the doorway.

'I was waiting for you both to come inside.'

'Oh,' said the boy and looked down at his shoes.

Wearing the ghost of a smile, the lady sat in the armchair next to the telephone. She opened a drawer in the table and removed what looked like a blank canvas and a glass paintbrush with a slim, sharp handle. Then she took a tiny bottle from a secret pocket in her dress.

Metty watched in fascination as Madame LeBeau uncorked the bottle, then used a dropper to remove one deep blue pearl of ink. She fed it to the tip of her paintbrush, and the mysterious liquid ran along the shaft.

It wasn't ordinary ink. Metty knew by the tingle on the back of her neck that it was something rare, something deeply magical. The sort of ink she'd learned about in school, that flowed in secret caves, or was hidden inside the heart of mountains, or pooled underground in sparkling lakes. The sort that could make trains disappear under London, or jellyfish come alive on the ceiling, or even make a city fly.

Some people spent their whole lives hunting down reserves of magic ink, the way others used to dig for oil or gold. The lady's bottle might have been small, but Metty reckoned it was worth a fortune.

'We'll dispense with any boring chitchat,' Madame LeBeau said. 'My excellent intuition tells me that one of you is impatient to start, and that the other' – her gaze found Metty who blushed even harder – 'is simply impatient. So.' She placed the canvas on her lap. 'Let's begin, shall we?'

'I'll go first,' Benedict said, hurrying across the room. He ran onto the stage before Metty could protest and stood in front of the prophetess. Madame LeBeau observed him in thoughtful silence, then sighed.

'Very well, Mr Finch. Hold out your hand.'

Unlike Metty, Benedict seemed to know what to expect. He gave the lady his index finger, then screwed up his face as though waiting for something bad to happen.

Even so, he gasped when Madame LeBeau stabbed the tip of his finger with the sharp end of her paintbrush.

A droplet of blood hung there, looking like it might drip off at any second. Instead, the blood sank into the brush and ran along it in a thin red line, like the strip inside a thermometer, mixing with the blue ink until the colour became indigo. A moment later, the ink-and-blood mixture reached the glass bristles.

Madame LeBeau inspected her brush, gave a satisfied nod, then started to paint on the canvas. Her head tipped back as she did, her eyes rolling like she was in some kind of trance.

Alarmed, Metty took a step away, but the lady didn't seem to notice. She swept the paintbrush back and forth without even looking at the canvas. Metty was surprised by how much liquid there was considering Madame LeBeau had only started with two drops of ink and blood.

Benedict frowned and sucked his finger. And then spat it out to howl in pain, clutching the back of his hand.

A dark mark was spreading on his skin. Metty watched with mounting dread, suddenly wishing she'd gone first and got the whole thing over with. Madame LeBeau seemed unconcerned by Benedict's agony, humming to herself as she flashed the paintbrush back and forth, until finally she lifted the bristles and sat forward, her gaze steady. The canvas was blank once more.

'There. All done.'

It seemed Benedict's ordeal was over. Blinking away tears, he stared at the tattoo on his hand.

'It's gold!' he said in delight, waving his fist at Madame LeBeau. 'It's a bag of gold – I know it is! My father has one just like it.'

Metty frowned at Benedict's fate. It wasn't the easiest shape to make out, a sort of blob with a funny lump at the top. To her, it looked more like a meteor than a sack of money, but she decided to keep that observation to herself.

'That means I'm going to be rich and successful, doesn't it?' Benedict said, beaming at Madame LeBeau, who shrugged lazily.

'Interpreting fates isn't part of the service.'

Benedict seemed taken aback. 'But – but you *chose* it for me, didn't you? Isn't that the whole point of elite fatings?'

'It's a little more complicated than that,' the lady said in a bored voice. Then she turned to Metty, beckoning her over with a curled finger. 'Your turn, Miss Jones.'

CHAPTER FOUR

Metty's Fate

Metty's heart thumped into her stomach like a brick dropped from a skyscraper as she dragged herself across the stage towards Madame LeBeau's armchair. Just as Benedict's fate had vanished from the canvas, leaving it white as snow, the glass paintbrush was clear now too, and ready for its next victim. Metty had to remind herself that this was what she wanted, what she'd dreamed about for years.

Madame LeBeau extracted another drop of magic ink, refilling the paintbrush. Then she leaned forward. Her hair shifted as she did and revealed her sparkling earrings shaped like a pair of black butterflies.

'Left-handed?' she asked. People's fates were always tattooed on the hand they favoured.

'Right.'

'Pity,' the lady said mysteriously, then raised an eyebrow. 'Any requests?'

'You didn't ask me that,' said Benedict sulkily.

The prophetess ignored him, gazing up at Metty, who chewed her lip. Could Madame LeBeau really influence her fate? Surely it was impossible to actually change the future.

'Nothing boring, please,' she said.

A smirk spread across the lady's face as she reached for Metty's right hand.

'I believe we can manage that.'

The jab of the paintbrush was worse than Metty expected. She put her bleeding finger in her mouth like Benedict had, glaring at the ruby bead hanging from the brush. Within seconds, the paintbrush had sucked it in. Her blood slid along the glass shaft, turning purple as it mixed with the ink, then reached the bristles at the other end.

Madame LeBeau touched the brush to the canvas. Her eyes rolled once again. And then the real pain began.

Metty's skin was flaming. She couldn't pay any attention to Madame LeBeau, too distracted by the unbearable sensation. It was like being branded with a white-hot iron, like holding her fist in the heart of a fire. Tears swam in her eyes, blurring her vision, as a roundish shape appeared on the back of her hand. Metty stared at it, willing herself to concentrate on her fate and ignore the excruciating pain.

At first, she thought it might be a keyhole, but the bottom wasn't flat enough and there were dark spots growing in the middle. A purple shape curved beneath it.

She sighed in relief when the scorching in her hand eased to a dull burn. Madame LeBeau sat back again, the canvas on her lap clear; only this time she didn't look half as satisfied, frowning at the tattoo below Metty's knuckles.

Benedict peered over her shoulder. 'What'd you get?' he said, his breath warm on Metty's neck.

She didn't answer, staring at her fate in stunned silence. It was quite clear, unlike Benedict's: an ink-black skull. But that was only half the tattoo. Holding the skull from underneath was a hand in a violet glove.

'Oh dear,' Benedict murmured. His voice sounded far away. 'That can't be good.'

Metty glanced at the prophetess, who met her gaze with a crooked smile.

'You did say nothing boring.'

Benedict disappeared at once to find his parents and show off his fate. No doubt they would put an announcement in the newspapers tomorrow morning like the rich and famous always did. Metty could see it now:

24th October

BENEDICT FINCH fated with a sack of gold, predicting a life of wealth and prosperity.

Somehow, she didn't think her parents would do the same. Metty didn't run downstairs like Benedict, instead hovering outside the seance room. She took out her *Dictionary of Fates* and thumbed through the pages, heart galloping in her chest. Benedict's was easy to find.

GOLD: *associated with banking, hoarding wealth, or piracy*

A few pages before that, there was a picture of a glove. She read the meaning underneath it, tracing the words with her finger.

GLOVES: *associated with magic*

Associated with magic? Breathing even more heavily, Metty kept searching until she found the entry she was looking for, near the end of the dictionary.

SKULLS: *associated with death, or foul murder*

Death. The word repeated itself in Metty's head, ricocheting like a bullet. The glove meant magic; the skull meant death. Or foul murder. Was murder ever not foul? And what did the two fates mean combined?

She closed her dictionary with a loud snap. Maybe the book was wrong and there was some other explanation. Maybe there was a way of erasing fates, and somebody else could do her a new one. If so, she'd have to speak to her parents, but the thought of facing Daphne and the captain made her squirm. It felt as though she'd done something terrible, like she'd let everyone down. They would be so disappointed.

Metty dragged herself downstairs. She hid her fate with a sweaty palm, not wanting anyone to see it. Her parents were waiting for her in the drawing room where she'd left them.

'Hello, Met! How'd it go?' The captain grinned, rising from the sofa. Daphne was sitting as far away from him as possible and holding a compact mirror. She seemed to be having a lively discussion with her reflection. For a second, Metty thought her mother had gone mad, then she realised there was another person inside the little mirror.

'Sorry, darling, must dash, but I'll tell you everything later,' Daphne said to the stranger, then shut the compact and dropped it in her handbag. 'There you are!' she said, getting up and hurrying over to Metty. 'Aren't you glad I warned you about the pain? Poor baby. At least you only have to do it once.'

Metty didn't say anything. Her heart felt like it might shatter any moment. She couldn't bring herself to look up into her parents' happy faces, to see the proud excitement shining in their eyes as they waited to find out what their only child would become.

Hanging her head, Metty lifted her palm. Her parents leaned in to see her fate.

There was a terrible silence.

'Oh no,' Daphne croaked at last. Her face had turned white as bone. Even the captain looked pale and drawn beside her and had to steady himself on the wall.

'It's bad, isn't it?' Metty said.

'It's not . . .' Her father shook his head and hooked a finger under his collar. 'It's not what I, uh . . .'

'Oh, sweetheart,' Daphne cried, spreading her fingers on her cheeks. 'You're a murderer!'

A *murderer*?

But that was ridiculous. A hysterical laugh wormed up Metty's throat.

'But I haven't murdered anyone!'

'No, not yet,' Daphne said, glancing fretfully at the captain. She began to pace back and forth, her heels leaving dents in the plush carpet. 'That's what it means though, doesn't it? Look at that hideous skull – that's murder! And the glove, that means—'

'Magic,' Metty said, feeling utterly wretched.

'This is worse than anything I imagined,' Daphne gabbled. 'What was Fayola *thinking*? A skull! After we paid all that money . . . Isn't there something – there *must* be something we can do about this? Moral!'

'Let's just try and keep our heads,' the captain said in a hoarse voice. Metty stared up at him in dismay. She'd never seen her father look so hollowed out, so *old*, like her fate had drained all the life from him.

'Maybe I'm not a murderer,' she said in a feeble whisper. 'Maybe it means I'll die in a magical accident or something.'

'Oh well, that's much better,' Daphne snapped, then softened her tone. 'No, honey, there's no mistaking it. If it was just the skull by itself . . . but look at the glove, the way it's holding it. Don't you understand what this means? You're going to do something dangerous, something *deadly* – with magic! Oh, how could this even happen? How did *we* raise an ill-fated child – a murderer, Moral? We're such *good* people!'

'Couldn't I . . .' Metty had to stop and cough, tears thickening her throat. 'Couldn't I just choose not to hurt anyone?'

'Who's to say you won't do it by accident?' Daphne said, fanning herself with a hand. 'I just don't understand it. I don't sin that much. I don't steal – I hardly ever lie. I know my commandments, the important ones anyway. That's got to count for something. My only child, a stone-cold killer . . . I'm going to ruin Fayola for this! Wait, you don't think it'll end up in the papers?'

'Shut up, Daph,' the captain muttered.

He'd been staring into space, lost in a maze of troubling thoughts. Now he returned his attention to Metty and crouched before her, reaching into his coat for something. He took a handkerchief from his pocket and wrapped it round Metty's hand as though tying a bandage.

'Too tight,' she said, and he loosened it a bit. Metty tried to prise her hand away, but her father held on to it.

'Look at me,' he said gently, and mustered a smile, though his kind brown eyes glistened with some emotion Metty didn't recognise. She had a nasty feeling that it was fear. 'Everything's going to be all right. But this . . .' The captain paused, pressing her hand. 'This has to stay hidden, do you understand? You must never show anybody.'

Metty nodded stiffly. Why would she? She didn't want people knowing the truth about her, that somewhere deep inside her was a black seed that would grow over time into something evil and twisted. That one dark day she would do something terrible with magic, that she would take another person's life.

How could she ever tell anyone her fate?

ONE YEAR LATER

CHAPTER FIVE

Murderous Jones

There were only ten toxic plants on Metty's list. She'd wanted eleven in honour of her birthday, but researching poisons wasn't easy in the middle of the Welsh countryside with no access to libraries or bookshops.

'Deadly nightshade,' Mrs Pope read aloud, holding the page in her skeletal hand. 'Foxglove, poison hemlock, wolfsbane . . .' The housekeeper paused to sneer down at Metty, her eyes magnified by a large pair of spectacles. 'You *have* been thorough. I had no idea you were so interested in botany. Of course, I'm sure you know that white snakeroot only grows in North America.'

'I'll have to send for it in the post then,' Metty muttered, glaring at her feet.

Mrs Pope's nostrils became slits. Maybe she paled a little.

It was hard to tell, as the woman's face was already the colour of watery porridge.

'I wonder, Meticulous, if you truly understand the gravity of this situation. Mr Ratchet's handing in his notice. Again.'

Metty pursed her lips, failing to look sorry. The stupid gardener had quit five times already this year. He always turned up a few days later and asked for his job back, having decided that his life wasn't in danger after all.

'Mr Ratchet is under the impression that *you* wish to poison him.'

'Then he's an idiot,' Metty said, crossing her arms, 'because my fate's got nothing to do with poison. It means I'll murder someone with magic.'

The housekeeper sniffed. 'Well, you needn't sound so pleased about it.'

Metty wasn't pleased in the least. In fact, she'd spent the last twelve months trying to figure out how to make sure her fate never happened, which mostly meant staying as far away from magic as possible. Although that didn't stop the staff treating her like an escaped convict. Metty heard them whispering about her sometimes, calling her Murderous Jones, which was clever but not appreciated.

Her Murder Lists had become a tradition since the captain had sold their townhouse in Old London and moved them to Wales, this month's theme being poisons, of course. The first time, Metty had simply written down the names of everyone in the household, including two cats and a budgie, and placed them in order of who she'd most like to get rid of, adding descriptive notes to some.

Strangle with own hair, she'd put next to Mrs Pope, who'd been right at the top of the list. Mr Ratchet was normally a close second. Then Metty made sure to place the lists wherever they were sure to be found. The staff treated her so badly these days, she felt the least they deserved was a good scare.

'And don't think I haven't seen you scribbling in that nasty little book,' Mrs Pope said, glaring at the pocket where Metty kept her *Dictionary of Fates*. It was like she'd read her mind. 'We all know what you're up to. We've seen you plotting.'

'Plotting? You're paranoid!'

Mrs Pope went red at that, and her chest swelled with an angry breath. Fortunately, the living-room door opened before she could start ranting and the captain appeared. He was in the middle of buttoning his coat, one of his shoes still unlaced.

'Is everything all right? There seems to be a tremendous fuss.'

'There you are, Captain Jones,' Mrs Pope said with a sly glance at Metty. 'I know you're in a hurry, but I suspect you'll want to see this.'

She held out the list of toxic plants. The captain took it with a sigh.

'Not another one.'

Metty felt a stab of guilt, although it faded at Mrs Pope's smugness.

'Yes, indeed. *Another* one. Mr Ratchet is quite distressed, you know. I fear he'll leave for good this time. Obviously, we all sympathise with your daughter's condition, poor dear—'

Metty's hands curled into fists. Mrs Pope made it sound like she was diseased or something.

'—but you did promise to keep her in check. We have health and safety to consider. Why, this morning I found her wandering the kitchen completely unattended!'

'It's my birthday,' Metty snapped. 'I was looking for cake.'

The captain raised his head, doing his best to sound patient. 'She is allowed in the kitchen, Mrs Pope.'

'But Captain, there are *knives* in there.'

Metty ground her teeth. According to their housekeeper, the living room was out of bounds because of the fire poker, and the curtain ties, which could be used to choke somebody. The garden was full of dangerous weapons, from rakes to rusty shears, and the kitchen was obviously a murderer's paradise: knives, corkscrews, rolling pins, pots and pans and, of course, deadly vegetable peelers.

Mrs Pope clearly believed that Metty spent her entire life

just itching to pounce on her first victim, as though she was destined to go around attacking people like a gleeful lunatic. Everyone always focused on the skull part of her fate and forgot about the glove. If Metty *did* become a murderer one day, magic would have to be involved somehow, which meant she wasn't very likely to go after someone with a frying pan.

The captain frowned and folded the sheet of paper.

'Right, well, thanks for bringing this to my attention, but now I really must—'

'You can't leave!' Metty cried. Her voice dropped to a guilty murmur. 'Not – not when everyone's so upset. Mr Ratchet's handing in his notice. Tell him, Mrs Pope.'

The housekeeper stared at her with dawning horror. 'You . . . planned this, didn't you? Captain Jones, surely now you see what I mean! If your daughter—'

'Thank you, Mrs Pope,' the captain said stiffly. 'I'd like a quick word with Metty, if you don't mind. In private.'

'Of course,' Mrs Pope said, looking deliciously snubbed. 'But what should I say to Mr Ratchet? He's packing his bags right this minute. Should I convince him to stay?'

'I doubt there's any need. He'll probably be back this time tomorrow.' The captain raised his eyebrows when the housekeeper lingered like a bad smell. *'Thank you, Mrs Pope.'*

Metty watched her leave with a smouldering sense of hatred. Mrs Pope hadn't always been horrible, back when they lived in London. It was only since Metty's fating that the woman had become so vile. If Metty asked her father, he would probably hire another housekeeper, but that would mean revealing her secret to somebody new.

On this they were agreed: the fewer people who knew about Metty's fate, the better.

'Evil old witch,' she whispered once Mrs Pope was out of earshot.

'Metty.'

'Well, she is! I hate her. And she hates me too.'

'I doubt that very much.' The captain held up the list of poisons. 'Though this won't help matters. I suppose it's pure coincidence that this fell into the wrong hands just as I was about to leave.'

'Where are you even going?'

'To meet somebody. There's, uh, something important I have to do, and I'm afraid it can't wait.'

'Why not?' Metty said with a sharp pang of betrayal. Her father hadn't left her once since they'd moved to Wales. She couldn't imagine what would be so important to make him leave today of all days. 'Who are you meeting? Let me come with you.'

The captain shook his head. 'Too dangerous. Anyway, you'd be bored stiff.'

'How can something be dangerous *and* boring at the same

time? Please, Captain, you can't just leave. It's my birthday!'

'I'm sorry, darling. I know the timing's awful, but I don't plan to be gone for long. A few days at the most.'

'Days!'

'Come here.' Taking Metty's hand, he led her into the gloomy hallway with scabby wallpaper and spots of condensation on the ceiling. They stopped in front of a brass mirror, the captain's hands resting on her shoulders. 'See this? At exactly eight o'clock tonight, I'll be in this mirror. You just come and wait for me here.'

'You mean you'll use magic?' Metty said, staring at her father in alarm.

'Yes, and there's no need to look so worried. Magic isn't dangerous, Met. I've told you that a thousand times.'

'Maybe not when *you* use it,' she muttered.

The captain didn't seem to hear. 'Blimey, look at the time. Now I really must go.'

'But what about the staff?' Metty said desperately. 'They're all going mad.'

'Are they really?' Her father sighed, bending to tie his shoe. 'I wonder why.'

He and Mrs Pope were right: she *had* left out her list of poisons in the hope that it would stop him leaving. He'd had a mysterious phone call twenty minutes earlier, then suddenly announced that he had to go, stranding Metty in the middle of Wales. She was furious with him, and worried too. The captain would never abandon her like this for no reason. And she had a funny feeling that the phone call had been about her.

'Listen, Met,' he said, stretching back to his feet, 'I know you find these lists of yours funny, but you really must stop terrifying the staff. What will we do if they all quit?'

'It's not my fault they keep leaving,' Metty said. Her father pursed his lips. 'All right, it is a bit. But you know what the dictionary says about my fate.'

'I don't care what the— Oh, for heaven's sake.'

Metty took out her beloved dictionary, full of notes about people's fates and Murder Lists scribbled in the margins. The book fell open on the exact page she wanted, the one she returned to most often.

'Look,' she said, showing it to her father. 'It says so right there. Skull fates mean death or foul murder. See, M-U-R-D—'

'Thank you, Metty, I can spell. Darling, you're not a murderer.'

'If *you* don't think I'm dangerous, then why are we living all the way out here? Why do we have to hide from everyone? You're just trying to make me feel better.'

'Of course I am. That's my job. That and keeping you safe.' The captain took Metty's shoulders and gave her a tiny shake. 'That doesn't mean I'm lying. And I've told you, we don't know *exactly* what your fate means. Not every tattoo has a simple meaning, and even then they're not always right. Look at mine.'

Her father held out his hand, showing her his proud ship.

'I was miserable in the navy, constantly seasick, dreadful at taking orders. It's a wonder they ever made me captain. When I decided to come home and look after you, everyone warned me not to go against my fate, but my only regret is that I didn't leave sooner. You are a thousand times more meaningful than some silly tattoo.'

'Maybe yours has another meaning,' Metty suggested. 'One you haven't figured out yet.'

'Maybe, but – truth be told – I stopped paying attention to it years ago. I know you, Met. I know that you're a good person, and you would never harm anyone.'

'Well, no,' she said quietly. 'Not on purpose, but what if . . .'

She looked at the tattoo on her own hand, then took a nervous breath. Surely if she kept away from magic then her fate could never come true.

'Sorry, darling, but I really do have to go,' the captain said, grabbing an umbrella from the stand by the door. Metty frowned in confusion and glanced at the window. It was a miserable grey day, but it wasn't raining outside.

The wind swept in when her father opened the front door. He hovered there, looking back at her apologetically. 'But we'll speak again tonight in the mirror. I promise.'

'Eight o'clock,' Metty said firmly. 'Don't forget.'

The captain smiled. 'Eight o'clock.'

Metty's heart sank when her father left, the wind banging the door behind him. It was her birthday and she was stuck with Mrs Pope. Daphne hadn't even remembered to call, too busy enjoying herself in New Madrid or New Monaco or wherever she happened to be, drinking cocktails and shopping all day and forgetting that she'd ever had a daughter.

Metty smothered the hurt inside her and ran upstairs to her father's bedroom at the front of the house. From there, she could watch him drive away.

Only the captain didn't get into their car. Instead, he set out for the hills circling the farmhouse, still clutching the umbrella. A frown puckered Metty's forehead. Surely he wasn't planning to walk – there was nothing for miles around.

She stayed by the window, watching her father's tiny figure make its way up an enormous hill. The captain must have been exhausted, but he didn't rest, only stopping when he reached the peak. Metty had to squint to see him, standing like a king atop a grassy mountain. It was hard to tell, but she thought he was holding something up.

Her nerves leaped when the sky suddenly darkened, a pool of indigo storm clouds swirling right above his head. A growl of thunder seemed to shake the entire farmhouse, sending shivers through Metty's bones. She put her forehead to the window, breathless with fear. What was her father doing? He was going to get hit by lightning, standing out in the open like that!

Just as she thought those words, a bolt forked from the clouds and struck the captain, piercing right through him.

Metty shrieked, jumping back from the window. When she looked out again, her father had disappeared and the sky was smooth and clear, like the storm had never happened.

'Lightning travel,' she whispered to herself, relief pulsing through her.

Of course the captain wasn't hurt. He'd used magic to summon the storm and had teleported to wherever he was going.

Metty let out a slow breath, watching the hill just in case her father came back. He wouldn't, she realised, dragging herself away from the window. She really was on her own.

She'd heard about lightning travel – it was expensive, stupidly dangerous, and probably illegal – but she'd never seen someone use it. Whatever that phone call was about earlier, it must have been urgent for the captain to do something so risky. Which meant he needed to get somewhere fast. But why?

She glanced at her fate. The black skull leered up at her as though it had a nasty secret, and didn't want to tell.

CHAPTER SIX

Pumpkin

The mirror was empty.

Metty waited in the hallway as eight chimes rang through the house, her eyes fixed on the glass. But her father didn't appear.

She held her breath, then let it out in a disappointed huff when the clock fell silent. She didn't understand. The captain had sworn he would be in the mirror at exactly eight o'clock, and he always kept his word. It was her birthday. He knew she'd be waiting for him; he knew she would worry if he didn't show up.

Metty would have stayed in the hallway and watched the mirror all night, but Mrs Pope bullied her upstairs. She went to bed with a cold, clammy feeling that had nothing to do with the damp weather. She couldn't sleep, too busy thinking about the captain, remembering how the lightning had struck him atop the hill. Why had he left her, and where was he now?

If her father had broken his promise, then something had surely gone wrong. Terribly wrong.

'But he must have mentioned something about where he was going?' Metty said, trailing after Mrs Pope, who was hanging wet clothes out on a washing line, even though it was late autumn and freezing. 'Isn't there *some* way to contact him? It's been days.'

'Hardly.' The housekeeper checked her watch. 'Less than forty-eight hours by my reckoning. Perhaps Captain Jones is enjoying some time away from the house.'

Away from Metty, she meant.

'Aren't you worried? Don't you think it's strange he hasn't got in touch, not even a quick phone call? He promised he would.'

'Meticulous,' Mrs Pope snapped, 'I'm sure your father is quite well and that he's simply busy – *too* busy to waste every second of the day thinking about you.'

'What about Daphne?' Metty said, desperation bubbling up inside her. 'Couldn't we speak to her, tell her what's happened?'

Mrs Pope laughed coldly. 'I can't imagine why you'd want to talk to *her*. That woman is the worst—'

Metty refused to hear another word, spinning on her heel and storming back to the house. Anger surged through her as she ran upstairs to her room and threw herself down on the bed. Daphne might have forgotten her birthday, but she was still her mother, and Metty wasn't going to stand there while Mrs Pope ranted about her.

Why wouldn't anyone listen? None of the staff seemed to care that her father had vanished, acting as though everything was normal, as though he wasn't out there somewhere, possibly in danger with no one to help him. Metty *had* to find out where he was.

She frowned as a voice boomed through the floorboards: '*. . . former civil servant accused of embezzling ink worth £300,000 from government reserves . . .*'

Mr Ratchet must have put the radio on downstairs (sadly, he'd decided not to quit after all). The old man always listened to the news, blasting it at top volume through the house.

'Turn it down!' Metty bellowed pointlessly. He never did.

She was tempted to stuff a pillow over her head. Instead, she sat up and took out her *Dictionary of Fates*, opening it in her lap. She thumbed through it until she found Mr Ratchet's fate.

TURNIPS: *associated with gardening, or a lack of intelligence*

She'd scribbled his name in the corner of the page, then written below it:

Reasons for being 'THE ONE'
Snores too loudly
Annoying whistle
Shouts whenever I go in the garden
Calls me Murderous Jones
Hides the cutlery (then pretends he doesn't)

Blasts the stupid radio, she wrote now, adding it to the list.

Not that she really believed she would end up murdering Mr Ratchet – not on purpose anyway, but her fate seemed to imply that if she ever used magic, and it got out of control, then *somebody* would get hurt. She'd started thinking of this vague, unfortunate person as 'the one'.

'*In other news, New London's governor urges caution in the wake of another magical attack. These assaults are rumoured to be the work of terrorist organisation the Black Moths, whose recent activity has raised concerns about Governor Finch's plans to . . .*'

Ignoring the radio, Metty flicked through her dictionary again, this time stopping on Mrs Pope's fate.

THISTLES: *associated with Scottishness, goat-farming or prickly personalities*

The list of reasons for being 'the one' under *her* name was extremely long. Metty was about to add to it further when there came a sudden tap at the window. Leering at her with his snout pressed to the glass was a small gargoyle. He looked rather like a capuchin monkey, only winged and ugly, and a lot more demonic. And made of stone.

'Pumpkin!' Metty ran to the window, throwing it open. A breeze rushed against her face and blew back her dark hair. 'Quick, come inside before someone sees you.'

The gargoyle stayed grinning on the windowsill, showing off two rows of lumpy fangs. There was something in his hand, a limp brown glove. Metty leaned back in shock: Pumpkin was holding a tether.

'*Where* did you get that?' she breathed, staring at the glove in his fist. It was smooth and velvety, like the pelt of a dark rabbit. 'Did you sneak into Mrs Pope's room?'

Pumpkin gurgled a laugh and hopped up and down.

Most people didn't even own a tether these days. There was no point when using magic was practically against the law, but Metty had discovered Mrs Pope's some time ago, a magical glove hidden at the bottom of her wardrobe.

In the old days, before magic became so restricted, children would get their first tether as soon as they were fated. The glove was worn on the same hand as their tattoo, and was activated by the drop of ink that had crept into their skin, connecting them to thousands of secret ink channels running underground.

Ink was everywhere really, flowing all over the world – if only you knew where to look. A famous explorer had discovered one of these channels back in the fifteenth century, but it wasn't until the Victorian era and the time of the great inventors, like Tesla and Edison, that people started realising just how much ink could do. Now all sorts of things were powered by it. Or at least they had been, before governments across the world decided that magic was dangerous and needed strict regulations. Metty was pretty sure that was why all the New Capitals had been created; spectacular cities that anyone could travel to, where ink wasn't limited by so many rules.

Pumpkin tipped his head to one side, still grinning.

'Eat?' he said in a crackly voice and shook the glove at her.

'Not eat. I said *not eat*! Oi, come back!'

He was off before she could catch him, scrambling away over the low rooftop, the tether clamped between his jaws.

'Get back here!' Metty hissed, leaning out of the window.

Pumpkin slowed as he neared the edge of the roof, then plonked down his rear end and gazed back at Metty. He knew just how to look at her with those soulful eyes of his.

'You little monster,' she said under her breath, then glanced anxiously at the garden below. Mrs Pope had finished hanging out the laundry, but she might return any second. Metty gripped the window frame and climbed onto the roof.

'Come here!' she called to Pumpkin, wobbling over the fragile slates. He didn't do as she said, but waited for her to reach him, then spat out the glove like a hairball.

'You're a nightmare, you know,' Metty said fondly and rubbed the stone skin between his ears. Pumpkin gave a gravelly chuckle as she sat down next to him with her legs dangling off the roof.

Metty had found him a few months ago, at a ruined abbey near the house, chasing after pigeons. Who knew where he'd come from before that: a living, breathing, ravenous gargoyle with a knack for thieving? He'd followed her back to the farmhouse, despite her efforts to shoo him away, and had stayed close ever since, like a stray puppy longing for an owner.

Metty was sure Pumpkin had been brought to life with magic, which was probably very illegal. If anyone found out, they might turn him back, so she'd kept him hidden for his own safety, even from the captain.

Pumpkin flicked one of his ears and pointed at the tether. 'Play?'

Metty's hand hovered over it. Part of her had always been curious about magic: how it would feel crackling through her fingers, what it would be like to change the world around her.

But a more sensible part knew it wasn't worth the risk. What if something went wrong and she ended up hurting 'the one'?

Then again, the captain had disappeared and nobody even cared. If she wanted to find him, she *could* use magic to do it. She could summon lightning like he had, and zap herself to New Cardiff, or even New London, then track him down from there.

She craned her neck, checking the garden. No one was around to get hurt apart from Pumpkin, and she didn't think lightning would do much to a gargoyle.

But this was the dangerous thing about her fate. She knew she would never intentionally murder someone, but when it happened, if it did, it would be unexpected, accidental, something she'd never see coming.

Biting her lip, Metty pulled back her fingers. 'Bad idea. Very bad idea.'

Pumpkin was stubborn. He picked up the glove and dropped it in her lap.

'Seriously, I can't. It's too dangerous.'

But even as Metty said it she was sliding her right hand into the glove, unable to resist. Her father was gone and if she didn't do something, he might not come back. Not if he really was in trouble like she feared. Surely if she kept her mind focused, if she only used a little magic . . .

Mrs Pope's tether was much too big, the fabric bunching

up around Metty's fingers, but there was a definite tingle on the back of her hand. From there, a thrum of magic coursed through her skin like an electric current. She flexed her fingers, then raised her head.

The late October sky glared back at her, grey clouds threatening rain. Pumpkin was excited, hopping up and down again. He clapped his hands with a stony *crack-crack-crack*.

'Play, play, play!'

A familiar feeling whirled around in Metty like a gathering storm. She knew it was reckless to use magic, but what was the point of being good when everyone already thought she was bad? She'd been a criminal since her tenth birthday. One day she would probably end up in prison, or worse. And if magic could bring her father home . . .

Metty stood up and aimed a finger at the sky.

'All right,' she said, steeling herself with a deep breath, 'let's play.'

CHAPTER SEVEN

Magnificent

Metty concentrated, picturing lightning, whispering the word in her mind like a silent wish. One brief blast of magic – surely that couldn't go too wrong.

A wave of prickly energy swept through her forearm and hand, numbing the very end of her fingers. The tether was working!

A drop of rain struck Metty's forehead like a tiny hammer. Another shattered on the end of her nose as she turned up her face, staring impatiently at the blackening clouds, waiting for the lightning. And then *whoosh!*

It was like someone had tipped a bucket of water over her head. Freezing rain pummelled Metty's bare skin, sinking into her clothes, sloshing into her shoes, turning her hair into long dark strings. It clattered on the roof, making a thunderous racket, and flowed into the groaning gutters. Pumpkin squealed and launched away from her, skidding across the slippery roof.

Metty gasped. She didn't understand. She'd been trying to summon lightning, not torrential rain. Now the blue skirt of her dress was clinging to her legs, and raindrops dripped from her eyelashes and nose.

It took her a minute to notice that the rain was falling in a focused column directly onto her. Intrigued, she stretched out her arms. Her fingers burst through a wall of water, finding dry air on the other side.

'Not what I had in mind,' she muttered, then took a large step to the left.

The pillar of rain followed her, as though each drop was magnetically attracted to her body. She shivered indignantly, glaring at the heavens.

'That's enough now!' she said and waved her hand. Mrs Pope's tether was loose on her fingers, no longer buzzing with magic. 'Come on, come on, work, you stupid thing.'

Metty tried everything she could think of: pointing, clicking, gesturing rudely at the clouds. None of it made a difference. If anything, the rain slammed down harder, sharpening into icy needles that stabbed her arms and face, making her skin pinken like raw chicken.

Her stomach twisted as a dark shape appeared on the

horizon, rolling along the distant hills. A car. Maybe it was the captain coming home after all? He'd left the family car on the drive, but he could be returning in a taxi.

Dread washed away any relief Metty felt. The car would reach the farmhouse any minute. What would her father think when he saw what she'd done? Stealing a tether, making it howl with rain – he'd be furious with her.

Crunching over the wet slates, Metty hurried to the window and swung into her bedroom feetfirst. The air inside was warm and dry. She heaved a sigh. And then a drop of water landed on her head with a slap.

Damp patches bubbled on the ceiling and turned into sagging pockets that swelled like blisters. They all seemed to pop at once and sent a torrent of water onto Metty. Her carpet became a fibrous swamp, slurping beneath her as she charged round the room, trying to keep the rain away from the furniture. Tearing off Mrs Pope's glove, she threw it into the corner, but that did nothing to stop the weather.

Nor did climbing into the wardrobe and shutting the doors.

Metty wailed in despair, flopping down on a pile of shoes. Rain trickled through the wardrobe, ruining all her neatly hung clothes, and splatted the top of her head. It ran beneath her collar and started pooling round her feet. Pretty soon the water would reach her ankles. Metty sniffed and hugged her knees, feeling intensely sorry for herself. At least if she drowned in the wardrobe, her father wouldn't have a chance to kill her.

She didn't hear anybody enter the room. The pounding rain muffled their footsteps, but then there was an unmistakable *snap*. And the downpour stopped.

Metty stiffened in the darkness. The rainwater hadn't vanished, still dripping from her clothes, but it was no longer filling the wardrobe like a fish tank. She held still, not quite daring to nudge open the doors and peek out. Somebody cleared their throat, and then came the squelch of approaching footsteps.

There was a sudden rap on the wardrobe door.

'Would you mind coming out? I'm on a tight schedule,' said a woman's clipped voice. 'Unless you've drowned. Then by all means stay inside.'

Swallowing her nerves, Metty climbed out of the wardrobe. The woman standing in the middle of the room, wearing a smart purple dress, was so like her father that it was impossible to mistake them as anything other than family.

She was younger, but had the same olive complexion and waves of thick black hair, tied in a braid over her shoulder. She even had the same eyes, only the expression in them was considerably cooler. In fact, she had the sort of joyless face that belonged on a statue decorating a graveyard.

'Aunt Mag,' Metty said in surprise, standing awkwardly on the sodden carpet. She managed a weak smile, remembering her manners.

Magnificent Jones flashed a smile back at her and, for a moment, at least, the statue cracked. But then her dark eyes chilled once more as her gaze crawled over the room. She was holding Mrs Pope's damp tether in one hand and a black cane in the other, topped with a silver octopus.

'This house is hideous,' she said in a voice that was surprisingly bright, given her severe appearance. 'There's not an interesting thing in it – apart from you. Don't know what my brother was thinking, shutting you up in such a frightful place. Never mind the appalling damp.'

'That's just because of the rain,' Metty said, feeling a tad defensive. The farmhouse wasn't *that* bad.

'Yes, about that: probably shouldn't tamper with the weather. That's illegal grade four magic, you know. You could get into quite a lot of trouble.'

'It was an accident,' Metty said, which wasn't a complete lie. She'd been trying to summon lightning, not make it rain indoors. Clearly, she'd been right to worry because she'd had no control over magic whatsoever. If her aunt hadn't shown up, she might have flooded the whole farmhouse and drowned everyone inside it.

'Hmm,' Aunt Mag said, unconvinced. 'Ah well, no harm

done. Except, of course, to the ceiling.'

She tossed the glove onto the bed, where it lay looking pathetic and limp like something dead. Aunt Mag was wearing a tether of her own, glossy black with a silver bone pattern running down the fingers and past the knuckles.

Metty realised, with a jolt, that she couldn't see her aunt's tattoo. There was no circle cut into her tether showing her fate, like most had. Instead, the glove was whole. Only people with terrible tattoos bothered to hide them. Had her aunt always been ill-fated, and Metty had simply forgotten?

'I'm surprised you remember me. It's been an awfully long time since we last met. You were smaller then. You've grown,' Aunt Mag said with faint astonishment, as though getting bigger was a remarkable feat accomplished by just a few clever children.

'Listen,' said Metty, 'not to be rude, but what are you doing here? And where's the captain?'

'Care for the short answer?'

Metty shook her head.

'Well, we haven't got time for the long one,' Aunt Mag said. 'Apparently, you're not safe here.'

'Not safe?' Metty spluttered. 'What are you talking about? And what's happened to my dad? Do you know where he is or not?'

Her aunt was silent a moment. 'Not exactly,' she admitted.

'He was supposed to contact me this morning, but he never showed up.'

'Is he missing?' Metty said, having to prise her voice from the back of her throat where it was stuck like a piece of gum.

'That's a big question – too big for right now – and anyway you're the one I'm most worried about. It seems somebody's found out where you are and they're coming for you.'

'Coming for me? Who?'

'Nobody you'd care to meet,' her aunt said, smiling grimly. 'The good news is you'll be perfectly fine.'

'How do you know that?'

Aunt Mag looked down at Metty, determination blazing in her dark eyes.

'Because I promised your father that if anything happened to him, I would take care of you. And I never lie. My word is quite indestructible. Now there must be something I can do to conceal this place from outsiders. I need a moment to think, that's all.'

'Wait, you can't just hide me here,' Metty said.

'Best way to keep you safe.'

Metty shook her head again. 'I'm coming with you.'

Aunt Mag arched an eyebrow. 'Are you indeed? And where are we going?'

'I don't know, but I can't stay here and do nothing. I need to find my dad. You have to take me with you.'

'What a preposterous idea,' her aunt said flatly.

Metty was stung. 'It's not. I mean, surely I'd be safer with you.'

'That's highly doubtful, given recent events and—'

'What recent events?'

'And as we're short on time—'

'Listen, if you leave me behind, I'll just run away. Couldn't I help you look for the captain? I'll be useful, I swear. Just take me with you, please.'

There was an excruciating silence while Aunt Mag considered. Then her nostrils flared with a sigh.

'Very well, if you're determined to be a nuisance about it. Pack a bag, essentials only – I can buy anything else you need – and meet me downstairs in three minutes. Oh, and I'm afraid that this uniquely charming creature' – she jabbed her cane at Pumpkin who'd crawled out from under the bed and was chomping happily on one of the posts – 'will have to stay here. And don't bother getting changed. You'll dry off on the way.'

'Wait,' Metty said before her aunt could leave the room.

She paused in the doorway. 'Yes?'

'Where *are* we going?'

Aunt Mag's eyebrows met in a bemused frown.

'New London, obviously,' she said, then stepped onto the landing, letting the door snap shut behind her.

CHAPTER EIGHT

Lightning Travel

M etty's rucksack was soaked, like everything else in the wardrobe. She wrung it out, creating another puddle on the floor, then started packing the bag with soggy clothes. She didn't bother folding them.

A hundred thoughts whizzed through her mind, so many it was impossible to focus on just one. Where was her father? Who was coming to the farmhouse, and why did they want *her*? Metty had a horrible feeling it was connected to her fate, though she couldn't think why.

Once she'd dumped enough clothes in the rucksack, she grabbed a few other things: an old teddy, a hairbrush and the music box the captain had given her last Christmas. She usually kept it pinned shut. Otherwise, the box would pop open in the dead of night and belt out a rendition of 'What

Shall We Do With the Drunken Sailor?' that got louder and more slurred with every verse.

She took down all her mother's postcards, tacked to a board above her desk, and placed them carefully in the bag. Some were from New Paris where Daphne had been staying with her latest admirer, but there were ones from different cities too: New Oslo, New Boston, New Amsterdam. Metty's heart hurt to look at them. She didn't even know where Daphne was right now; her mother was always moving around. Just then, Metty missed her with a physical ache. But she squashed that feeling away. Never mind Daphne. Metty needed to focus on the captain.

She found some gloves in a drawer and put them on to hide her fate. Her bag was almost full by then. Pumpkin hopped onto the bed and watched her with a plaintive expression, nibbling his claws.

'That's it,' she said. 'I'd better go downstairs.'

Pumpkin held up his stony arms.

'You want to come with me?'

'Meh!' he said, which seemed to be his name for her.

Metty rolled her eyes and opened the rucksack wider. 'Are you completely daft or what? Like I'd leave you behind. Get in, but make sure you keep still.'

She waited for Pumpkin to tuck away his wings and get

settled, then pulled the zip. Fortunately, pet gargoyles were hard to suffocate. Although they were also rather heavy.

Aunt Mag was downstairs, waiting at the front door beside Mrs Pope, who seemed torn between disapproval and relief at the prospect of Metty's departure. Metty put on her coat and shoes, then followed her aunt outside into the blustery afternoon.

She thought Aunt Mag would unlock the car she'd arrived in. Instead, she strolled right past it and aimed for the hills lying on the horizon like mossy rocks, just like the captain had two days earlier.

'Keep up!' she called to Metty, who was already jogging.

'I hope you don't expect me to walk all the way to New London.'

'Ha! That would be a clever trick,' said Aunt Mag, grinning back at her. 'Don't be ridiculous. Walking would take far too long, and neither of us has appropriate footwear.'

'Will we try and find the captain?' Metty panted. 'D'you think he's somewhere in New London?'

'I think he would want you safe and sound, and to leave any worrying to me.'

Not a chance, Metty thought, although there was no point arguing.

The freezing wind did little to dry her clothes, even after fifty minutes climbing a steep hill. She shivered and hugged herself once they reached the peak. From up there, they had a view of the farmhouse and lots of green and brown fields stretched out beneath the sky like a patchwork quilt.

'What now?' Metty said, watching her aunt warily.

'Now,' Aunt Mag replied at length, 'we find ourselves a taller hill.'

'*What?* Why?'

'Because this one's clearly a hazard. It's much too small.'

'It's huge!' Metty cried, although she followed her aunt back downhill, ignoring the ache in her legs.

Aunt Mag dragged her up an even larger one, and still she was dissatisfied. By then, the sun was sinking fast, making the clouds blush along the horizon and the wind blow even colder.

'I thought you were on a tight schedule,' Metty said, stuffing her hands in her coat pockets as they tramped up their third hill, which was really more of a mountain.

'I am,' said Aunt Mag without looking back at her. 'I'm expecting an important phone call. But, much as I'd like to hurry, I'd sooner not disintegrate on the way.'

'Disintegrate?'

'No doubt a highly unpleasant experience. Look over there,' Aunt Mag said, and raised her hand, pointing into the distance. A string of lights floated along a road that flowed between the hills like a smooth black river. 'Here they come.'

Metty squinted at the cars, trying to count them. There must have been at least six.

'Who are they?' she asked Aunt Mag, who'd already set off, taking humungous strides with her long legs. 'That's who's coming for me? You don't think they've got the captain?'

'*Now* we really must hurry. No more dawdling, Metty.'

'I wasn't daw—'

Metty shook her head, abandoning the protest. She chased after Aunt Mag, keeping an eye on the cars. Unease was like a thistle in her throat. Whoever those people were, she hoped they couldn't see them on the hill, silhouetted against the dusky sky.

'Ah yes. This should do,' Aunt Mag said when they finally reached the top. She placed her hands on her hips and surveyed the view. 'Lightning travel works best the higher up you get. Much less chance of dying horribly. Right then.'

Aunt Mag gripped the top of her cane. Metty watched, fascinated, as the silver octopus began to glow, only dimly at first and then a stronger shine. One of its metal tentacles shifted, then another. Soon all of them were wriggling.

Aunt Mag waited until the octopus was glowing so fiercely that it gave off waves of heat, and then she thrust the cane into the air as high as it would go. The sky responded with a deafening growl, and the clouds turned a deep, stormy purple, just as they had above the captain.

But then came a loud thrum and the squelch of tyres on mud.

'They're here,' Metty said, peering down the hillside.

The cars had reached them and were circling the base of the hill. One began to power up the slope. Aunt Mag threw a worried look at the sky, then groaned through her teeth.

'Not enough time.' She glanced at Metty. 'Chuck some magic at them, would you? We only need to hold them off for a minute.'

'How?' said Metty, raising her hands. 'I don't have a tether.'

'*What?*' Aunt Mag's eyes swelled as though she'd never heard anything so ridiculous. 'What about the one you used before, to make it rain?'

'Oh, that was Mrs Pope's. I just . . . borrowed it. But I don't have it now – I left it back at the house.'

'Why on earth . . . Never mind, change of plan. You take this and I'll deal with them.'

She thrust the cane at Metty, who stared at it in dismay.

'What am I meant to do with this?'

'Hold it up!' said Aunt Mag as though that should have been obvious.

'That's probably not the best idea,' Metty said, thinking again of the disastrous rain. Surely she was the last person who should be in control of powerful magic. 'Maybe *you* should . . .'

But Aunt Mag wasn't listening, rolling up her sleeves and marching over to the lip of the hill. She held out her right hand, encased in its black tether. Suddenly there was a bubbling sound loud enough to rival the thunder, like a cauldron of scorching water about to froth over.

Metty was dying to see what her aunt had done to the cars below, but instead she concentrated on holding up the cane. The clouds were still darkening above her. Lightning began to streak across them like silvery veins.

'Aunt Mag!' she called as a shiver ran along the cane and into her hand. She had a feeling something was about to happen.

'Ha! Let's see you drive through that,' Aunt Mag said triumphantly, black braid flying in the wind. If she didn't hurry, she would be left behind on the hill.

'Aunt Mag, I really think—'

'You want some more, do you?'

The lightning was getting fiercer. It knifed across the clouds, the flash of it stinging Metty's eyes. There was a furious clap of thunder. The octopus shone even brighter, turning a blinding shade of white.

'MAG!'

Still brandishing the cane, Metty ran and grabbed her aunt's hand. The cars at the bottom of the hill were drowning in a sea of mud. One was stuck halfway up the slope, and the men inside it were trying desperately to open the doors. Aunt Mag looked at Metty in surprise and parted her lips to speak.

She didn't get the chance. A bolt of lightning shot from the clouds and speared towards them, striking the octopus.

Metty's head filled with thunder. It roared through her in deafening waves, threatening to burst her eardrums. It was impossible to tell if her eyes were open or shut, for the whole world had become a dizzying smear, so bright it didn't even have a colour. Her cheeks flapped; her bones snapped. It felt like she was wrapped up in chains and was being pulled in twelve directions by wild horses.

Just when she thought she couldn't stand it any longer, as her fingers began to slip from the cane, the terror stopped.

Still squeezing Aunt Mag's hand, she opened her eyes (they'd been shut after all). The searing brightness from before had softened to the deep red glow of sunset. Metty had a fleeting impression of ruby clouds drifting across a navy sky scattered with stars.

And then she plummeted.

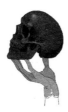

CHAPTER NINE

Arrival

They were only falling for three seconds, but it was probably the worst three seconds of Metty's life. Her eyes streamed, the wind almost ripped the hair from her scalp, and her internal organs tried very hard to eject themselves from her body.

She let out an *oof!* as they came to a sudden stop. It was like they'd crashed into an invisible mattress, and now they were floating gently in mid-air. She looked down and discovered that her dress had ballooned round her legs. She hadn't dropped the cane, thank goodness. The octopus head was no longer glowing.

'Don't worry,' Aunt Mag said in a pained voice. It seemed Metty was crushing her hand. 'You can let go now. They've got us.'

'*Who's* got us?' Metty rasped. It felt like her throat had been sanded.

Aunt Mag nodded at their feet. Swallowing, Metty looked down. The sight was enough to steal the air from her lungs.

Hovering about five hundred feet below them, and several thousand feet above the ocean, was the city of New London: a gigantic, floating, bell-shaped metropolis that narrowed the higher it climbed. At the very top was an incredible cathedral with silver spires poking like needles into the clouds and stained-glass windows of red, amber and gold. Beneath the cathedral were great winding streets lined with brick buildings, their windows shining like beacons in the gathering twilight.

Metty could see patches of greenery, the faint shapes of trees and lampposts, and huge curved bridges that seemed to drift like boats, connecting different parts of the city. An indigo river swirled through the top half of New London like a glass serpent, reflecting the twinkling stars.

Magic-powered gondolas rowed through mid-air, carrying passengers from district to district. One was gliding away from the city to get a good look at the sunset. It was close enough to Metty and Aunt Mag for the people inside it to turn their heads and give them a friendly wave.

Metty was so distracted by the incredible vista that it took her a moment to realise they were still descending. It was like the city was reeling them in. The lower they got, the sharper the buildings became. People were soon visible, walking along the spiralling streets or riding strange bicycles with colourful umbrellas attached.

'Metty, love, you might loosen your grip,' Aunt Mag said. 'I promise you won't fall.'

'Sorry,' said Metty, though she couldn't quite bring herself to let go. After all, they were still thousands of feet in the air. With some reluctance, she dropped Aunt Mag's hand and stretched out her arms experimentally. She did feel sort of weightless, like she was bobbing on a vast lake.

'Where are we?' she stammered, peering down at New London. It was the only thing she could think to say.

Aunt Mag frowned thoughtfully. 'About halfway across the Atlantic, I'd hazard. In a fortnight or so, we'll probably see the coast of Ireland.' She gave Metty a bemused look. 'You did know the city flies? All the New Capitals do.'

'Of course I knew,' said Metty with a touch of indignation. 'I'd forgotten, that's all.'

'Funny. You'd think it would be quite memorable. Good work back there, by the way. I'm afraid I got a bit carried away – unfortunate habit. If you hadn't come and grabbed my hand, you might have flashed off without me.'

'Thanks,' Metty mumbled, slightly embarrassed.

'Ah, feel that? We're coming down faster now. I expect we'll arrive in a few minutes.'

'Arrive? You mean land?'

'In a manner of speaking. I'll have that back now,' Aunt Mag said, reaching for the cane. 'Oh, and you might want to take my hand again.'

Metty did, squeezing so tightly that her aunt made a noise of discomfort. They were indeed descending faster. There was a horrid fluttering in Metty's tummy like she'd swallowed a load of flies.

Now they were drawing level with the cathedral, thankfully avoiding its spires. They glided in a diagonal path over the tops of trees and slate rooftops, garnering curious looks from the people in the streets below. Soon they were drifting towards a golden building that looked like a train station with a large chimney on top of it. Metty stared past her shoes at the pavement, which still seemed very far away.

'Aunt Mag, how exactly do we get—'

Before she could finish her question, they floated over the station chimney. And gravity latched onto them like a giant hook.

A scream burst from Metty's lips. She felt like a rock being dropped down an impossibly deep well. Warm air whooshed against her face, and her dress flapped wildly as they hurtled through a tunnel of perfect darkness.

When she and Aunt Mag finally impacted, they hit the ground with enough force that they should have broken all the bones in their bodies. Instead, they met a soft landing, bounced a couple of times, then flopped onto the squishy floor. Metty moved shakily to her hands and knees, then tried to stand up. The ground gurgled and rippled underneath her like a waterbed.

'Up you get,' said Aunt Mag, who'd already found her footing. She reached down to help Metty.

'You could have warned me about the chimney.'

There was a mischievous glint in Aunt Mag's eye. 'I thought it best not to alarm you.'

Metty rubbed her aching back, then looked around curiously. They were standing inside a chamber lit by blue lanterns that gave the whole place an underwater atmosphere. Curling from the chimney above their heads was a network of glass pipes, with strange indigo liquid flowing through them.

There was only one door inside the chamber. Aunt Mag opened it, then paused, looking back at Metty, who was still piecing together her shattered nerves. 'I really wouldn't go on standing there. Someone else might arrive any moment and crush you.'

Metty gulped, throwing an anxious glance at the funnel above her head. Then she adjusted her rucksack and wobbled over to Aunt Mag. Her aunt held the door open, and Metty slipped under her arm, emerging into a far brighter room.

The station was much larger and cleaner than any public

place she'd ever visited in Old London, apart from one corner where the wall tiles looked blistered and chipped, like there'd been an explosion. People were queueing along the many platforms, waiting to board blue and pink gondolas that were flying in and out of the building through an archway in the furthest wall. BLACK INK STREET read a large plaque above it.

Aunt Mag steered Metty away from the lightning chamber and led her deeper into the station.

'What's that over there?' Metty asked, pointing at a shadow on the floor. It was hard to make out at first, a hazy shape with triangular wings gliding round the damaged part of the station. Other people had noticed it too. They kept glancing at the shadow and whispering to each other, but nobody dared go near it. 'Is it meant to be a butterfly?'

'Moth,' Aunt Mag said with a grim expression.

'What's it doing, floating around like that?'

'Making everyone very uncomfortable. Shame they can't get rid of the horrid thing – but that's not for you to worry about. We'll take a gondola up to the house, I think. I don't know about you, but my feet could use a rest.'

Metty didn't answer, concentrating on putting one foot in front of the other. Her legs felt like matchsticks that might snap at any second. Aunt Mag laughed at her, not unkindly.

'Oh dear, wobbly legs? Being struck by lightning does

make one feel rather odd, but the effects usually wear off. For most people. Ah well, try and keep up,' she said, then strolled off before Metty could even catch her breath.

She paused to lean against a vending machine, keeping an eye on her aunt, who was heading for one of the platforms and seemed to have forgotten her. Something winked in the corner of Metty's eye. The vending machine wasn't full of snacks as she'd assumed, but rows of small silver bells.

"Scuse,' said a bald man, bustling her aside. The tattoo on his hand was a lump of Swiss cheese. Metty subtly consulted her dictionary.

CHEESES: *associated with cheesemaking, rat-catchers, or pungent body odour*

She grimaced and leaned away from the gentleman, holding her breath just in case. He fed some money into a slot in the machine, and a bell clanged into the drawer at the bottom. The man pulled it out and gave it a good shake as he walked off. He didn't seem concerned that the bell made no sound.

Metty looked up at the vending machine. DIRECTION BELLS, it said at the top.

'Metty!' her aunt called impatiently.

She put away her dictionary and tottered over to Aunt

Mag, who took out her purse, along with a silver gadget that resembled a pocket watch.

'That's a magic meter, isn't it?' Metty said, rising on her tiptoes to see inside it. Aunt Mag checked the meter, then frowned and snapped it shut.

'Hmm. Looks like I'm strapped for cash *and* running low on magic. Lightning travel – bloody extortionate. How do you feel about walking after all? I suppose it'll give you a chance to sightsee. Come along then. And do keep up!'

CHAPTER TEN

New London

Metty was not enthused about walking, even after her legs firmed up. She was exhausted, starving, windswept, not to mention alarmed by the whole situation, the captain's disappearance and the fact that someone was after her. The last thing she wanted was to embark on another long hike after trudging up and down hills all afternoon.

But then they set off, and it was like the city had cast a spell on her.

Nowhere was level in New London. All the roads slanted, climbing towards the cathedral at its peak, and there were no cars. Instead, gondolas glided above the pavements, and all the stations had magical chimneys to catch anyone arriving by lightning.

Pedestrians made their way on foot or raced by on those

funny bicycles with giant parasols attached to their seats – wind bikes, according to Aunt Mag. They seemed to give the riders a speedy boost no matter which direction they travelled in.

Metty kept her eyes peeled for the captain, hoping to glimpse him turning a corner or crossing the road. She got excited when she spotted a tall man in a trilby, but then her heart deflated. Of course the man wasn't her father. It was probably stupid to think that she might just run into him, although she didn't stop looking as Aunt Mag led her through the city.

New London had many districts, some just a single street, others much larger. They were all linked to fates, Metty realised, wandering from Crust Corner – full of bakeries and pie shops and people with tattoos like baguettes and cakes – to Stamp Square – where the post office was, and everyone had letter-themed fates – to Cheddar Close, a tight, rather pungent coil of a street full of cheese merchants. She wondered if the man she'd seen at the station worked there.

Metty glanced at her gloved hand, thinking about her own fate. She didn't expect to find a district for potential murderers, although there was probably a prison somewhere.

'What's wrong with all the streetlamps?' she asked Aunt Mag, noticing the metal posts lining the pavements. At least, she assumed they were streetlamps, only they seemed to be missing their heads.

Aunt Mag frowned at the dark ruby clouds. 'Too early for them yet. Now hurry along or we'll miss the bridge.'

Soon they came to a chasm that ran like an almighty crack through the city, cutting New London in half. They'd just missed a red bridge that was moving quite fast, floating westward and knocking against both banks.

'Never mind. Tesla's rather excitable anyway. We'll wait for the next one,' Aunt Mag said, then pointed with her cane. 'Ah, here comes Edison, nice and sturdy.'

It took the next bridge (a solid grey one) a good five minutes to drift along the bank. Metty felt like she was waiting for an elderly train to chug into a station.

'Aunt Mag?' she said while they were standing on the pavement. Other people were waiting too, but they weren't close enough to eavesdrop. 'Did the captain ever tell you about . . .?' Metty paused, a hot, prickly feeling spreading through her. She had to clear her throat. 'Do you, uh, know about my fate?'

'I do,' Aunt Mag said quietly.

Metty was taken aback. She'd felt certain the captain would never share her darkest secret. Even more surprising, though, was the sympathy in her aunt's face.

'But then aren't you worried I might . . .?'

'Might what?'

Aunt Mag was going to make her say it.

'That I might, you know' – Metty dropped her voice to a whisper – *'murder you.'*

Amusement sparkled in her aunt's eyes. 'No, dear. Not in the least.'

'Oh,' said Metty, distracted by a new feeling in her stomach. It was a sort of tingly warmth, like she'd just drunk hot cocoa. Aunt Mag wasn't afraid of her. She knew about her fate, and yet she *wasn't* afraid.

They crossed Edison Bridge once it drew near enough to hop aboard, and entered an even higher part of the city on the far side of the chasm.

WELCOME TO INKRIVER MARKET read an archway, changing colour every few seconds. The market was the best place Metty had seen yet. Signs advertised buttons, hairbrushes, false teeth, pet lizards, lucky stars, enchanted footwear and (for some reason) unsolvable riddles. New London's river, which she'd spotted while she and Aunt Mag were flying over the city, wove through the district, then ran into a large dark hole somewhere in the middle, like water disappearing down a sink.

But it wasn't water, Metty realised, frowning at the river. The liquid was too thick, its colour too rich and dark, threaded with bits of silver and gold.

'Is that . . .?'

'Ink,' Aunt Mag said.

Metty stared at the ink river in astonishment. She was looking at pure magic.

'Shockingly valuable, of course,' her aunt continued. 'A single drop has tremendous power.'

'Don't people try and steal it then?'

'Oh, they certainly try, but the river's protected by strong enchantments. It's what keeps us afloat, you know – ink runs through the whole city and powers the core at the heart of New London. That's how *all* the New Capitals fly.'

'But why?' Metty said, watching the river ripple and shine like purple silk. 'What's the point of them? The flying cities, I mean. If they need so much ink, aren't they sort of . . . wasteful?'

'Well, yes, but . . .' Aunt Mag frowned. 'Didn't my brother explain any of this? He must have told you about growing up in New London?'

Metty shook her head.

'How forgetful of him,' Aunt Mag said, looking rather unimpressed. 'Well, it's quite simple really. This city only exists because, years ago, the British government began controlling ink, making up ridiculous rules about who could use it, and when, and how. New London was created by a group of visionaries and freethinkers to be a sort of magical haven, without any restrictions at all.

'And then, once the city was a roaring success, the other New Capitals started appearing: New Paris over the Channel, New Tokyo above the Sea of Japan, New Washington DC over the Potomac and so forth. Suddenly the world had all these independent utopias where people – *rich* people, at least – could buy ink and use magic to their heart's content.'

'But what about . . .'

Metty lost track of her thought as a powerful smell hit her, wafting from a pink shop shaped like a perfume bottle. Her eyelids sank in a dreamy expression, and she breathed in a scrumptious scent of chocolate that morphed into spicy honey, then a sharper tang of fresh lime.

'Watch it,' Aunt Mag said, grabbing the back of her coat. Metty had started drifting towards the perfume shop without even noticing. 'Set foot in there and I'll never get you out again. Come on. Home's not too much further.'

As they were leaving Inkriver Market, Metty spotted a tether shop. She stopped opposite the window, observing all the gloves on display. A blue tether embroidered with white birds drew her eye in particular. Beside it, stuck to the store window, was a poster depicting a dark moth, reminding Metty of the shadow she'd seen back at the station.

FREE NEW LONDON FROM TERROR!

Something about the poster felt familiar, tugging at a faint memory. She couldn't think why.

'Keep up, Metty!' Aunt Mag called.

She stepped back from the glass, throwing a final glance at the blue silk glove. If she ever had her own tether, she would want one just like that. But obviously it would never be safe for her to use magic.

They left Inkriver Market and, a few streets later, came to another flashing sign: WELCOME TO HIGHFATE.

'Home sweet home,' said Aunt Mag, leading Metty past beautiful houses covered in Halloween decorations. The streets were wider in Highfate, with glorious autumn trees lining the cobbled pavements. Aunt Mag raised her hand suddenly, drawing Metty's attention to one of the strange lampposts. 'Here they come now. Look up.'

Metty did, tipping back her head. A shiver of delight ran along her spine. Swooping from the darkening heavens were golden birds, dozens of them, hundreds even, shining against the clouds like curls of fire. Some were as large as eagles, others as small as sparrows, and they flew through the streets of New London, settling on top of the many lampposts as if they were great metal perches. The birds' feathers were bright liquid gold, their eyes fierce beads of light, bathing the roads in a rich honey glow as they folded away their wings.

'Solar-powered,' Aunt Mag explained, steering Metty along the pavement again. 'They fly around all day, soaking up the sun, then swoop down at dusk. Remarkable inventions.'

'Inventions? You mean they're not real birds?'

'Real? I suppose they are in a sense, if you want to get philosophical, but they used to be plain old statues. At one point, the governor was keen to disenchant the poor things, but New Londoners have grown quite fond of them. Hardly surprising. They are delightful.'

Metty frowned at the nearest lamppost. Three robin-sized birds were huddled together, expelling light with their bright little chests. Why would anyone want to destroy such beautiful creations, to rob them of their magic? She couldn't understand it.

She could feel Pumpkin getting restless as they tramped up the last few streets. He wriggled inside Metty's rucksack and kept tugging on the zip, trying to let himself out. She held it shut and hoped he would get the message.

Finally, they arrived at a courtyard bordered by seven grand manors.

'Right, this is us,' Aunt Mag said, marching over to the biggest and most forbidding of the houses. She pointed at the blue front door. 'And this is home – for now, at least. Welcome to Winter's Knock.'

CHAPTER ELEVEN

Winter's Knock

'Word of advice. Be extremely careful about what you touch in this house,' Aunt Mag warned as she closed the heavy front door and twisted all nine of the locks. 'Unless you want to suffer a highly unpleasant and entirely avoidable death.'

Metty thought she must be joking, but Aunt Mag's eyes were stonier than ever. She was about to ask why, then abandoned the question for the answer was obvious, if disheartening.

Winter's Knock was chock-full of cursed objects, at least according to the danger sign hanging in the entrance hall. Six glass cabinets flanked the majestic staircase, casting thick shadows on the floor. Inside them were clocks, bells, tribal masks, old coins, dolls with cracked faces and all sorts of sinister trinkets, most of them labelled and oozing a peppery smell of dark magic.

'Why do you collect all this stuff?' Metty asked, peering at a tiger's claw from a safe distance. According to the note beneath it, whoever held the claw would feel like a hunted animal. Beside that was a bell made to deafen the ringer and a Victorian camera that blinded whoever it photographed.

She glanced back at Aunt Mag, wrinkling her nose. 'A necklace that makes people's teeth fall out? That's just evil.'

'Yes, it is a bit grisly. But don't you think a *nice* curse would defeat the point? I have no intention of using these charming creations myself, quite the opposite. My goal is to remove as many of them from society as possible, then disenchant them if I can. Unfortunately, that's easier said than done.'

'So you're a professional curse hunter?' Metty said, standing up straight.

Aunt Mag shrugged, trying not to look pleased with herself. 'Not *professional*. It's more of an addictive hobby. Anyway, you'll be glad to know that the real monstrosities are locked downstairs in the vault, but you'll still want to be careful. The rule is, if it's labelled, don't touch.' Aunt Mag cocked her head to one side. 'Is there something wrong with your bag? Only it appears to be giving you some trouble.'

Metty wheezed an awkward laugh and gripped the straps of her rucksack. Pumpkin was getting quite boisterous.

'It's heavy, that's all,' she said quickly. 'And my back's tired, you know, from the lightning travel.'

Aunt Mag clapped her hands together. 'Of course! You must be exhausted. Come on, let's find you a room.'

'You mean I get my own?' Metty said, following her upstairs.

Aunt Mag wore a baffled smile. 'Did you think I'd lock you away like one of my deadly curses? You're a Jones. This house belongs to you as much as to me. Neither of us paid for it, we probably don't deserve it, but somebody ought to put it to good use.'

'Did the captain ever live here?' Metty asked.

'For a while, when we were children. After our parents died.'

Strange to think of him wandering these hallways, breathing in the same smell of marble dust and rich old wood. It reminded Metty of a church. A feeling of dread travelled through her, turning her insides to stone when she thought about her father.

'So when can we start looking for him?' she asked the back of Aunt Mag's head. 'What did he say the last time you spoke? If he asked you to take care of me, then he must've known something bad might happen. D'you think it's connected to those people back in Wales, the ones in the cars?'

'All excellent questions,' her aunt said.

'Maybe you could give me some excellent answers. Or any answers at all would be nice.'

Aunt Mag threw a sharp look backwards. 'Quite confident, aren't you, for such a young person? Perhaps my brother should've called you Impertinent Jones. I'll be generous and put it down to tiredness.'

'So where do we even begin?' Metty said, ignoring her. 'Should we tell the police what's happened? Maybe you could try tracking him with magic.'

'If it was that simple, you and I wouldn't be having this conversation. Not that we should be having it at all. I told you already: leave your father to me.'

'But—'

'Ah, this one'll do.'

They'd come to a solitary door in the hallway. Aunt Mag went to open it, then stopped.

'Before we go in, I'd better warn you that the room isn't quite . . . ready. Obviously, we had no idea you were coming, so there hasn't been any opportunity to tidy up. The important thing is to keep away from the wardrobe. And the mirror. And certainly the desk. Don't touch any of the toys on the windowsill either. You needn't look so mortified. I'll have Rupert tackle the room tomorrow.'

'Rupert?' Metty frowned. Why did that name sound familiar? 'Wait, you don't mean Uncle Monot—'

'Don't call him that,' Aunt Mag said with a slight shudder, 'or you'll never hear the end of it. Although imagine how boring life would be if all us Joneses went by our middle names. People would have to work so much harder to tease us.'

It's all right for some, Metty thought. She wouldn't mind being called Magnificent.

'Right then. Let's get you settled,' Aunt Mag said and threw open the door to Metty's new room.

The first thing that struck her was the dreadful atmosphere, rolling over her like a bad stench. Metty screwed up her face, appalled. Every inch of the bedroom was crammed with cursed furniture, all labelled like parcels in a post office. There was hardly anywhere to step safely or put down her bag.

'Remember,' Aunt Mag said brightly from the doorway, 'don't touch anything and you'll be absolutely fine. Sleep tight!'

'Wait,' Metty said before she could march off. 'I know you don't want my help, but I can't just sit around doing nothing. My dad . . . he's just *gone*. He would never leave me, I know he wouldn't, so that means he must be hurt, or stuck somewhere. What if he's . . .?'

Aunt Mag gave her a pitying look. 'He's not dead, Metty. I know that much.'

'How?'

'Long story, too long for tonight. You'll just have to trust me.'

Metty pursed her lips. 'But what if you're only saying that to make me feel better?'

'I've told you already: I never lie,' Aunt Mag said, gaze inspecting her. 'Look at you – practically dead on your feet. What you need is a good night's rest. Although do watch out for the bed. It's rather malicious. I'd stick to the right side.'

'But—'

'Goodnight,' Aunt Mag said briskly, and closed the bedroom door.

Metty glared at it for a moment, then shrugged off her rucksack and set Pumpkin free. He flew straight to the chandelier and dangled from it by his feet.

'Play?' he croaked with a sleepy smile.

Metty shook her head, then perched on the very edge of the bed. She didn't care what her aunt said. She had to find the captain – for all she knew, his life might depend on her.

She pulled out her *Dictionary of Fates* and went to the very back of the book, past the section for brand-new fates that had been discovered since the previous edition. There was a blank page at the end. Metty grabbed a pen from her rucksack.

Magnificent Jones. Fate unknown, she put down, then thought for a second before adding:

Reasons for being 'THE ONE'
Too secretive

Annoyingly stubborn

They weren't very good reasons, which was a relief. Obviously, Metty didn't want to hurt anybody, but especially not a family member. Although it was hard to imagine Aunt Mag being anyone's victim.

She found the captain's fate after that.

SHIPS: *associated with the navy, adventurous spirits, or drinking too much rum*

Reasons for being 'THE ONE', she'd written under his name, then: *Never, never, never!*

Metty closed the book and pressed it to her chest, trying not to cry. She would find her father. She'd do anything to get him back.

Metty didn't try to sleep. Instead, she waited for Aunt Mag to go to bed while her new bedroom ticked and groaned around her like a giant bomb. It was impossible to tell whether anyone was still awake in the house. Eventually, she decided to chance it, grabbing her rucksack from the floor.

'Pumpkin, come down,' she hissed, holding open the bag, but Pumpkin was stubborn, still hanging from the chandelier like a petrified bat. He didn't really need to sleep, being a gargoyle, but lightning travel seemed to have worn him out too. 'Look, if you don't fly down, I'll have to leave you behind.'

'Sleep,' Pumpkin grumbled and wrapped his wings tighter round himself.

'All right,' Metty said, zipping up her bag. 'Stay behind then, but you cannot leave this room. No one can know you're here, all right? I'll come back for you soon, I promise.'

Her stomach gurgled as she slipped into the hallway. The captain would never have forgotten to feed her. He loved cooking, and he always let Metty choose whatever they ate for dinner, no matter what Mrs Pope had to say on the subject. It was usually the highlight of Metty's day, tasting her father's bold new recipes, making fun of his appalling singing while he cooked, then washing up together afterwards.

She just *had* to go out and look for him. It would be dangerous wandering New London on her own, but if Aunt Mag refused to trust her, then she would find her father by herself. She'd search every street if she had to.

A river of moonlight led her to the grand staircase and from there Metty descended to the entrance hall. The front door was locked, and there was no sign of a key anywhere. She would have to find another exit.

Metty searched the downstairs rooms, poking her head through the doors in the hallway. She was startled to discover an indoor swimming pool. The pool itself was shaped like an hourglass, with a slender tunnel connecting the halves and small white fish swimming in the water. They vanished when Metty approached, darting into hidden alcoves in the sides of the pool, and wouldn't come out again.

After that, she found a broom cupboard, a library spanning three floors and a drawing room with grand portraits hanging on the walls. Metty inspected the paintings, reading the names at the bottom of each one. Masterful, Maudlin, Majestic . . . They were all Joneses, including a portrait of Aunt Mag and the captain as children alongside their baby brother Monotonous. Metty's father looked tidy and smiling, her aunt scruffy and cross, and her uncle rather dribbly. Metty noticed that quite a few Joneses had whole tethers covering up their fates like Aunt Mag. Perhaps being ill-fated ran in the family.

She returned to the hallway. The final door opened into a study, with framed certificates on the walls. Aunt Mag's desk was a complete mess, covered in books and papers. Metty rifled through a bunch of newspaper clippings, accidentally knocking over a photo of a boy and a woman eating ice cream on one of the New London bridges.

Two words kept leaping out at her: Black Moths. They were printed everywhere, stamping every headline Aunt Mag had cut out.

FINALLY COMING OUT OF THE COCOON? RUMOURS OF THE BLACK MOTHS' RETURN.

ARE BLACK MOTHS TO BLAME FOR MAGIC STRIKES IN NEW LONDON?

BLACK MOTHS ON THE BRINK OF EXTINCTION PROMISES GOVERNOR FINCH.

The Black Moths . . . Why did that name sound familiar? It must be connected to her father's disappearance. Why else would Aunt Mag keep so many articles about the same thing? Clearly, she knew more than she was letting on.

A hissing noise grabbed Metty's attention. She left the newspapers and turned to look at something else on Aunt Mag's desk. In the middle of all the chaos was a device she'd seen once before: an old copper telephone. Purple mist rippled from the mouthpiece. If Metty listened carefully, she could just make out the scratch of whispering voices.

She ran her fingers along the telephone's spine. It trembled like something alive. Wetting her lips, she slowly picked up the receiver and brought it to her ear. She'd thought the whispers would sharpen, that she'd be able to hear actual words, but the phone only crackled like white noise.

'Hello . . .?' she said into the mouthpiece and waited, heart thumping.

Is that you? said a voice so deep and gravelly, so dripping with spite that her courage popped like a balloon. She almost dropped the handset.

Are you there, child? the voice continued in a rasping breath. Metty could practically smell its foulness. *Have they found you yet . . .? The men with chains and sticks . . . They know what you are . . . Oh yes, they know what you are . . . And they'll come for you soon . . . They'll drag you out of your warm little bed, oh yes, and there's nothing you can do to stop them . . . They'll drag you all the way to—*

'Wrong number!' she squeaked and slammed down the telephone.

Metty stepped back from the desk, flattening a hand over her heart. That awful voice echoed in her mind: *They'll drag you out of your warm little bed . . . The men with chains and sticks . . .*

Surely the voice hadn't meant those people chasing her and Aunt Mag in Wales?

Metty swallowed, feeling queasy. Then dread prickled on the back of her neck. Something was watching her from the doorway.

She spun round and there was a skinny boy with eyes like black pearls shining in the darkness.

'Who are—' Metty began to say, but the boy turned and ran.

CHAPTER TWELVE

The Ghost

Metty chased the boy along the corridor to a flight of stairs at the back of the house. He was faster than her, his footsteps silent as he skidded over the waxed floorboards and down the narrow staircase. He had disappeared by the time Metty reached the kitchen below. She paused in the doorway and thumped the light switch.

Eight or nine lamps flickered to life along the walls and filled the room with golden warmth. The kitchen was surprisingly modern, with white marble worktops and sleek black cupboards. Pots and pans dangled from hooks on the ceiling, and a large round table stood in the middle of the room, draped in a cloth.

The boy was nowhere to be seen. Suspicious, Metty prowled round the kitchen, opening cupboards. Most were empty. Even the ginormous fridge didn't appear to have much food inside it. Anyone would think Aunt Mag didn't need to eat.

A soft squeal drew her attention back to the table. It sounded like a shoe rubbing on the floor. Metty frowned, eyeing the cloth.

'I know you're under there,' she said in her fiercest voice, pressing her knuckles to her hips so her hands wouldn't shake. 'So you'd better come out.'

There was a long silence, and then the tablecloth rippled.

'Go away,' said a muffled voice. It sounded more timid than threatening.

Metty made a disgruntled face. 'No!'

Another anxious pause. *'Please,'* whispered the voice.

'Not until you come out. Or maybe you want me to come under there instead.'

'No,' the boy snapped and yanked the tablecloth out of Metty's hand as she bent down and grabbed it.

A few seconds later, a head emerged from the shadow of the table. The boy looked up at her with a strange expression that was half surly, half terrified. He had reddish-brown skin, black curls and the longest eyelashes Metty had ever seen.

'Are you a-a ghost?' he asked in a wobbly voice, not daring to take his eyes off her. They were beautiful eyes, she noted, reflecting golden jewels of lamplight.

'Am *I* a ghost?' Metty scoffed. 'Course not. Are you?'

The boy considered, then shook his head.

She softened a bit. 'Well, that's all right then, isn't it? What are you— Oh, get out from under there, won't you? I feel stupid talking to a floating head. What are you doing at Winter's Knock?'

The boy crawled out from beneath the table and got to his feet. He was a little shorter than Metty, the silk of his navy pyjamas shimmering in the light. He put his hands in his pockets, so she didn't get a chance to see his fate.

'I live here,' he said, to her surprise.

'What, permanently? Are we cousins or something?'

Surely she would know if Aunt Mag had a son.

The boy shook his head. 'Mag took me in after I lost my family. She's my guardian.'

'Oh,' Metty said, taken aback. She suddenly realised why the boy looked familiar: she'd seen him in the photograph on Aunt Mag's desk, the one she'd knocked over before. 'She's my aunt.'

'Then you must be Metty.'

'Of course I am. Who did you think I was?'

The boy shrugged. 'A ghost. You *were* talking on the spirit phone.'

'The what?' said Metty.

'The spirit phone. You shouldn't mess around with it, you know. Mag'll get annoyed – she says it confuses the dead, and they're already unreliable. I mean, sometimes *I* use it if there's no one home and I'm really bored, but—'

'Wait, what?' Metty muttered, scrunching up her forehead. 'You mean that *thing*, it lets you speak to the . . . dead?'

'Well, yeah,' said the boy.

A chill crept into Metty's bones. 'So that voice was actually . . . I was speaking to a-a dead man?'

'It wasn't Terry, was it?' the boy said with a pained face. 'Sounds ancient, like he's swallowed a bucket of gravel?'

Metty nodded weakly.

'Yeah, he's horrible. Next time, I'd ask for Frank, or Miss Sharma's pretty nice.'

'Next time? No thanks. How does Aunt Mag even get away with having all this cursed stuff? Does no one care?'

Metty knew there were practically no magic laws in the flying cities, but hoarding dangerous cursed items was surely illegal, even in New London.

'Nobody knows, otherwise she'd be in a whole load of trouble. I think she's meant to hand over most of the cursed things she finds, like the spirit phone, but . . . Well, you know Mag.'

'Not as well as you, apparently. What's your name, by the way?'

'Sundar,' the boy said, smiling shyly as he held out his hand. Metty shook it, relieved to find his palm warm and solid and not at all ghostlike.

Sundar frowned at her rucksack. 'Are you going somewhere?'

'That's the plan, if I ever find a way out. I'm looking for . . .' Metty paused, unsure whether she ought to tell the boy about her father. She didn't know if she could trust him yet, and he might run and fetch Aunt Mag. Her stomach gave a loud rumble.

Sundar laughed. 'Hungry?'

'A bit,' she admitted.

'You won't find much to eat,' he said, scratching his ear. 'Mag's a rubbish cook, and Rupert's too lazy to bother half the time. They eat out normally. Or use the snack pocket.'

'The what pocket?'

Sundar grinned at Metty. 'The snack pocket. C'mon, I'll show you how it works.'

He led her over to a metal box on one of the worktops. It looked like a steel breadbin with a drawer at the front and a small round handle.

'Put your thumb on the button,' he said. Metty did, startled by a sudden zap like a tiny electric shock. 'That's it. Now all you have to do is think about whatever you fancy and wait for the ping. Oh, but picture it nice and clear in your mind, otherwise things can get a bit messy.'

'What, you mean anything?'

Sundar's smile broadened. 'Yep.'

'Even ice cream?'

'Ice cream's easy. If you're going for that, at least pick an interesting flavour.'

'All right,' Metty said, chewing her lip as she summoned a hazy memory.

On her seventh birthday, the captain and Daphne had taken her to the biggest teashop in Old London where they'd ordered magnificent ice-cream sundaes with zingy chunks of mango and straws made from chocolate wafers. It was the best birthday she'd ever had, and one of those special occasions when her parents were still together and acting like a real family. Metty had only seen Daphne a few times after that, and then not at all after her fating.

She was so busy concentrating on the memory of her parents that she was caught off-guard by the sudden *ping!* She flinched and took her thumb off the button.

Sundar was waiting for her. 'Go on then,' he said, waggling his eyebrows.

Metty grabbed the handle and pulled up the metal door. Inside the machine was an almost perfect replica of the ice cream she'd remembered, with a few imagined extras like sprinkles and a dollop of whipped cream. Her mouth watered as she reached into the snack pocket and pulled out the mango sundae, carrying it over to the table. Sundar grabbed a spoon from one of the drawers and pressed it into her hand.

'Good?' he said when Metty scooped out a generous portion. The ice cream fizzed on her tongue, deliciously sweet and sharp all at once.

"Ood.' She swallowed a second mouthful, then threw down her spoon and stared at Sundar. 'Better than good. That's amazing! Can I make something else, d'you think? Where do all the ingredients come from?'

Sundar shrugged. 'I dunno,' he said. 'It's just magic.'

Metty bounded across the kitchen and put her thumb on the button again. This time, she was ready for the zap. After a few seconds, there was another *ping!* and a plate of steaming waffles appeared inside the machine. Metty gave them to Sundar while she worked on a Black Forest gateau.

Soon the kitchen table was groaning under the weight of several cakes, a treacle tart, a bowl of profiteroles, seven types of ice cream, toffee apples, Turkish delight, a cherry pie and a whole platoon of gingerbread soldiers, not to mention two enormous jugs of strawberry milk and hot cocoa, the latter topped with whipped cream and bumblebee-shaped marshmallows.

'Don't you think that's enough now?' Sundar asked as Metty discarded a plate of doughnuts with mustard fillings and a liver-flavoured jelly pudding. Her imagination seemed to be wearing thin, or perhaps the opposite was true. Either way, her creations were getting less edible by the minute.

'Why?'

Sundar pointed at the snack pocket's round handle. 'Look, it's getting low on uses. There's only five left.'

'Wait, you mean it doesn't just make food forever?'

Metty gulped, squinting at the button. There was indeed a tiny five engraved on the handle. She hadn't even noticed, too busy dreaming up snacks.

'Oh dear,' she said, looking over her shoulder at the table. She'd created quite a midnight feast. 'I'm guessing none of that can go back in the machine. You don't think Aunt Mag'll be angry?'

'Probably not. Not with you anyway, although she might be a bit annoyed with me. The snack pocket's not broken or anything. Mag or Rupert can refill it with ink tomorrow, get back all its uses. It's just expensive.'

Metty drifted back to the table, frowning at all the food. She was supposed to be looking for the captain, not messing around with magical inventions, but her stomach was still grumbling.

'In that case, I really shouldn't let all this go to waste,' she said, then glanced at Sundar. 'Want to help me eat it?'

The boy shook his head, though he pulled out a chair. 'Not got much of a sweet tooth. Anyway, aren't you meant to be running away?'

'I am,' Metty said with a flash of determination. 'I mean, I will. Just not on an empty stomach.'

She quickly gave up trying to eat all the snacks, realising they would make her extremely sick, and settled for nibbling everything instead. She took small bites from the pastries, cut thin slices from each cake, and washed them down with gulps of strawberry milk. Some of the marshmallows in the hot cocoa had buzzed to life and flown out of the jug. Now they were circling the ceiling lamp like real bumblebees.

'You and Aunt Mag must be pretty close,' Metty said to Sundar through a mouthful of cherry pie.

The boy shrugged. 'She takes care of me.'

'Does she ever, uh, tell you things?'

'Like what?'

Metty tried to look casual, licking chocolate sauce off her finger. 'I don't know. Has she mentioned me?'

'Sure, once or twice.'

'What about my dad?'

'You mean Captain Jones?'

Metty's chair made a noise as she sat bolt upright. 'You know him?'

'We've met,' Sundar replied, watching her with an uneasy expression. His eyes were so dark, they were like drops of ink on white paper.

'And have you heard my aunt . . . has she mentioned anything about what might've happened to him?'

'No, but he was here the day before yesterday, and I know he was stressed about something.'

'About what?' Metty said, chest tightening. The day before yesterday was her birthday – so surely that meant the captain must have lightning travelled to New London, then gone straight to Winter's Knock. It gave her a funny shiver to think that her father had been here so recently. Perhaps he'd sat in this very room.

'I dunno. Some people. I think they were following him.' Sundar paused, watching the marshmallow bees floating above them. Metty could tell he didn't want to say any more in case he got in trouble.

'I'm really worried about him, you know,' she said quietly. 'I think he might be in danger. Listen, if you *did* know something . . .'

'I don't think those people were after the captain,' the boy blurted out. 'At least, not exactly. He's not what they really want.'

'What *do* they really want?' Metty asked in a tremulous voice. *The men with chains and sticks . . .*

Sundar's gaze slid to her hands, which fortunately were still wearing gloves.

Of course. It was just as she'd suspected. It was all to do with her fate.

'They want *me*. But why? I haven't even done anything.'

Yet . . .

There it was: the awful, unspoken word that had haunted her ever since Darkwell.

'I don't know,' Sundar said, 'but I'm sure Mag'll keep you safe now you're here. She's good at that sort of thing.'

'I don't want to be safe,' Metty grumbled. 'I want – I need to find the captain and make sure nothing's happened to him.' She looked up suddenly, shaking off her bad temper. 'Would *you* help me? I don't know this city at all, but if you've been living here a while then . . . Hey, you could come with me now!'

Sundar shook his head. 'I can't. I want to help, really, but . . . I don't get out much.'

'What do you mean? Why not?'

The boy only shrugged, glancing away.

'All right,' Metty said, trying to hide her disappointment. 'I guess I'll just manage on my own.'

Sundar grimaced. 'Look, please don't run away. I'm sure if you talk to Mag in the morning—'

'No point. She won't listen. Unless . . .'

An idea was taking shape in Metty's mind. It was a terrible thought, bound to fail, not to mention pretty despicable. But then, as she'd wondered a thousand times before: why bother being good when the skull on her hand reminded her every day that she was destined to be bad?

Plus, it *would* mean not having to sneak off in the middle of the night.

Metty leaned forward, placing her palms on the table. 'Sundar, what d'you think would happen if the police found out about Aunt Mag's curse collection?'

CHAPTER THIRTEEN

A Monstrous Plan

When Metty first woke up, she thought she must have fallen asleep outside. Hard bits of dirt were stuck to her cheek, digging in like shrapnel. There was a loud crunch somewhere nearby.

Alarmed, she jerked upright and blinked in confusion. She was, in fact, not outside, but still sitting at the kitchen table, surrounded by bowls of melted ice cream and stale cakes. Now pink beams of early-morning sunshine rippled through the high windows, and Sundar was nowhere to be seen. In his place, watching Metty with amused blue eyes, was a man who looked around thirty, and was munching his way through a large and sticky toffee apple.

Tattooed on his right hand was a golden mask with dark blue ribbons, the sort you might wear to a masquerade ball.

Metty frowned at it, wondering what such a fate could mean, and wished she could pull out her dictionary without seeming rude. Maybe the man was an actor or somebody good at donning disguises.

'Morning.' He grinned, showing off slightly crooked teeth. 'I see you've been making yourself at home.' He winked at Metty, then pointed to her rucksack dumped by the table. 'Sneaking off somewhere?'

'Uncle Monot— I mean Uncle Rupert,' she said, colouring a bit. She rubbed her cheek, and chocolate sprinkles clattered onto the table like hail. She hadn't seen her father's younger brother in so long that she could barely remember him, although he did look a lot like the captain and Aunt Mag.

He chuffed a laugh, taking another bite from the toffee apple. 'I appreciate the effort. I suppose being called Rupert is slightly less embarrassing than the alternative. But you'd know all about that, wouldn't you, *Meticulous?* Gawd, our family's dreadful.'

'It's a tradition, isn't it, the stupid names?'

'Can't see how that makes it better. You hungry? No, I expect not after stuffing yourself with sugar all night. Blueberry ice cream's not bad, by the way, but lemon and cheddar?' Rupert made a disgusted face. 'That's adventurous, even for my tastes.'

'I got the flavours muddled up,' Metty replied defensively.

She hadn't thought the ice cream too bad herself, although it did admittedly leave a funny aftertaste.

'Yeah, the snack pocket can be tricky to get the hang of, although you've clearly had some practice.' Rupert paused to stare at Metty as though he'd only just really noticed her. 'Blimey, you've shot up. Last time I saw you, you were small enough to carry on my shoulders. If I remember rightly, you took great pleasure in pulling my hair. I think you were trying to give me a bald patch.'

'Doesn't seem to have done any lasting damage,' Metty said, nodding at Rupert's black ponytail that flowed to the middle of his back. That and the blue feather hanging from his ear lent him the air of a well-mannered pirate.

'Anyway,' he said, crunching on the apple again, 'you'd best run upstairs. The chief's after you, and she doesn't like to be kept waiting. Frightful temper, that one, especially in the morning.'

Metty leaped up from her chair. Aunt Mag was looking for her? Surely the first place she'd check was Metty's bedroom where she'd left Pumpkin dangling from the chandelier.

Grabbing her bag, she raced out of the kitchen and hurried through the house (which was quite beautiful in the daylight, sunshine rippling on the marble floors and mahogany walls). She was halfway up the staircase when a voice on the floor above roared: 'METICULOUS JONES!'

Metty froze, gripping the banister. She'd never heard her name spoken with such blistering rage before and had to drag herself up the rest of the stairs, nerves weighing her down like a pile of rocks.

Aunt Mag was standing outside her bedroom. She looked phenomenally tall in a Persian blue trouser suit with her braid coiled like a snake atop her head.

'Might I have a quick word?' she said icily, then pushed open the door.

Swallowing, Metty peered into her room. Pumpkin was no longer hanging from the chandelier, but had parked himself on the windowsill next to a row of horrible toys and was sniffing each one in turn. He perked up when he saw Metty, flashing her his toothiest grin, then poked a large (and probably cursed) nutcracker soldier.

'Eat?' he asked in a hopeful voice.

'I wouldn't recommend it,' Aunt Mag said curtly, then snapped the door shut and turned her ferocious gaze onto Metty. 'Just out of curiosity, are you planning to obey any of my rules?'

'Definitely,' Metty said. 'Some of them. Probably.'

Aunt Mag rolled her eyes, then pointed sternly at the bedroom door. 'That creature stays inside this house. Do you understand, or must I make myself clearer?'

'His *name* is Pumpkin.'

'His name won't be anything if the police get wind of him,' Aunt Mag said, then frowned at Metty's rucksack. 'Running away already? That didn't take long.'

'I'm not actually,' Metty said, dropping the bag at her feet. 'At least not if you agree to my conditions.'

'Oh? How intriguing. Let's hear them then.'

'All right,' Metty said, swallowing nervously again. 'I want to look for my dad, and I know you're not telling me everything.'

'Funny, I thought we discussed this last night,' said Aunt Mag.

'Yes, but last night I didn't know about this house.'

'This house?'

'What's in it, I mean. All the cursed things you've collected. The *illegal* curses.'

Aunt Mag's eyes began to bulge, but then she crossed her arms and smoothed out her expression.

'Are you actually attempting to blackmail me?' she said in a voice so chilling that Metty almost shivered.

'No,' she lied, then squirmed guiltily. 'Well, yes, I suppose I am. But only because I have no choice. And because I'm, um . . . well, evil.'

'Evil?' Aunt Mag repeated, sounding even frostier, if that was possible.

'Yeah,' said Metty, glancing at her fate-hand. Her tattoo

was still hidden under the glove. 'If I'm destined to be a murderer, then I'm probably bad already, aren't I? Deep down, I mean. It just makes sense.'

'What a load of rot,' Aunt Mag snapped. 'You, Miss Jones, are about as evil as that gormless gargoyle of yours. Although I'll admit you are monstrously bold. Trying to blackmail your own aunt. Honestly. Now come on,' she added and strode off down the hallway. 'There's something I need to show you.'

Metty didn't expect the gondola to feel quite so wobbly. After all, it was floating in mid-air, not rocking on a choppy sea. She clung to the side as they set off, gliding up from the pavement, and hardly dared look down at the ground shrinking underneath them.

Aunt Mag seemed perfectly at ease, sitting opposite her on one of the little benches. At the back of the gondola was a man in a pink uniform with golden frills, and he used a long wooden oar to steer them through the air.

When Metty did get up the courage to look over the side, she was rewarded with a spectacular view of the district's Halloween decorations. Giant sparkling spiders crawled over the rooftops of Highfate. Round orange pumpkins with faces carved into them rolled along the pavements, the littlest ones trying to escape the bigger hungry ones.

Winding lazily through the district was the wide ink river.

Metty was surprised to see that it wasn't indigo any more, but soft lilac dappled with silver and pearly blue.

The view almost distracted her from thinking about the captain, but then that awful feeling settled in her stomach again: a leaden sense of dread. Where was he? Hiding, or captured, in danger somewhere? She couldn't bear to imagine him hurt.

Forcing those thoughts away, she took out her dictionary and a pencil. She hadn't seen Sundar's fate the night before, so she scribbled his name on the blank back page. She really hoped the boy wouldn't turn out to be 'the one'. At the moment, she couldn't think of any reasons to write beneath his name.

Stupidly bossy, she added to the list under Aunt Mag, then *Doesn't like Pumpkin*.

After that, Metty wrote down her uncle's name and searched the book for his fate too.

MASKS: *associated with the theatre, or deceptive tendencies*

Deceptive tendencies? She chewed the end of her pencil. Did that mean lying?

'What are you writing, Metty?' Aunt Mag said.

'Nothing!' she replied, shutting the dictionary.

Her aunt gave her a suspicious look, but then her gaze

dropped to Metty's rucksack and became pensive. Suddenly she raised her hand and pointed skyward to the cathedral at the very top of New London. It was dark and ugly in the morning light, like a burn mark on the fluffy white clouds.

'*That* is what I wanted you to see,' Aunt Mag said. 'Know what we call it?'

Metty shook her head.

'The Naked Cathedral.'

'Why?' she asked, wondering why on earth her aunt wanted to show her some old church.

'Because of something that happened there before you were born, a very nasty rebellion.' Aunt Mag's gaze became even more serious, and her lips hardly moved as she said: 'I take it you've heard of the Black Moths?'

CHAPTER FOURTEEN

The Naked Cathedral

The Black Moths. There was that name again, echoed last night in a dozen headlines.

Metty swallowed, feeling nervous, though she wasn't sure why.

'Yeah, I think so. There's been stuff about them on the news, and I saw all those articles in your study last night.'

'Did you indeed?' said Aunt Mag, pinching her lips. 'Well, the Black Moths were the ones behind the rebellion. The Naked Cathedral used to be covered in statues, you see, hundreds of angels and demons, gargoyles on every roof and turret, and now there aren't any at all.'

'What happened to them?' Metty asked uneasily.

'They came to life,' Aunt Mag said. 'Specifically, they

were brought to life with magic, then used to attack a square full of innocent people.'

'But why would anyone do that?'

'It was a protest, Metty, a violent, cowardly protest against those in charge of this city, and it got a lot of people hurt, even killed.'

'But you said this happened ages ago, right, before I was even born?' Metty said, thinking of the posters she'd seen around New London and the shadow moth in the station last night. 'So how come they're back now? What are they even protesting?'

'Magic laws, mostly. The Black Moths believe everyone should have access to ink, not just the rich and powerful. And many people happen to agree with that principle, myself included. It's their methods I find indefensible.

'Magic is unlimited in New London, you understand – that's the whole *point* of the city, why it was built in the first place. But back then we had a governor who was proposing laws to control the use of ink, just like down in the Old Capitals. Fortunately, those laws never came into power, so one could argue that the Cathedral Rebellion achieved its purpose. Not that that justifies the damage it caused, or the lives lost. Anyway, the reason I'm telling you this is that, right now, there are almost no magic restrictions in New London. But there *are* a handful, and the most important one – the one *you* need to know about – is the Pinocchio Law.'

'The Pinocchio Law?' Metty said with a slight scoff.

'I know, stupid name, but this is serious and I need you to listen. It's been illegal to bring inanimate objects to life in New London for nearly fifteen years – ever since the attack on the cathedral. That means statues, furniture, decorations. Anyone caught using magic that way could end up in jail for a very long time. I hope you understand what I'm saying.'

She flashed a pointed look at Metty's rucksack, where Pumpkin had been stashed the night before.

'But I didn't . . .' Metty stopped and glanced at the gondolier. He'd turned his head and was pretending not to eavesdrop. '*I* haven't brought anything to life. I don't even have a tether.'

'Doesn't matter,' Aunt Mag said quietly. 'My point is that any such *illegal creatures* would be disenchanted on the spot if they were ever discovered. And disenchantment is a lot like death, you understand? So we have to be very careful about always obeying the law.'

'But what about those?' Metty said, pointing at the Halloween decorations tearing through the streets.

'Oh, they're not alive, not really. They're just enchanted to behave a certain way. If you look closely, you'll notice them repeating the same actions over and over like the little figures inside a clock. See?'

Aunt Mag was right. Metty watched one of the purple spiders scuttle around a rooftop. Eventually, it climbed onto the chimney and wriggled a few of its twinkly legs. Sure enough, it seemed to reset after that and started retracing its steps, moving in the exact same pattern. It was all just a clever illusion.

'All right, then what about the birds?' Metty said, looking down at the lampposts. They were plain black poles again like when she'd first arrived in New London. All the solar birds must have flown off at dawn. 'They're definitely alive.'

'Well, yes, but they're an exception,' said Aunt Mag. 'I told you about them last night. The birds were almost disenchanted after the rebellion, but the citizens of New London put up a good fight and the governor agreed to keep them. Anyway, I happen to know that the man who made them is extremely dead, so it would be an awful bother to send him to prison. Unlike certain other people.'

Metty nibbled her lip and stared at her knees. She knew what Aunt Mag was trying to tell her. But Pumpkin wasn't like those Halloween decorations, pretending to be alive just to entertain people in the streets. He wasn't artwork or a mindless toy – he was real. He was hers, and the thought of him being disenchanted made her stomach churn. She had to protect him.

'Listen,' Aunt Mag said, reaching out and patting Metty's

gloved hand. 'It just means being careful, that's all. We can do that, can't we?'

Metty gave an anxious nod. 'But,' she said, her mind returning to the newspaper cuttings on Aunt Mag's desk, 'if the Black Moths got what they wanted last time, then why are they back now?'

'Because we have a new governor. One who keeps threatening to bring in absurd laws to restrict the use of magic, even stricter than those proposed last time – but that's a conversation for another day,' Aunt Mag said, and leaned over the side of the gondola. 'Perfect, we're flying up to the Gold District now. I need to stop by the bank.'

Metty felt her head spin. She wanted to finish talking about the Black Moths, suspicious of why her aunt was so keen to change the subject. 'But what about the captain? We can't just—'

'Try to be patient, Metty.' Aunt Mag sighed. 'I've got a plan to find your father. Trust me.'

The Gold District was a stately part of the city, a winding street full of accountants and moneylenders. The Bank of New London stood at the very top, casting an impressive shadow on the pavement.

The building was even grander inside. Metty's footsteps echoed on the marble floor, and pillars of pure gold stretched up to the ceiling. It was mostly like an ordinary bank with counters where people could ask for money, doorways leading to offices and safes built into the walls. But there was also a row of mysterious tubs at the back of the hall shaped like hourglasses. Pipes ran into the glass tubs from the ceiling, filling them up with golden liquid.

'That's . . . that's ink, isn't it?' Metty said as she and Aunt Mag approached them.

She could tell the ink was magical by its thickness and the way it gleamed, catching the sunlight pouring through the bank's stained-glass windows. But this sort wasn't indigo or lilac like New London's river. Instead, it was the colour of honey.

Metty frowned, noticing the signs on each hourglass.

WORLD'S PUREST PERUVIAN INK said one.

EXTRACTED FROM THE LOCHS OF SCOTLAND said the next.

MINED FROM THE HIMALAYAS read a third.

They were each priced by the drop, the Himalayan the cheapest, the Peruvian the most expensive.

'What's the difference between them?' Metty asked Aunt Mag, who'd taken out her magic meter, the one that looked like a pocket watch.

'Some ink isn't as pure as others,' she explained, pulling Metty over to one of the counters, where they joined the back of a short queue. 'It'll still do the job, but it's not as powerful and runs out more quickly. The less pure sort is cheaper,

141

of course. You remember I told you that ink keeps the city flying?'

Metty nodded, her eyes drifting back to the shimmering tubs.

'There's a core at the centre of New London – a big mechanical heart that ink flows in and out of like blood. That's why we have the river, to keep it churning, and that same ink powers our magic meters too.'

Metty was quiet for a moment, imagining the ink river coursing through the heart of New London. 'Hang on. If ink makes the city fly, then what happens if it ever runs out? Would we drop out of the sky?'

'You don't need to worry about that. Our ink stores never run low. New London gets a top-up, at least once a year, from the finest ink reserves in the world, straight into the river. Then that flows through the core and keeps everything powered: the gondolas, the lightning chambers—'

'Can I help you, Ms Jones?' a bank teller said suddenly. They'd reached the front of the queue.

'Here for a refill,' Aunt Mag replied and handed over her magic meter. 'The Peruvian ink, if you'd be so kind. Fill her up to the top.'

'Right away, Ms Jones.'

'That's the strongest sort, isn't it?' Metty whispered as the bank teller stepped out from behind the counter and made his way to the big glass tubs at the back of the hall.

She watched, fascinated, as the man turned a key in a lock on the Peruvian hourglass, making a small tap appear. Then he unstoppered Aunt Mag's magic meter and attached it to the tap. Peruvian ink began to flow into the meter, but the bank teller was quick to turn the key once it was full, careful not to waste a single drop. He stoppered the meter and returned to the desk.

Metty gasped when she heard how much it had cost to refill. She'd had no idea that magic was so expensive. She wanted to peek at Aunt Mag's meter and see the ink glistening inside it, but her aunt put it away once she'd finished paying the teller.

'I hope you're ready,' she said, sparkling at Metty as she steered her back towards the doors.

'Ready for what?'

'I'm taking you to buy your first tether.'

Metty's blood ran cold. 'But you can't! It's not safe.'

'What, giving you access to unpredictable and catastrophically dangerous magic? Yes, it is a bold choice on my part, but, after some careful consideration, I've decided that it's necessary. You need to be able to protect yourself, and I might not always be around to do it.'

'But Aunt Mag . . . I can't use magic. What about my fate?

What about what happened in Wales with the rain? Someone could've died!'

'From a bit of drizzle? I doubt it. Don't be silly, Metty. Of course you need a tether. Frankly, it's ridiculous that you don't have one already.'

Metty's jaw tightened stubbornly. 'It's to keep everyone safe.'

'Safe from what?'

'From *me*!'

Aunt Mag only snorted and propelled her through the station doors, into the sunshine. 'Terrifying as you are, I think we'll all survive.'

CHAPTER FIFTEEN

Tethers

The aromas wafting from the perfume shop in Inkriver Market had changed overnight. This time, Metty breathed in a smell of clean sheets that turned into lavender soap, just like the kind they'd used in their Old London townhouse. The last notes were sweet and familiar, a fruity blend of apricot and vanilla – her mother's favourite perfume.

'Wrong direction!' Aunt Mag sighed. She caught the belt on Metty's coat and reined her in like a wild horse before she could drift away across the square. 'Carry on like this and I'll make you wear a peg on your nose. Come on.'

She led Metty to the tether tailor and threw open the door. The room beyond was colourful and welcoming, with lots of gloves displayed on mannequins and a counter in the middle shaped like a crescent moon. A balcony ran round the whole shop.

On the counter was a large grey cat. Metty stopped when it narrowed its emerald eyes and growled.

'Play nice, Cleo,' said a voice from above.

Leaning over the balcony was a woman with dark brown skin wearing a yellow bohemian dress that flowed all the way to her ankles. A voluminous Afro haloed her face, and her smile seemed to radiate light like the brightest sunbeam.

'Ignore her,' she added to Metty as she came down the spiralling staircase and joined them on the shop floor. 'She's funny around new customers, but I've got a good feeling about you.'

'Uh, thanks,' Metty said, edging away from the cat, which shot her a hateful look, then started grooming itself with vicious displeasure.

'Care to introduce me, Mag?' the woman said.

'Oh yes, how rude of me. This is Metty, my clever, charming and annoyingly disobedient niece. And *this* is Kiki Darego, also clever and charming and the best tether tailor in all of New London. And probably the whole world.'

Kiki laughed, putting her hands on her hips. 'I think you might be a little biased.'

'Well, maybe, but I bet it's true,' Aunt Mag said. Then she added, for Metty's benefit, 'Kiki and I are old friends.'

'Friends?' Kiki said, raising an eyebrow at Aunt Mag, whose face turned rosy.

Metty stared at her aunt in astonishment. She hadn't thought anything could make Magnificent Jones blush.

'Anyway,' she said, briskly changing the subject, 'exciting day – Metty's come for her first tether, and I wouldn't dream of taking her elsewhere.'

'I hope you're not angling for a discount,' Kiki said. She winked at Metty as she led her to the mannequin hands in the shop window. 'Now then, did any of these catch your eye from outside? You should go with your gut, you know, pick whichever one makes your heart sing.'

'None of them,' Metty said firmly, frowning at the display. There were gloves of every colour imaginable, made from silk, satin, cotton, velvet, wool and lace. Her eye was drawn to the blue one she'd seen last night, with the pattern of white birds, though she tried to hide it.

'Hmm, it'll have to be something from the back then.'

'Hang on.' Aunt Mag sighed, folding her arms. 'Don't be stubborn, Metty. You need a tether, whether you like it or not.'

'A reluctant customer?' said Kiki in surprise. 'That's new.'

'Show her your fate,' Aunt Mag said gently.

Metty scowled and shook her head. Had her aunt gone mad? It was supposed to be a secret. Her father had warned her never to show anybody.

147

'It's all right, Metty. I trust Kiki with my life and, more importantly, I trust her with yours. You can let her see.'

Kiki gave Metty an encouraging grin. Her own tattoo was a multicoloured tether, rather fittingly.

'Discretion's my policy. And I've seen more fates in this store than I can count.'

Not one like this, Metty thought as she eased off her right glove, holding it self-consciously in front of her stomach. The smile vanished from Kiki's face like a handprint wiped from a window. It was replaced by an expression Metty knew only too well. Fear and distrust.

'Statistically speaking, it's not likely to be you,' Metty said quietly, fighting an urge to bury her hands in her coat pockets.

Kiki frowned. 'What's not?'

'Whoever I murder.'

'Oh, child.' A kind smile restored the light to Kiki's face, and she took Metty's fated hand, pressing it between her own. 'You're not the only one cursed by fate. Trust me.'

Metty felt a little better after that. Perhaps not everyone was quite so unforgiving as Mrs Pope and Mr Ratchet.

'Look, why don't we start slowly?' Kiki said. 'Try one on and see how you feel?'

'All right,' Metty agreed with the tiniest flutter of excitement. She pointed at the blue tether with the white birds. 'What about that one?'

To her disappointment, the glove she'd chosen didn't fit well. It was too small and kept biting into her wrist.

'Definitely not,' Kiki said, tugging it off Metty's hand.

'But aren't you a tailor? Couldn't you adjust it or something?'

'No, no, no, that's not how this works. The right tether – *your* tether – will fit like . . . well, like a glove. You'll see. Let's try another.'

They went through eight potential tethers in all sorts of colours and patterns, but none were quite right. Some were baggy or tight, others too long in the fingers or too short; some itched and others were slippery. Metty blanched when Kiki presented her with a violet tether that looked eerily like the glove holding the skull in Metty's fate. She refused to even try it on.

'Why don't the tethers have holes in them?' she asked. 'Most do, don't they, to show a person's fate?'

'That's part of my job,' Kiki said. 'I cut the hole afterwards, once you've found the right tether.' She threw a glance at Aunt Mag. 'Unless a person wants to keep their fate hidden for some reason. Then I leave the glove whole. Hold on, I've just had a thought.'

Kiki disappeared into the back of the store. When she returned, she was holding a box with a pale grey glove inside it.

Metty knew she'd found her tether the moment her fingers brushed the fabric, which was not quite velvet or cotton. A funny tingle ran through her like the pleasant shiver you get when you step into cold water on a scorching day. Although . . . her heart sank. The glove was terribly plain and such a boring colour. She'd hoped for something interesting like Aunt Mag's bone pattern, or vibrant like Kiki's lime-green tether.

But then she slid her hand into the grey glove and it was . . . perfect. Like wearing a second skin.

Metty flipped over her hand. To her surprise, the tether wasn't plain at all. Hidden on the palm was a raven with its wings spread in flight. Real feathers were sewn into the fabric, tiny and dark as night.

'It's beautiful,' she breathed, trying to ignore the dread knotting tighter round her heart. Wearing the tether felt so right, but what if buying it made her fate come true?

'Looks like we've found our winner,' Kiki said.

Metty felt a swell of sadness as she looked down at her glove. The captain should have been here with her – both her parents should. Getting your first tether was supposed to be special, one of those moments you cherished forever, like a person's fating. She wondered what her father would say if he was there. Probably something to make her laugh and stop fretting. Just then, she missed him more than anything.

'Right, Kiki,' Aunt Mag said, whipping out her purse. 'How much is this going to cost me?'

Metty fidgeted while her aunt paid for the glove, rocking on her heels.

'Look, if I do decide to use the tether—'

'You *will* use it,' Aunt Mag said, shooting her a firm look.

'Then won't I need a magic meter too? Tethers don't work without one, do they?'

'I'll put you on mine once we're back at Winter's Knock.'

'But that makes it even more dangerous! How am I meant to know how much ink I'm using if *you've* got the meter?'

'Good question. You won't, but I have faith in you,' Aunt Mag said as she finished counting out banknotes, then put away her purse. 'So, if that's all sorted, we'll be off.'

Kiki showed them both to the door. 'Don't forget about Halloween, Mag. You promised me dinner.'

'Yes, well, we'll have to get through the conference first,' Aunt Mag said, then grimaced as though she'd misspoken.

Metty stopped in the doorway, frowning up at her aunt. 'What conference? Is it something to do with the Black Moths?'

Kiki shushed her, putting a finger to her lips.

'It's nothing to concern *you* at all,' Aunt Mag said, nudging Metty through the door. 'Now come along. It's about time we—'

'Hey!' Metty cried.

She'd hardly stepped outside when somebody barged into her and snatched the brand-new tether, packaged in a smart blue box, from her hand. Her jaw dropped in outrage. The thief was a red-haired child wearing a shabby coat with an old fleece collar, and she was already darting away across Inkriver Market.

'Oi! Give that back!' Metty bellowed and charged after her without a second thought. Aunt Mag tried to grab her, but Metty was too quick, her eyes fixed on the girl's back.

'Thief!' she shouted as she ran.

A few people turned to stare, but none of them were fast enough to catch the girl, who paused as she reached the mouth of an alleyway and smirked back at Metty. Her face was pale and smothered in freckles, her nose snubbed and her hazel eyes small and mean.

She shook the tether box like a victorious taunt, then disappeared.

CHAPTER SIXTEEN

The Magic Thief

Rage sparked in Metty's belly, then roared up into a fire. She may not have wanted a tether, but that one was hers. It might as well have been moulded to her hand, and she wasn't going to let some sneering pickpocket run off with it.

The girl was still in sight when Metty reached the alleyway, although she was about to vanish round another corner. Metty chased after her, ignoring the prickly feeling in her lungs and the slam of her heart. The child was fast, but *she* was determined, and she followed the girl along three more alleyways and across another square. By then, Metty had no idea where she was, but she'd run too far to give up and turn back. She wanted her tether.

The thief shot an anxious glance over her shoulder. Seeing her panic filled Metty with grim satisfaction and helped her push through the ache in her legs and the rub of her leather shoes. She was gaining on the girl, almost close enough to hear her panting breaths, when she threw herself round a corner and—

The thief was gone.

Metty frowned in despair at the brick wall in front of her. The passage she'd chased the girl into was a dead end, but that didn't make any sense . . .

'Miss Jones?' said a husky voice behind her.

Metty jumped and spun round. A man was standing on the other side of the alleyway, blocking her route to the street. He was tall with a sallow complexion and a flop of dark, greasy hair. The body of a dead animal was slung round his shoulders. It looked like a pale fox, its eyes glassy in the sunlight.

'Miss Jones, is that you?' he went on, moving closer to Metty.

She opened her mouth to reply, but her voice had deserted her. She felt very alone suddenly, glancing left and right. Would anyone hear in the street if she screamed? Would they come?

'Don't be afraid,' the man said. He held up his palms.

He wore a leather tether on his right hand. She could just see something small and black pinned inside his sleeve. It looked like a tiny butterfly.

Or a moth.

'I'm a friend of your aunt's, and she's dreadful worried about you. A kid like you shouldn't run off on your own, not in this city.' The man extended his hand to Metty. The fate in the hole of his tether was hard to make out, some kind of wild animal with large teeth. 'Why don't you come with me, eh? I'll see you back to your aunt. C'mere.'

Metty took a step back, shaking her head.

'It's all right,' the man said softly, coaxingly, closing the gap between them. 'I'm trying to look after you. You can trust me – I know who you are. Meticulous Jones, ain't that right? Quite a mouthful, that is.'

He smiled at her, baring his sharp teeth. There was something wolfish about him, something that made her skin crawl.

'There's dangerous sorts about,' he went on. 'Men you wouldn't like to run into.'

'Please, I can find my own way.'

'Let's not risk it.' Still grinning, he grabbed at Metty's hand. His dirty fingers brushed her skin, almost catching her wrist. She jumped back just in time, and the man's face contorted in anger, making him twice as ugly. 'I said come here!'

He dived towards Metty again, but stopped when something hit him in the chest – a fistful of copper pennies. They exploded as they struck him, bursting into flames, and the man threw up his arms to protect his face. One coin bounced off Metty's foot and rolled away over the cobblestones, spitting sparks like a firework. She watched it spin and then transform into an ordinary penny as it clunked sideways onto the ground.

Metty twisted round to see who'd thrown the coins and found herself staring into a pair of hazel eyes, surrounded by clouds of red hair.

'Come on,' snapped the magic thief, and then she grabbed Metty's hand.

The girl dragged her towards the end of the passageway. Metty glanced over her shoulder, checking on the man who was frantically patting out the flames on his chest, then turned round in the nick of time. Her nose was almost grazing the brick wall. What on earth were they going to do, climb over it?

'Come *on*,' the thief groaned again, then charged straight ahead. Instead of smacking into the wall, the girl passed right through it like a ghost.

Metty dug her heels in, refusing to follow, and stared dumbfounded at the bricks in front of her. They looked so solid and real.

'Oi!' the man bellowed, lumbering after her. 'Don't you move!'

There wasn't time to be cautious. Shutting her eyes, Metty inhaled sharply and ran forward. She expected to hear a loud crack, to feel pain in her forehead, but instead there was a rush of wind and a tinkling chorus of bells.

Metty opened her eyes. She was standing in a street packed with cyclists, flying up and downhill on wind bikes and ringing their bells aggressively at any pedestrians in their way. The red-haired thief was waiting for her. Astonished, Metty turned to look back at the wall just in time to see a filthy hand burst through the bricks. Its fingers scraped along her shoulder, but Metty wriggled away before they could find purchase.

'Move, *now!*' the magic thief said.

She ran into the road, dodging all the bicycles with their bright umbrellas. Metty sprinted after her. She hadn't much choice. She stopped to avoid being hit by a raging cyclist and then another a few seconds later. The breeze from their umbrellas slapped her in the face, making her hair flap.

The man with the dead fox on his shoulders had come through the wall now, and was chasing them across the road, his eyes narrowed in determination. Metty knew at once that she would rather be knocked down by a wind bike than fall into his clutches.

'This way!' said the thief.

She was leading Metty towards a gap between two shopfronts and another dead end. There was nothing beyond the short passageway but clear blue sky and wisps of cloud, and yet the girl didn't seem afraid, bounding towards it.

'Wait!' Metty cried as they finally crossed the road and sprinted between the stores. The edge of the city was fast approaching – they would surely fall right off the street and plunge to their deaths.

'Just trust me,' the girl said.

Metty might have laughed and called her crazy, but there was no time. They only had seconds before they ran out of cobblestones, and the man was still coming after them.

'Get ready to grab on,' the thief panted. She wasn't slowing down.

'To *what?*' said Metty shrilly.

The girl didn't answer. Instead, she rushed off the edge of the pavement as though expecting the clouds to firm up beneath her. Metty's heart faltered, and a breath caught in her throat. But the girl didn't drop through the air like a rock. For a second, she just floated, like she was held by an invisible hand, and then she began to rise, drifting up at a rapid pace.

The girl twirled round like a ballerina as she soared and gazed down at Metty.

'Hurry!' she hissed.

Metty swallowed, looking back at the road. The man would reach her any second. She had to do *something*.

'*Oh God, oh God,*' she muttered, screwing up one eye. She lifted her right foot and placed it tentatively out in front of her. The air felt horribly thin, like she would fall right through it if she leaned forward.

'Come on!' Metty told herself in a furious whisper. Footsteps pounded the cobblestones behind her. 'Come on, come on! Please don't die . . .'

Just as the man's shadow cooled the back of her head and she heard his rasping breath, Metty seized her courage and leaped off the side of New London.

CHAPTER SEVENTEEN

Ill-fated

Metty was falling for a heartbeat, then hovering in mid-air just like when she'd travelled by lightning with Aunt Mag. She looked down. It wasn't a sheer drop to the ocean, but the bottom half of the city was far enough away that she was certain she would die if she impacted those scruffy buildings below.

The man caught himself before he could tumble off the edge of the pavement, then lunged for Metty with an animal grunt. He couldn't quite reach her, and she was already shooting skyward. She tore her eyes from the stranger and glanced up at the clouds and the blindingly blue sky.

The magic thief was waiting for her on the nearest rooftop, holding a rope that was looped round the chimney. She stuck out her hand.

'Thanks,' Metty said, grabbing it. The girl pulled her in, still clinging to the frayed rope.

Gravity weighed Metty down as soon as her feet touched the rooftop. Relieved, she let go of the girl's hand and peered at the street below. The building they were on was four-storeyed and the man was an ominous shadow on the pavement, staring up at them.

'Don't worry. He can't fly up here.'

'How do you know?' Metty asked, watching the man anxiously.

'Too heavy. Only kids'll float if they fall off New London. It's some old enchantment to stop toddlers wandering off the edge while their daft parents aren't looking. Although we'd better move before that bloke comes after us another way.'

With that, the girl set off along the rooftop, treading carefully on the crumbly slates. The blue box with the tether inside it was sticking out of her coat pocket.

'Wait,' Metty said, trotting after her. She wasn't half as confident walking over the lopsided roof. 'Do you know that man down there?'

'Nope,' said the girl without a backward glance.

'But you came back to help me.'

'Well, I could tell he was dodgy. Don't you know how to recognise scum?'

'He had something hidden in his sleeve. A pin or something,'

Metty said, peeking over the side of the roof again. The man was stalking them in the street below, prowling along the pavement like a scabby old dog. 'I think he might be one of those people . . . a Black Moth.'

The girl paused and scrunched up her nose. 'Well, that's just brilliant. What you got yourself mixed up with that lot for?'

'You know who they are?'

'Who the Moths are? Course I do. I ain't stupid. What does a bunch of crazy terrorists want with you?'

'No idea,' Metty said.

The thief hummed distrustfully, then carried on marching over the rooftop. Most of the buildings were terraced in New London, and their connected roofs snaked along like a bumpy road. They were heading slowly back downhill, in the direction of Inkriver Market, passing from Wheel Street, full of stores selling wind bikes, helmets and spare parts, to Blotter Square, crammed with bookshops, stationery suppliers and the New London Library shaped like a giant clock. Metty knew that if they followed the ink river they would get back to the market and hopefully find Aunt Mag.

'Did you use magic on that brick wall back there?' she called to the thief. 'So we could get through it?'

'Nope. Just knew it was there, that's all. I know lots of things. Have we got rid of him yet?'

Metty stopped and frowned at the street. She couldn't see the man slinking along the pavement any more.

'Think so,' she said.

The girl raised her lip, dissatisfied. 'We'll go a bit further just in case. Keep up, all right? I got stuff to do.'

'Stealing, you mean?' growled Metty.

'Yeah, exactly.'

'Maybe you could give me back my tether.'

The thief ignored her, swinging nimbly round a chimney. Perched on top of it was one of those enchanted spiders, but it didn't seem interested in them. Metty hurried past it. Arachnids were not her favourite thing, even when they were purple and glittery and not really alive.

After several more rooftops, they came to a building with a fire escape and climbed down to the street, the magic thief leading the way. Metty paused when her feet hit the pavement and glanced left and right. The stranger was nowhere to be seen, though she had an unshakable sense of being watched.

Metty frowned as something glided past her foot: a shadow that crept up the wall of the building next to her, spreading tar-black wings.

'Another one?' she muttered, watching the shadow of the moth float down the street. 'What are those things?'

'Reminders,' the girl said impatiently. There were so many

ginger freckles on her face, they formed a constellation. 'Black Moths send 'em after an attack, so people know it was them what did it.'

'What sort of attacks?'

The thief shrugged. 'Explosions. Buildings vanishing overnight. Dark magic stuff, like making it rain blood on Red Ink Street the other week.'

'That's awful.'

'Yeah, well, the Moths ain't known for being cuddly. Right, can you find your way back to Inkriver Market from here?' the girl said, her eyes darting round the street.

'Wait, you're not just swanning off with my tether,' Metty snapped, crossing her arms.

The girl only snorted, then turned round and walked off. Metty chased after her, half jogging to keep up.

'Give it back!'

'You're going in the wrong direction,' the thief said without slowing down.

'I don't care. Give me back my tether.'

'Can't. I need it. Anyway, you owe me. I saved your life, remember?'

'You *might* have saved my life,' Metty said, jumping sideways to avoid a wind bike that came racing towards her. 'I don't know what that man wanted.'

'Nothing good if he's a Moth.'

'Anyway, that's not the point. Look, that tether you stole, it's *mine*, the first one I've ever had! And it's not connected to a meter right now. It can't even do magic.'

'Don't matter. Still worth something. And you've got big hands for a kid – that'll bring up the price. You ain't a leftie, are you?'

'Give me back my tether!' Metty said in a dangerous voice and made a grab for the box. The thief was too quick. She seized Metty's wrist.

'Listen, you ain't getting it back. I got brothers and sisters at home, lots of 'em, and some'll go hungry tonight if I don't bring back the goods.'

'Have you considered finding an honest profession?' Metty asked icily.

The girl looked scornful. 'How many honest, well-paying jobs d'you reckon there are for a kid, specially a girl?'

'You could sell newspapers or shine shoes or—'

'Do you want to shine shoes day in, day out?'

Metty tossed her head. '*I* don't need—'

'Exactly. *You* don't need, and I do.' The girl's eyes crawled over Metty, taking in everything about her, from her neat brown hair to her smart leather shoes. 'Look at you in your pretty dress, not a mark on it,' she sneered. 'Don't tell me your ma can't afford another tether.'

'That was my aunt, not my mother.'

'Small difference.'

'There's an enormous difference, actually,' Metty said, trying to shake off the girl's hand. Her grip was strong for someone so bony. 'And you don't know anything about me.'

'Oh really?' the girl said. She tugged at the plain glove on Metty's hand. 'Bet you got an elite fate, didn't you? Bet your parents paid for something good. Let me guess: pot of gold, is it, or a fancy tiara, maybe a great big castle?'

'Let go of me!' Metty snarled, but it was too late. The thief had already torn off the glove, revealing her ugly fate. Surprise flashed across the girl's face and chased away her smugness, for a moment, at least.

'I ain't seen one like that before,' she said, dropping Metty's wrist. 'What's it mean?'

Metty snatched back her glove and put it on. 'It means I'm destined to be a stone-cold killer,' she said with great relish.

The girl laughed. 'You? Yeah, right.'

'And what are you fated to be? The foulest person who ever lived?'

'Nah, that would be my Uncle Doug. He eats his own toenails.'

Grinning, the girl bit off her glove. She wasn't wearing a tether but a pair of rust-coloured mittens. She waved her fist in front of Metty's nose. The girl's fate was a red hand holding a diamond ring between its finger and thumb.

'What's that then?' Metty said, unimpressed. 'You're destined to become a jeweller or something?'

'No, dummy. It means thief.' The girl pulled her mitten back on, then shrugged. 'Being ill-fated's not so bad. At least you don't have to bother with guilt. What's the point of feeling rubbish about something that ain't in your control? It'd be like being sorry for having red hair or too many freckles. Some of us are just born rotten. No use crying about it.'

'Well, you might not feel bad, but I do. And I don't care what my fate says,' Metty lied. 'I'm trying to be good.'

The girl looked at her in disgust. 'Why?'

'Because. That's the right thing to do.'

'Says who?'

Metty was still coming up with an answer when a piercing whistle sounded at the end of the street. The girl stiffened beside her and glanced urgently back and forth. Heading straight for them was a police officer in a navy uniform.

The thief started to back away, getting ready to bolt, but there was a second officer at the other end of the street, blocking her path to freedom. She and Metty were sandwiched between them, nowhere to run.

The girl swore under her breath, then shot Metty a look that was half fierce, half desperate. *Help me*, it seemed to say, *or else.*

'What have we here?' said the first police officer, his

shadow spilling over the thief like a bucket of oil. 'Thought I recognised your face. You brats from Sinner's Oak all have the same look. Bit high up in the city today, aren't we?'

'There's no law stopping me from coming up here,' the girl said moodily, scuffing the dusty pavement with her boot.

'Maybe not, but there's laws about grubby pickpockets. What's that box you got there? Hand it over.'

'Excuse me, that's mine,' Metty said as the girl surrendered the blue box.

The police officer frowned down at her, suspicious. 'That so?'

'Yes, it has my tether inside. I can prove it if you like – it fits my hand perfectly.'

'No need, miss. I believe you.' The officer's moustache bristled as his gaze shifted back to the thief. 'And if that's so, then perhaps you'd like to report a case of stolen property.'

Metty opened her mouth, getting ready to explain everything, about the magic thief and the sinister man. And then she glimpsed the girl in the corner of her eye.

Her freckly face was drawn in resignation, her eyes dull and fixed on the pavement, the corners of her mouth downturned. Metty's anger faded, replaced by a new feeling she couldn't quite name. Something like guilt, or even a prickle of shame. She turned back to the police officer who was waiting for her to speak.

'No, thank you,' she said, surprised by the strength of her own voice. The girl's head jerked towards her as the man's moustache twitched again.

'Really?' he said. 'In that case, might I ask why she was carrying *your* tether in her pocket?'

'I asked her to hold it for me.'

'I see. And you're sure about that? No one's making you feel threatened, like you have to lie?'

Metty adopted an innocent expression. 'I'm not sure what you mean, officer.'

The man harrumphed, sticking his thumbs through his belt loops. He glared down at the thief again.

'You'd best clear off then,' he growled, then slapped the tether box back into the girl's hands and gave her a push. 'And get back to your own district before you find yourself in serious trouble.'

'Right you are, officer. So long,' the thief called, thumbing her nose behind his back. The second policeman saw the rude gesture and stared at them coldly as the children inched round him and entered the next street.

They didn't speak at first, absorbing what had just happened.

Metty broke the silence. 'Are the police always—'

'Ignorant pigs? To me, yeah, pretty much. I doubt you've got anything to worry about.'

'Apart from becoming a murderer,' Metty muttered.

The girl looked at her strangely. 'It bothers you, don't it? Being ill-fated.'

'It seriously doesn't bother you?'

'Nah. But I guess killing someone's worse than thieving. You seem all right. I'm sure whoever you knock off has it coming to 'em. Most folks do.'

Metty was about to say something, then stopped, noticing a poster stuck to the side of a building. She grabbed it without thinking and stared at the picture in surprise. It was a portrait of Madame LeBeau, her elegant fingers resting on a spirit phone.

Madame Fayola LeBeau

in Conversation with the Spirits

Witness the World-renowned Prophetess and Medium

FOR ONE WEEK ONLY THIS HALLOWEEN

at the

Glass Peacock Theatre

Doors open at 7pm

'This is her,' Metty said, waving the poster. 'This is the woman who fated me. She's coming to New London.'

'Madame Fayola LeBeau. Sounds fancy. Hey, you could get her to rewrite your fate,' the girl said casually, as though suggesting Metty try out a different hairstyle.

'That's not a thing.'

'Sure it is. My cousin has a friend who knows someone what had it done. You just find the prophetess what fated you and make her change it, easy.'

'Easy?' Metty snorted. 'That's impossible. A person can't change their fate.'

The girl's eyes narrowed. 'Says who?'

They stopped as they came to the end of the bustling street. Metty vaguely recognised where they were; Inkriver Market was only a five-minute walk. Aunt Mag was probably wild with panic by now.

'Here,' the girl said. She held out the blue box.

Metty took it, trying to hide her surprise. 'Thanks. But what about your brothers and sisters? Won't they go hungry?'

'Oh, I'm sure I can nab something else.' The thief smirked and held up her fated hand. 'It's in my nature. And that makes us even anyway. Thanks for not ratting me out back there.'

'It's nothing.'

'It ain't nothing,' the girl said. 'Really, it ain't. I'm Faith, by the way. Faith O'Connell.'

'Metty Jones.'

'Metty? That French or something?'

'No, er, Welsh actually.'

'Oh right. Well, anyway, I'd best be off,' Faith said. She took a step backwards, suddenly shy. 'You can find your way, can't you? The market ain't far.'

'I'll manage,' Metty replied.

'Wait,' the girl said before they could part ways. 'Be careful, okay? That guy from before, he was following you for a while, even when you was up in the gondola.'

'How do you know?'

Faith rolled her eyes. 'Cos I was following you too, dummy. Thought you'd make an easy mark. Guess I got that one wrong.'

'I'll be careful,' Metty said, ignoring a shivery feeling. 'Take care, Faith.'

'You too,' said the magic thief.

Then, with a final wave, she darted down the street and vanished into a crowd of shoppers with armfuls of bright paper bags. Metty sighed as she turned round and followed a hand-shaped signpost pointing her to Inkriver Market. Aunt Mag was going to kill her – if the man from earlier didn't beat her to it.

Metty almost stopped walking as a thought flashed into her head. Maybe *they* were the ones who'd taken her father – the

Black Moths. But what would a bunch of terrorists want with the captain? Surely they wouldn't hurt him if Metty was the one they were actually after. Just thinking about it made her insides twist.

She glanced at her hand, remembering the way Sundar had looked at it the night before. Did the captain's disappearance really have something to do with her tattoo? If so, then how on earth was she supposed to save him?

Faith's words repeated in her mind like a secret spell: *You could get her to rewrite your fate.*

But that was impossible.

Wasn't it?

CHAPTER EIGHTEEN

The Grades of Magic

Aunt Mag didn't kill Metty, but she did become grave and marble-eyed when she heard about the man in the alleyway. Metty described him as best she could, but if her aunt knew who the stranger was, she hid it well.

She was determined to keep Metty close after that and insisted they take a gondola back to the house. Metty was disappointed. She'd wanted to search for the Black Moths, to find more of those awful shadows in case they led her to wherever the Moths were keeping her father (if they really had taken him). But she didn't argue, reluctant to use their name out in the open where she might be overheard.

'I think I know who's after me now,' Metty said the

moment she and Aunt Mag were safely inside Winter's Knock. 'Who was following the captain and chasing us back in Wales. It's the Black Moths! They're the . . .' Her sentence trailed off as she stared at Aunt Mag, whose face was still and unsurprised. 'You knew,' Metty breathed. 'You did, didn't you? You already knew.'

'Yes,' her aunt said quietly.

Metty felt like she'd swallowed a hot coal. 'Then why didn't you tell me?'

'Because it didn't seem necessary, and the situation's complex.'

Metty clenched her hands. What else was Aunt Mag keeping from her?

'Do you know *why* they want me?' she asked thinly. 'They're terrorists!'

'They are now, yes,' Aunt Mag said, watching her carefully. 'But they weren't always. The Moths are a very old organisation, one that's been around almost as long as this city. I told you earlier, their original purpose was to make sure everyone in New London had equal access to magic. Obviously, anyone can *buy* ink in the New Capitals – it's not restricted here like in the cities below – but it's still expensive. It still means some people have more opportunities than others.'

'But doesn't that make the Moths sort of . . . good?' Metty

said. 'I mean, why *should* people have to pay for ink if there's enough to go around?'

'That's an excellent question. Like I said before, many of us share the Moths' ideals and find the thought of ink being reserved for the rich morally despicable. Trouble is, over time, they've become more violent and started opposing *all* restrictions on magic, whatever the rationale for them. I'm pretty sure the Moths' current leader doesn't care about equality in the slightest. They simply want power, and whoever gets in their way . . . well, that's just collateral damage.'

Metty paused for a moment, shivering as she remembered the story about the Naked Cathedral: all the statues the Black Moths had brought to life and used to attack innocent people.

'Hold on though. What's any of that got to do with *me*? If they want free ink for everyone, or even just power . . . how does going after *me* help with that? Or kidnapping the captain?' She hesitated, studying her aunt's face. 'You know that too, don't you? Is it something to do with my fate? Aunt Mag, just tell me!'

'Metty,' Aunt Mag said, her tone sharp as a knife, 'I can't.'

'Why not?'

'Because I swore not to. But' – her aunt took Metty's hands and pressed them – 'I swear that if you ever *need* to know, I will tell you everything. For now, you'll just have to trust me.'

'Who made you swear?'

Aunt Mag only shook her head, refusing to say another word. Scowling, Metty reached into her pocket and took out the poster for Madame LeBeau's show.

'I found this earlier near Inkriver Market. That's the prophetess who fated me, and she's coming to New London on Halloween.'

'I dread to think where you're going with this,' Aunt Mag said, taking the poster from Metty's hand. She held it up, inspecting it.

'Maybe she could help us find the captain. Prophetesses are really powerful, aren't they? And listen, I had an idea before – there's something I want to try. Have you ever heard of a person getting their fate rewritten?'

Aunt Mag lowered the poster and sighed. 'Oh, Metty. You don't need to change your fate. Honestly, you're perfectly fine the way you are.'

Frustration swelled in Metty's chest like a balloon full of hot air. 'How can you say that? How do you expect me to use magic if I'm always scared I'll murder someone? You know what I am, what I'm fated to do.'

Aunt Mag gave her a serious look. 'You are whatever you decide to be. Nobody controls your actions. Nobody but you.'

'But—'

'And I don't want to hear another word about it,' she said, crumpling the poster into a ball. 'I mean it, Metty. Going down that path won't bring you anything but trouble and disappointment. Trust me, I know.'

'*How* do you know?'

Aunt Mag's eyes cooled and her lips drew into a familiar pout. Metty knew what that face meant.

More secrets.

She didn't care what her aunt said. She was determined to track down Madame LeBeau on Halloween night. The prophetess might be able to find the captain. After all, she knew him and Daphne. And maybe Madame LeBeau really could rewrite Metty's fate.

Halloween was only four days away. Metty couldn't ignore such a perfect opportunity, and now she had a tether. If magic was as powerful as everyone said, then surely it could help locate her father. Although using it filled her with dread. She was scared just to wear her glove, especially around other people, and it spent a couple of days tucked safely inside its little box.

'Right, that's enough moping,' Aunt Mag said three days before Halloween, dragging Metty into her study. 'I'm teaching you the grades of magic. If you understand how magic works, then you needn't be afraid of it. You just have to take control, Metty, that's all.'

There were five grades, according to Aunt Mag, one being the least powerful and five the most. The higher the grade of magic you used, the more ink you needed.

'Let me show you,' Aunt Mag said, getting out her magic meter. Golden ink filled a glass tube inside it, although at least a third had disappeared since they'd visited the bank.

'See these lines?' Aunt Mag pointed to the numbered markers inside the meter. There were five altogether. 'These measure how much ink you have left. So long as the ink stays above this top line, that means I can do grade five magic. Once it dips under, then I'll only have enough for grade four, or grade three – you get the picture.'

'So, if the ink's all the way down here . . .' Metty said, putting her thumb on the marker labelled 1.

'That means I can only do grade one magic, very minor stuff. Does that make sense?'

'Sort of. But how do you know which grade does what?'

'It's something of a knack. You'll get a feel for it over time, but there are charts for new magic users. I'll dig one out for you, see if that helps.'

A GUIDE TO THE GRADES OF MAGIC

All acts of magic can be measured by how much ink they require. No measurement is exact, but below you will find some useful estimates. Remember to always use magic responsibly!

GRADE ONE
moving small objects, folding clothes, opening doors, etc.

GRADE TWO
charging up magical appliances, creating a flame, communicating via mirror, etc.

GRADE THREE
animating furniture, changing a person's hair or eye colour, moving heavy objects, etc.

GRADE FOUR
(use with adult supervision)
transforming materials, e.g. stone to sand, disrupting the weather (not recommended), lightning travel, etc.

GRADE FIVE
large acts of destruction
(not encouraged)

The guide was an ancient booklet with the words PROPERTY OF MORAL JONES printed in the top corner. A young Aunt Mag seemed to have crossed her brother's name out and replaced it with her own, then covered the guide in doodles. There was a note at the bottom, in the captain's handwriting: MAGNIFICENT JONES IS A LARGE ACT OF DESTRUCTION.

'Thirty years out of date, but it's better than nothing,' Aunt Mag said, her eyes creasing with a sad smile when she saw her brother's message. Metty realised that her aunt must be missing him too. It made her feel better somehow.

She tried to memorise the booklet, then put it in her dictionary for safekeeping. That evening, she only attempted safe bits of magic – boring grade one stuff. Instead of putting her clothes away, she snapped her fingers and had them fold themselves, and used her tether to make objects fly to her rather than getting up and grabbing them.

'You'll get bored of that pretty quick,' Rupert chuckled as he watched her make a glass of water fill itself at the tap, then float across the kitchen into her open hand.

Metty thought she'd been alone. She was so startled by her uncle's voice that she clenched her fist, and the glass shattered halfway across the room.

'Sorry,' she mumbled, watching Rupert brush shards off his clothes.

'S'all right. Accidents happen. When I got my first tether, I turned our cat into a tarantula. Never could get rid of all those extra legs, poor puss.'

Metty practised in her bedroom after that, away from the others so she wouldn't risk hurting them. She changed the colour of her walls so they reflected whatever mood she was in: sunny yellow when she was happy, bubble-gum pink if she got excited, and a surly charcoal grey whenever she was in a foul temper (which wasn't too often).

Feeling more confident the next day, she tried to liven up the entrance hall too, only to transform the whole area into a humid jungle. Vegetation bulged from the walls, vines coiled up the staircase like vicious green snakes, and tropical flowers kept popping up suddenly and spitting poisonous darts at everyone. They weren't deadly but left a spotty rash that itched for hours afterwards.

'It wasn't meant to be quite so . . . It got a bit out of control,' Metty said sheepishly as her aunt wasted an obscene amount of ink stripping the jungle from the hall.

'I know you're having tremendous fun,' Aunt Mag replied in her flintiest voice, 'and I'm glad you're finally using your tether, but you might have some care. Magic isn't cheap, you know. And it's not necessarily easy to fix.'

That night, once she was in bed, Metty flicked through her dictionary. She stopped when she reached a page with a glaring red eye. It looked identical to the tattoo she'd seen on Madame LeBeau's hand last year.

EYES: *associated with prophetesses, opticians, or having excellent vision*

Metty jotted down the lady's name, then:

Reasons for being 'THE ONE'
She chose my fate

It was a pretty good reason, probably the best in Metty's whole dictionary. She would have to be extra careful when she found Madame LeBeau, especially now that she had a tether. It would be disastrous if the prophetess turned out to be 'the one'. Metty was counting on Madame LeBeau being able to use her power and connections to track down the captain; and, if she was lucky, the woman would change her fate too. Then maybe the Black Moths wouldn't be interested in Metty any more, and they might let her father go.

She thumbed through the dictionary, so full of names and ideas about who she might accidentally . . . Her eyes filled with tears at the thought. How was she supposed to guess who 'the one' might be?

It could be anyone she'd ever met.

CHAPTER NINETEEN

Snakes and Ladders

Metty woke on the morning of Halloween with a heavy feeling, like she'd swallowed a bucket of lead. It had been a week since her birthday, seven whole days since her father had disappeared, and she felt no closer to finding him than when she'd first arrived in New London. Her only hope was tracking down Madame LeBeau, but to do that she would have to get past Aunt Mag, who'd been hellbent on keeping her inside the house ever since the incident with the Black Moth.

Sundar sprang into Metty's room that morning (which was much cosier now all the cursed furniture was gone). He was practically fizzing with excitement as he led her up a secret staircase to a playroom at the top of the house. It was a cheerful space with squishy chairs, a life-sized rocking horse in front of the window, and a thousand toys and games piled up on shelves. Some were ordinary, like chessboards and dolls' houses, while others had special packaging and required magic.

'I've never been able to play with any of these,' Sundar said, grabbing a pile of games from the shelves. 'Not without a tether, but I was thinking about it this morning, and I realised *you* can charge them up.'

'Why don't you have a tether?' Metty asked.

She'd spent a little time with Sundar, but felt like she knew nothing about him. Annoyingly, he made a point of always wearing gloves, so she still hadn't seen his fate. Metty was sure it must be something really bad for Sundar to keep it so well hidden. She wondered if it was as dreadful as her own.

'Haven't got one yet.' The boy shrugged, then pressed a box into Metty's hands. It was a game of snakes and ladders. *Grade Two Magic* read a gold star in the corner. 'You will charge it, won't you? I've always wanted to play.'

She looked at Sundar from the corner of her eye. It had only just occurred to her that she might persuade him to help her sneak out of the house.

'Go on then,' she said.

Aunt Mag had confiscated her tether after the jungle debacle, but she'd given it back that morning. Metty didn't think too much could go wrong if she only used grade two magic.

Inside the box was a plain wooden slab like a chopping board. She flipped it over and discovered a handprint on the other side.

'I think you should put it down,' Sundar said, taking a few steps back. He glanced around, chewing the inside of his cheek. 'I reckon we've got enough room in here.'

'Now what?' Metty said after she'd placed the board on the floor.

'Just hold your hand on top of it for a minute. You know, where the print is.'

Metty did, and a tingle spread through her palm, travelling in waves to the tips of her fingers. The board didn't change, apart from heating up beneath her tether, but she knew when to let go all the same. Her magical instincts were getting sharper every day.

Metty stumbled back, eyes fixed on the board as it swelled suddenly, broadening into a large wooden square that got bigger and bigger until it took up most of the floor. And then, with a cacophony of loud pops, the board sprouted poles like shiny metal limbs. Within seconds, it had grown into a climbing frame that practically touched the ceiling.

Metty stared up in awe at a humungous, three-dimensional board game with colourful numbered squares and real ladders running up and down the four tiers. Purple and red snakes curled round the framework, some short, others frighteningly long. They had heads at both ends instead of tails, and their amber eyes gleamed hungrily at Metty and Sundar as they flicked their tongues.

'We'll be needing this,' Sundar said, grabbing a massive dice that had appeared on the floor in front of them.

Metty didn't answer right away, inspecting the game.

'Is this thing safe?' she finally asked.

'Of course. I'll go first if you're nervous,' Sundar said. He shrugged off his jacket and dumped it on the floor.

Metty took off her cardigan while the boy rolled. She flung it down beside Sundar's jacket, then hesitated, spotting a name tag on his collar. To her surprise, it said *Arjun Singh*.

'Your go, Metty,' Sundar called to her, having already climbed onto the lowest level of the board game. He'd rolled a four and was standing safely on a blue square.

Metty tossed the dice and it landed on a six. She pulled herself onto the first square, then moved to the sixth, which happened to touch the bottom of a ladder.

'Lucky,' Sundar grumbled as she started to climb.

She soon arrived at the thirtieth square. 'Um, Sundar, can I ask you something?' she said, having to lean round the body of a snake that was dangling off the side of the framework like a long magenta rope. Its scales looked terrifyingly real.

The boy wasn't listening. 'Hang on a minute. How are we meant to keep rolling the dice if we have to climb? I guess you could use your tether and roll for me, but that's not really—'

'One sec,' Metty said. Sticking two fingers in her mouth, she whistled for Pumpkin who came gliding into the playroom a few seconds later. 'Pumpkin will roll, won't you, darling? Roll the dice for Sundar.'

Pumpkin seemed a tad confused, dropping onto the dice like a perch. He tucked away his stone wings and cocked his head to one side.

'Eat?'

'No, not eat.' Metty sighed, shaking her head. Really, did he think about anything else?

'He can't actually eat, can he?' Sundar asked.

'No, he just likes to chew things. Pumpkin, no! Not eat, *not* eat – you'll crack your teeth! Play. Pumpkin play with Meh and Sundar.'

'Play!' chanted the gargoyle, smiling gormlessly. 'Pum play!'

'That's right. Now roll the dice. Good boy, that's it.'

It took some coaxing, and quite a bit of patience, but eventually Pumpkin flipped the dice over. Sundar had his second turn, moving to square seven. Deciding that using Pumpkin every time would take far too long, Metty aimed a finger at the dice and rolled with her tether.

'Anyway,' she said, wobbling along to square thirty-five and narrowly avoiding a red snake. Its mouth stretched wide open, then snapped shut in disappointment. 'I was trying to ask before why you've got someone else's name in your jacket. Arjun's not your real name, is it?'

'No,' Sundar replied after a breath of silence. Metty couldn't see him from her current position.

'Who is he then?'

'My brother,' the boy said in a quiet voice. 'My twin. He died.'

'Oh.' Metty winced. 'Um, I'm really sorry. I shouldn't have—'

'It's fine. Honestly. It happened ages ago, and we weren't close.'

Metty wasn't sure she believed him. She thought of the photo on Aunt Mag's desk, the one of Sundar with a woman who she'd assumed was his mother. Had that been Sundar, or was it actually a picture of Arjun?

'It's my turn, isn't it?' the boy said, brightening again. 'Come on, Pumpkin. Do me a favour and roll a five.'

'I need your help with something,' Metty called across the board when they were nearing the end of the game. She'd been building up the courage to ask Sundar while they played, hoping he might warm to her as they got to know each other. He'd caught up to Metty after a few disastrous rolls, and now they were both closing in on the hundredth square.

'With what?' he said.

'Remember how you promised to help find the captain?'

'I'm not sure I promised . . .'

'Well, I think I've found a way and I need to get out of the house tonight. There's someone I have to meet at this theatre – it's called the Glass Peacock.'

'I know it,' Sundar said. 'It's right at the top of the city, but Mag's got some big meeting tonight and she'll never let me leave the house without her, even if it *is* Halloween. It's pretty much the only night I'm allowed out,' he added glumly.

'Wait, what?' Metty said, frowning in confusion. 'You make it sound like Aunt Mag's keeping you locked up or something.'

'She's not,' Sundar said quickly. 'It's for my own safety.'

'But . . . why? Is it because of your fate?'

The boy began to fidget, tucking his gloved hands behind his back as though afraid Metty might magically see through them. 'Look, it's a long story. I'd rather not talk about it, if you don't mind.'

'Okay . . .' she said slowly. 'But Aunt Mag wouldn't actually have to know we're going out.'

Sundar looked startled. 'You mean sneak off?'

'Just for a bit. We'd be quick, so she'd never find out. Even if she did, I'd take all the blame, I swear.'

'I don't know, Metty.'

'I thought you wanted to help me? Please, Sundar. This is my chance to look for my dad, the first proper one I've had, and he's been gone a whole week now. I'm scared if I don't find him soon then—'

'All right, all right, I'll help. But if Mag does find out—'

'She won't. Anyway, don't you want to go out for Halloween? How come you're allowed out for that, but not for—'

'I said I'd help!' Sundar said, beginning to look flustered. He wouldn't meet Metty's eye as he changed the subject. 'Stop stalling, by the way. I saw you roll a four. It's not so bad, you know. I've done it twice already.'

Metty exhaled through her nose and dragged herself over to the ninety-ninth square. A dark purple snake was waiting for her with a gleeful expression. It spread its jaws until they were wide enough to devour an adult. Metty gulped as she peered into the serpent's shadowy throat. It was the longest one on the whole board.

'Couldn't I just forfeit the game?' she said weakly.

'Well, you could,' said Sundar, 'but that would be extremely boring. Just jump in. Trust me, it's actually quite fun.'

Metty lowered herself into the snake's mouth, using its fangs as handholds.

'Here goes,' she muttered, clamping her eyes shut. Then she let go.

Darkness swallowed her up, and a shrill sound echoed round the tunnel. It took Metty a second to realise it was her own scream. Then, before she could truly panic, she whooshed towards a circle of light, punctuated by two long fangs. She flew out of the snake's second head and landed awkwardly on square five.

Groaning, she rubbed her lower back and glared up at Sundar, who was grinning over the side of the board game.

'See? Isn't it fun!'

'No,' Metty grumbled.

The snake behind her winked and playfully flicked its tongue.

CHAPTER TWENTY

Halloween

Metty itched with nerves as she watched the sky darken and the sunshine deepen to bronze, turning all the buildings in New London the colour of brass. This was it: her chance to get out and search for the captain. All she had to do was wait for Aunt Mag to leave Winter's Knock, then sneak outside.

She and Sundar hurried downstairs to the entrance hall as soon as her aunt called goodbye. Then they waited for an agonising ten minutes, making sure Aunt Mag was far enough away from the house that she wouldn't catch them leaving. At last, Metty gave a tremulous nod and moved to open the front door.

'Where are you two off to?' her uncle asked from the top of the stairs.

Panic scrambled Metty's thoughts. She glanced at Sundar who blurted out: 'Trick-or-treating.'

'Trick-or-treating?' Rupert said with a bemused smile, trotting down the staircase. For a moment, he looked just like the captain. 'Tonight?'

Metty bobbed her head. 'Aunt Mag said we could.'

'Really? Did you hex her or something?'

'No,' Sundar said. 'It's just that she knows how much it means to me, going out on Halloween. And Metty's never seen the parade before.'

Rupert still seemed unsure. 'Mag said the two of you could go out *on your own?*'

'Only for an hour,' Metty said quickly. 'And she told us to stay in Highfate.'

'I see. So . . . where are your costumes?'

'Our costumes?'

'Well, you can't go out on Halloween dressed like that, can you?' Rupert nodded at Sundar. 'Especially not you. Run upstairs and get changed while I find something to wear.'

'Wait,' Metty said, struggling not to grimace. 'You want to come with us?'

'Why not? The more the merrier.'

'But . . .'

'We'd be fine on our own,' Sundar said, exchanging a worried glance with Metty.

'Don't be daft. Now hurry, both of you, before we miss the parade.'

Metty felt rather deflated as she tramped upstairs with Sundar. The last thing they needed was her uncle tagging along, but she couldn't see how to get round Rupert without looking suspicious.

'You know he's going to say something to Mag later,' Sundar whispered. 'And she'll be livid.'

'I know,' Metty said, casting a miserable glance down the stairs. 'But we'll just have to deal with that afterwards. I told you, I'll take the blame for everything.'

She meant it, although the thought of facing a furious Aunt Mag made her belly twist into knots. Still, it would be worth it if going out tonight brought Metty even one step closer to finding the captain.

There was a chest full of costumes up in the playroom. Sundar decided to dress as a prince in a gold satin coat and a Venetian mask that looked like Rupert's fate. Metty chose Alice in Wonderland, using a magical comb to dye her hair blonde. They raced back downstairs as soon as they'd finished their costumes, hoping they might be able to slip out while Rupert was getting changed.

Unfortunately, her uncle was waiting for them in the hall. He'd dressed up like an actual pirate, complete with a wide hat and leather eyepatch, and excitedly ushered the children out of the house and into the colourful chaos.

The air was thick with the delicious smell of roasted meat, hot pies and doughnuts. Decorations had quadrupled overnight and covered every building. Flaming pumpkins bobbed up and down in mid-air, lighting the paths of passing gondolas. Skeletons on stilts drifted along the streets; a parade of zombies marched up and down, beating drums and blowing on trumpets; and vampires handed out free snacks to anyone who passed by. The ink river had turned burnished amber to match the festivities.

Metty looked around with a light-headed feeling. It was almost too much, all the noise and brightness, all the ghoulish spectacle, but she steadied herself with a deep breath. She needed to find Madame LeBeau as soon as possible. According to Sundar, her theatre was right at the top of the city next to some famous park.

'Um, do you think we could go to Winter Park?' she asked Rupert, tugging on his sleeve. He frowned down at her in surprise.

'What on earth for? I thought you wanted to go trick-or-treating?'

'I do, but maybe we could go there first? Sundar mentioned something about it, and he said the view's amazing from the top of the city. Please, Rupert.'

'All right, if that's what you really want.' Rupert glanced at Sundar. The boy was distracted by a group of kids who were bouncing on a silk cobweb that had spun itself between two lampposts like a trampoline. 'You don't mind, do you, Sundar?'

'Hmm, what? Oh no, I don't mind at all. Come on, we should stop by Sinner's Oak first. It's not far.'

'We don't have time. The show starts at seven,' Metty hissed as Sundar grabbed her arm and pulled her down the street. They were going in the wrong direction.

'Course we do. It'll only take ten minutes. Anyway, Madame Whatsit will be at the theatre all night.'

'Shush! Don't let Rupert hear.'

'I wouldn't worry.' Sundar grinned. 'He's pretty relaxed.'

Rupert was indeed a lot more relaxed than Aunt Mag, even if he didn't like the children running too far ahead. The dying sun painted the sky crimson and cast a hellish glow as they made their way through the city.

They crossed one of the floating bridges and walked through several merchant districts before reaching an archway with thorny vines curled round it. They were quite far down the city by then, and Metty threw an anxious glance over her shoulder. They still had to get all the way to the top of New London, and she wanted to arrive before the start of Madame LeBeau's show.

WELCOME TO SINNER'S OAK read the archway.

'What is this place?' she whispered to Sundar. That name sounded familiar for some reason.

'It's the dodgiest part of New London,' he said in Metty's ear. 'Where all the ill-fated live. You know. Like future criminals, or people destined to be unlucky.'

Metty felt a nasty jolt in her stomach. Ill-fated. Surely that meant Sinner's Oak was where *she* belonged, where she might end up one day. Perhaps there was a special street just for murderers.

She glanced around. A steady stream of people was entering the district, and Metty could tell from their clothes that they probably didn't belong there. She wondered what they'd all come for, why Sundar had brought them here, and why Rupert hadn't objected. It didn't exactly seem like a safe place to visit.

'What sort of criminals?' she whispered to Sundar as they followed the crowd.

'Depends. The fancy kind live up in this nice bit: crime bosses, fraudsters, tax evaders, that sort of thing. I think the rougher ones live a bit further down where it's not as clean.'

'Why don't the police just arrest them all?' Metty said, although her throat went dry at the thought.

Sundar shushed her. Rupert leaned down and said in a quiet

voice: 'Not everyone from Sinner's Oak is fated to be a criminal, Metty. Some are just unfortunate, destined to gamble away all their money, or carry bad luck with them wherever they go. Even the ones that *do* have criminal fates . . . Well, most of them haven't actually done anything illegal – yet. And you can't arrest someone for having a tattoo that suggests they *might* break the law one day. Not in civilised places anyway.'

Yet. That word again.

Sundar jogged Metty's arm. 'Look, there it is!'

To her surprise, a majestic oak tree was growing right in the middle of the street. It wasn't tall but broad, and its sweeping canopy had leaves of cinnamon brown and tawny gold. A crowd of children was gathered round it. Some were trying to jump up and reach the lowest branches.

At first, Metty thought the oak was full of baubles like an overdressed Christmas tree. Then she realised the splashes of colour among its leaves were actually sweets, a whole range of them, from lollipops to chocolate pumpkins to jelly skulls and gobstoppers that looked like eyeballs.

'Wonder what I'll get this year,' Sundar said, joining the back of a snaking queue.

'We need to hurry, Sundar.'

'Oh, come on. Don't you want to have a go yourself?'

Metty was admittedly curious, watching children approach

the tree one by one. They appeared to be whispering something to it.

'All right, so long as we're quick. What are you even meant to do?'

'Don't worry, you'll see. I'll go first.'

Soon they were second in the queue. Metty watched the girl in front of them shuffle nervously up to the tree. She touched its trunk, then said in an uncertain voice: 'The other day, I, uh, told my sister that she has really disgusting dog-breath.'

There was a pause while the tree contemplated, rustling its leaves. Then one of its branches uncurled from the rest and drooped towards the girl. Her face flushed pink with relief, and she took a jelly spider from the branch before scampering off.

'Hope I can do better than that,' Sundar said to Metty, then stepped up to the tree himself. He approached it with surprising confidence, planting his hand on the bark. 'Two weeks ago, I swapped my guardian's teapot for a cursed one and it turned her morning cuppa into blood.'

The tree didn't have to think hard this time, dropping one of its thicker branches almost at once. Sundar punched the air and grabbed a gobstopper eyeball, putting it in his pocket as he skipped back to Metty.

'Your turn.' He grinned at her.

'Did you really do that to Aunt Mag?' she whispered disapprovingly.

Sundar looked guilty. 'Well, I had to do something if I wanted to get anything decent off the tree. It's not like I let her drink it.'

Still shaking her head, Metty walked up and cautiously placed her hand on the old oak. She wondered what reward it might give someone utterly rotten like her.

'Let's see,' she muttered, thinking of all the villainous things she'd done recently. 'Last month, I put worms in my housekeeper's pillow, then I buried her favourite slippers in the garden. Oh, and I convinced all the staff that I was planning to murder them and—'

'One'll do!' Sundar laughed behind her.

She blushed, removing her hand from the tree. It considered a little longer than it had with Sundar's offering and then, with a creak, the oak lowered its thickest branch and presented a giant lollipop to Metty. She took it with a thrill of pleasure and joined the others.

'Well done,' said Rupert. 'I had no idea you were quite so wicked.'

Metty's smile wilted, and she looked at her gloved hands. Hadn't Aunt Mag told him about her dreadful fate?

'We should hurry up if you still want to visit Winter Park,' Rupert added, glancing at the sunset.

Alarm zapped through Metty. She couldn't believe she'd let herself get distracted. This was her one chance to look for the captain.

'We need to hurry!' she cried, grabbing Sundar's arm. 'Let's go, let's go!'

CHAPTER TWENTY-ONE

Winter Park

They left Sinner's Oak in a rush and started climbing the city, trying not to get swallowed up by the Halloween parade. Soon they'd reached Highfate again, and Metty was sure they were getting near the top of New London when she noticed something drifting through the sky.

'What's that over there?' she asked the others, pointing at the mysterious shadow. It was about to disappear behind a ruby veil of cloud.

'Hmm? Oh, that's the Ink Museum,' Rupert said. 'It flies round the city, although it's hard to spot through the clouds sometimes.'

Metty realised it was a tiny floating island, holding just one impressive building. Even from a distance, it reminded her of the British Museum in Old London with its triangular rooftop and large columns, only rather than being stone, they seemed to be made of solid glass. Something curled round the building, sparkling in the fading sunlight: a pool of ink like a glittering moat.

'The Ink Museum?' She frowned.

'Yep. It charts the history of all the flying capitals, starting with New London – how our founders used ink to create it last century.'

'But how come it's floating around on its own? Isn't it part of the city?'

'Well, sort of.' Rupert shrugged. 'The museum technically belongs to New London, but, to be honest, it's hardly ever here. The island's got its own core, you see, the first one ever invented, and it travels all over the world, visiting the other New Capitals. It's pretty famous: the very first bit of land flown up with magic! Well, the first bit that *stayed* up, so people like to go and see it. Of course, it's here right now because of the big anniversary.'

'Anniversary?'

Sundar laughed. 'Don't tell me you don't know about it!'

'Know about what?' Metty grumbled, beginning to lose patience.

'New London!' Sundar said. 'It turns one hundred next year. Anyway, the museum's brilliant. It's got all these weird machines, and you can play on some of them. Mag took me once, when it was here a few years ago.'

'I thought you weren't allowed out of the house?' Metty said, regarding him suspiciously.

'I'm not. I mean, Mag doesn't like me to go out *too* often, but . . . Look, just forget I said anything.'

Metty would do no such thing – in fact, she was increasingly desperate to find out Sundar's secret, why Aunt Mag was so determined to hide him from the world. But she could tell that if she pushed him now, she'd get no answers at all. Instead, she nodded at the floating island.

'But if it needs a core to fly, doesn't that waste loads of ink? What's the point, just for some museum?'

'You sound remarkably like our new governor,' Rupert said, chuckling at her disdainful expression. 'Finch keeps banging on about shutting the old place down – says it costs too much ink to run, even though the museum gets millions of visitors every year, and *we* get a whacking great pay cheque whenever it goes to another city. Personally, I reckon she just hates the thought of anyone having fun.'

'Still,' Metty said, frowning at the museum. It was almost invisible now. 'I bet it *is* expensive.'

'It's history, Metty. That matters to some people.' Rupert smiled suddenly, gesturing at a small crowd up ahead. 'Here we are, just in time.'

WELCOME TO INKSHIMMER read a pearl archway leading to

the uppermost district of the city. There were police officers on either side of it, checking people as they passed through the gate. Even though all the children seemed happy and excited, Metty noticed their parents whispering and looking around anxiously.

Inkshimmer was a wealthy district like Highfate, but it didn't seem to have many houses. Instead, it boasted the finest theatres, art galleries, restaurants and fashion boutiques in the whole city. The Naked Cathedral formed a severe pinnacle at the top, its spires knifing into the clouds and its windows flaming like fiery swords.

'This way,' Sundar said. 'We're nearly out of time.'

Suddenly there was the theatre: a golden building lit by rainbow lanterns, glowing like a gem on a cushion of red velvet sky. Next to it was Winter Park, and a toyshop one building along flanked by twelve-foot nutcracker soldiers. The park itself wasn't special in the least. As far as Metty could tell, it was a bog-standard green field bordered by a few trees and flowers. It wasn't even big or decorated for Halloween. She wondered why Rupert had agreed to bring them here when there wasn't anything to see. Hadn't he thought her request strange?

'We're here,' she whispered, nodding at the Glass Peacock Theatre, but Sundar didn't seem to care. He grabbed Metty's arm when she moved forward.

'Just wait,' he muttered. 'Any second now.'

'Any second what? Sundar, we're *here*.'

'Trust me, Metty. This is our way in.'

The transformation began once the last of the sunlight faded from the park. A crunching noise filled the air as a sparkling silver frost spread from the entrance, creeping over the grass and the flowers and climbing up all the trees, crystallising their autumn leaves. Within ten seconds, every inch of Winter Park was a magical frozen landscape, glittering in the lamplight.

'Wow,' Metty whispered, astonished when she breathed out steam. Glancing down, she realised that ice had reached the points of her shoes, chilling her toes.

'Amazing, isn't it?' Sundar said, stepping into the park. The ground crackled under his feet. He spun round, looking back at Metty and Rupert.

'Does it do this—'

'Every night at dusk,' said Rupert. His gaze ran over all the frozen flowers, their petals glinting like diamonds. 'Even at the height of summer.'

'Come on,' Sundar said, moving deeper into the park. He waved Metty over, giving her a meaningful look. 'You're allowed to walk through.'

She glanced anxiously at the theatre. How were they supposed to get inside while Rupert was breathing down their necks?

'Aren't you coming?' Metty asked him as she stepped onto the ice.

Her uncle shook his head with a rueful smile, brushing his elbow. 'Had a nasty fall a few years back. You two go ahead. I'll wait for you out here.'

The frost on the grass was so thin in places that it shattered underfoot, then smoothed out again, becoming a clean white sheet. Metty slipped and slid her way over to Sundar, who'd gone to admire the glassy flowers twinkling under a lamppost. One of the solar-powered birds was perched on top of it, its heart pulsing like a fireball.

'What now?' she whispered, staring at the theatre through a gap in the fence. A side entrance was visible from where they stood, a scruffy red door. 'I need to get inside. There's no one queueing, so I think the show must've already started.'

'If we cut through the park, then we can probably sneak round the back,' Sundar said. 'Although we won't have long before Rupert catches on. Maybe a couple of minutes. I can create a distraction for you.'

'Thanks. Maybe if we—'

Metty jumped as the red door opened with a creak. She pulled Sundar behind one of the bushes, peeking round it to see who'd appeared. There were two men – no, three, she realised – wearing lion masks. The third man was limp like a rag doll, having to be dragged along by the other two.

209

Metty turned and frowned at Sundar, who looked just as baffled.

Is he drunk? she mouthed and the boy shrugged.

Metty returned her attention to the men. For some reason, they were waiting in the shadowy alley that ran alongside the theatre, as though they didn't dare step out into the open. Then the limp man's right arm swung free. Metty glimpsed something on his hand, and her heart shrivelled.

She knew that fate. She'd seen it a thousand times before. A neat ship with a proud white sail.

'Dad,' whispered Metty.

CHAPTER TWENTY-TWO

The Black Moths

How was this possible? How could the captain be here, now?

Metty stepped out from behind the icy bush, then froze as a noise screeched through the park.

It was louder than a siren, shriller than any whistle or alarm, like the anguished howls of a spirit, like something that had crawled up from hell. She gasped, clapping her hands over her ears, and glanced around in fear. Where was that *sound* coming from?

'Metty! Sundar! Move!' Rupert yelled, charging towards them across the ice.

Metty turned to look at the men from the theatre, but they were dragging her father down the alleyway. She tried to follow, crunching over the frozen ground, then ran headlong into Rupert, who grabbed her shoulders, breathing hard.

There was a second of tense silence, broken by a high-pitched shattering sound. Then every window in the toyshop next to Winter Park exploded.

Metty looked up just in time to see a rainstorm of glass flying towards her and Rupert. She lifted her right hand instinctively, revealing the raven embroidered on her tether, and the shards softened to curls of black feather. They fluttered harmlessly past her and settled on the icy ground.

Metty stared down at them in shock. Her throat was dry as dirt. That awful noise still rang inside her head, bouncing around like a shrill echo. There were more screams coming from nearby, more explosive crashes as windows smashed and showered people with knives of glass. She tried to look for her father and those men through the gaps in the fence, but they'd vanished.

'Good reflexes,' Rupert said. All the blood had drained from his face, and he looked scarily alert. His hand landed on Metty's shoulder again, anchoring her to the ice.

'I saw my dad,' she said breathlessly. 'I saw him just now – he was coming out of the theatre. These men had him and—'

'Hold on, what do you—'

Before Rupert could finish his sentence, there was a shuddery creak of wood. One of the enormous nutcracker soldiers in front of the toyshop rocked forward and toppled, impacting the cobblestones with a deafening crunch. Blood pumped in Metty's ears, roaring like the sea as she spun round, trying to figure out exactly what was happening. It was as if the city was under attack.

And then all the noise cut out again, the desperate cries and crashes of glass. A smothering silence descended. Somehow that was even more frightening than the shrieking chaos. Sundar appeared just behind Metty, and she reached for his hand.

'It's them,' Rupert murmured, then raised his head.

Metty glanced up too, heart punching her ribcage. The sky was no longer red but murky blue and laced with clouds. The moon was a sneering crescent, low on the horizon. With a rumble of thunder, the clouds began to swirl, deepening from grey to black. They came together in a tar-like mass above the city. The darkness was becoming a shape, turning into a winged creature silhouetted against the sky.

Recognition shivered through Metty, making goosepimples rise on her arms.

The sky flashed as a hundred small lightning bolts crackled round the black moth, creating a blinding halo. Metty winced and began to look away, but then the brightness faded. Tiny gaps appeared in the shadow, pinpricks of sky, as the moth slowly disintegrated, turning into black powder that rained onto New London and filled the air with a cindery smell. A flake landed on Metty's cheek and left a stinging kiss.

'Ouch,' she muttered, brushing it away. It smeared her fingertips like ash.

'Here,' Rupert said, shrugging off his pirate coat. He held it in his tethered hand, and it swelled into an umbrella large enough to protect all three of them if they huddled in close. But Metty wasn't interested in standing still. She tried to run for the park entrance.

'Where are you going?' Rupert said, grabbing her arm.

'To look for my dad. I told you, he was just here!'

'Are you sure? It couldn't have been someone else?'

'No.' Metty groaned. 'It was him, I know it. I recognised his fate, and those men – I bet they were Black Moths. Sundar, you saw him too, right?'

'Um, sort of,' Sundar replied with an apologetic grimace. 'Although I didn't really see his face. They were all wearing masks.'

'I told you both, I recognised his fate. I know it was him!'

Her uncle seemed unconvinced. 'I think we'd better go home.'

'We can't leave yet!' Metty cried with a fretful glance at the theatre.

'Don't argue,' Rupert said, shepherding her and Sundar across the park. 'It's not safe any more. We can't stay.'

'But what about the captain? We need to go after him!'

'Listen, even if you're right and somebody did take him, we have no idea where they are now. I say we concentrate on getting home before something else happens, then we'll talk to Mag. She'll know what to do.'

Metty reluctantly followed Rupert out of Winter Park. About a third of the buildings in Inkshimmer had lost their windows. Soot blanketed the streets, rising in dusty swirls.

'Why would the Moths do this?' she muttered.

'You mean, apart from to spread misery and fear?' Rupert whispered, glancing warily at everyone nearby. Most people seemed as frightened and confused as they were, hurrying along the dusty pavements.

'They're terrorists, aren't they?' Sundar said, frowning when Rupert shushed him.

'Not here. Wait till we get home. And stay close, both of you.'

The mood was sombre in Winter's Knock that night. Rupert went off to make a mysterious phone call as soon as they arrived home, and Sundar crept away to his room, looking utterly dejected. It was like someone had taken a pin to his high spirits, but that was hardly surprising if Halloween really was the one time he ever got to leave the house.

The attack on Inkshimmer had left Metty shaken. She could still hear that blood-chilling screech inside her head, could still see her father being pulled along by those men in masks. The thought made her stomach churn.

She remembered the night of her fating, after they'd left Darkwell and said goodbye to Daphne, who was still fretting about the newspapers. Metty hadn't wanted to eat dinner that evening, or talk, or do anything at all. Ignoring her birthday presents, she'd climbed into bed and cried like she never had before, or since. It had felt as if her whole life was over, that the world had ended. All she'd wanted was to make her parents proud, and instead she was nothing but a disappointment. Fated to be a cold-hearted killer.

The captain had brought her hot chocolate and a disgraceful amount of biscuits, then sat with Metty for hours, trying to make her laugh and refusing to go away until she wasn't so upset.

'It'll be all right,' he'd told her again and again, his hand warm on her back through the covers. 'Look at me, Met.' She had, rolling over in bed and pulling the duvet off her head, staring into her father's brown eyes shimmering with fierce love. 'I know this isn't what you wanted. I know you're scared about what might happen, but everything will be fine, I swear. Even if it doesn't feel like it right now.'

'How can you swear?' she'd whispered, her throat thick.

'Because.' Her father's expression had changed then, turning serious. 'Because it's my job to keep you safe, and I will *never* let anyone hurt you. That's a promise.'

Metty had felt comforted at the time, although afterwards she'd realised that the captain had it upside down. *She* wasn't the one who needed protecting. Surely everyone else was in danger from her.

Aunt Mag didn't come home for hours. Metty waited for her in the entrance hall, determined not to go to bed until they'd spoken. She didn't care that she might be in trouble when her aunt found out that they'd left the house. It felt like all the thoughts in Metty's head would come frothing out of her ears if she didn't get a chance to voice them soon, and the longer Aunt Mag was gone, the more restless she became. She tried to distract herself, reading her dictionary for the thousandth time.

At last, a key rattled in the front door. Metty threw aside her book and jumped up from the stairs. Her aunt came in, looking weary and windswept but still striking in a long black dress that paled to shimmery gold as it flowed to her ankles. Her waist-length hair was let down, and she gathered it over one shoulder as she closed the door behind her.

'You're still up,' she said to Metty in a yawn. 'I thought you'd be exhausted after tonight's excitement. I heard about your little outing, by the way. What my ridiculous brother was thinking, letting you both—'

'Where were you?' Metty cut in shrilly. 'I've been waiting ages. Did you not hear about the attack?'

'Of course I did. That's why I'm so late.'

Metty felt a twinge of hurt. 'Didn't you care about what happened to us, if we were even okay?'

'That's a highly insulting question,' Aunt Mag replied, pinching her lips. 'Obviously, you and Sundar were my first concern – although I *was* under the impression that the two of you were safe at home until Rupert phoned and told me otherwise. Kiki and I had to stay and help the authorities tidy up the city.'

Tiredness seemed to wash away Aunt Mag's frustration, and she yawned again. 'Really, Metty, you ought to go to bed. You look dead on your feet.'

'So do you.'

'Do I?' said Aunt Mag, glancing down at her slinky dress. 'Actually, I believe I look rather fabulous.'

'Aunt Mag, please be serious. I need to talk to you.'

'Right this second?'

'Yes!' Metty groaned, knitting her fingers to keep them still. 'I saw the captain tonight, coming out of the theatre next to Winter Park. They've got him. The Black Moths have got him.'

Aunt Mag sobered at once. 'Rupert told me. Did they see you?'

Metty shook her head. 'It happened so fast. I don't think they had a chance to notice me and Sundar before the explosion. Everything was crazy after that.'

'We thought the Moths might attack tonight because of the conference – everyone with half a brain has been telling the governor to change the date. A protest was inevitable. I suppose the chaos was a perfect distraction while they moved your father.'

'I don't understand. Was the conference about them or something?'

'It's complicated.' Aunt Mag closed her eyes, squeezing the sides of her forehead. 'Remember I told you about our new governor? Nadiya Finch. She has some very old-fashioned ideas about magic and she's pushing for the laws to get a lot stricter in New London, like they are in the cities below. Ink is getting more expensive every day, and Finch made it clear at the conference tonight that she intends to keep it that way. Then there's talk about raising the age of fating, so children won't be able to use tethers any more, and that's just the start of her plans.'

'But why does she even want that?' Metty said. 'It sounds awful.'

'It's about fear. Magic is unpredictable. It makes things complicated for the governments in charge, and it makes people hard to control. Nothing Finch is planning has come into effect yet, but it's only a matter of time and the Moths aren't happy. They oppose *any* rules around magic, and Nadiya Finch wants to bring in dozens.'

'But then why . . .' Metty shook her head in frustration. It felt like they were going round in circles and, despite everything that had happened tonight, she was hardly closer to saving her father. 'I don't get it! Why not go after Finch herself, or some other politician, someone who could actually change things? Why do the Black Moths want *us*?'

Aunt Mag sighed through her nose.

'Let me guess,' said Metty. 'You can't say.'

'I did promise not to.'

'*Who* did you promise? The captain, right? I bet you knew they had him all along.'

Aunt Mag shook her head. 'I suspected as much, but I didn't know for certain. I didn't lie to you, Metty. I never lie.'

'Keeping secrets is the same as lying! You never tell me the truth. Not about my dad, or why Sundar has to stay in the house, or why you're . . .'

Metty's sentence trailed off, her boldness fading as she stared at Aunt Mag's right hand, at the dark tether concealing her fate. She didn't know for certain that her aunt was ill-fated, but why else would she hide her tattoo?

Aunt Mag raised an eyebrow. 'Why I'm what?'

'It doesn't matter. Look, you said you'd explain things if I ever needed to know, and now they've got the captain, so *I need to know*. You promised.'

'Metty, believe me when I say it's not that simple.'

'Please, Aunt Mag! What if they do something to him? What if they've already hurt him tonight, and that's why they were taking him away? What if they're planning to—'

'I've told you already. We'd know if he was dead.'

'*How?*'

Aunt Mag paused to consider, then held out her hand. 'I'll show you.'

CHAPTER TWENTY-THREE

The Jones Family

When they set off along the hallway, Metty assumed they were heading for her aunt's study. Instead, they arrived at the swimming pool.

Aunt Mag turned on the light, startling all the little white fish. The poor things froze like they'd been electrocuted, but then most went back to swimming. A few hid in those strange alcoves built into the walls of the pool. Metty frowned and tucked a strand of hair behind her ear. The magic from the comb was wearing off now, the blonde fading.

'One minute,' Aunt Mag said, then pressed a second button under the light switch. The rosy lamps in the pool began to flash, and a quiet whistle sounded in the room.

The fish gave another funny start, then made their way to the tunnel separating both halves of the hourglass swimming pool. Soon they had all emptied out of the left side and were swimming around the right side instead.

Aunt Mag jabbed the button again and a metal lid snapped over the mouth of the tunnel, sealing off one section of the pool. Then she turned the knob several times until it stopped clicking and a tremendous rumble made the floor vibrate beneath their feet.

Metty crept forward to see what was happening inside the pool. To her surprise, all the water in the left half was draining into those holes in the walls with an echoing *glug-glug-glug*. Soon there was just a thin puddle glittering on the tiles at the bottom.

'There we are,' Aunt Mag said, lowering her hand. She crossed the room and climbed into the pool, using the ladder on the wall, then glanced back at Metty. 'Come along then. Aren't you curious?'

'What are we doing?' Metty asked, using the ladder herself. She hopped off near the bottom and landed on the floor with a slap. As far as she could tell, there was nothing inside the pool itself, just pearly tiles and pink lamps. The puddle on the ground squelched under her shoes.

Aunt Mag didn't bother to explain. She moved into the centre of the drained swimming pool and crouched down. Then she flattened her hand on one of the tiles.

'Stand back,' she warned Metty.

Metty walked backwards until she bumped into the wall of the pool. There was another rumble, then the tiles on the floor began to sink, one row then the next. They became a shallow staircase that led down into a mysterious cavelike room. Metty waited for the growling to stop, then peeled herself off the wall.

Aunt Mag stood up with a satisfied smile. 'Welcome to the family vault.' Then she added more sternly, 'Put your hands in your pockets – and keep them there.'

'Why?' Metty asked, although she did as she was told.

'You'll see. Come along then – let's not stand around like lemons.'

Metty followed her down the staircase, treading carefully as the tiles were still damp. She found herself in a shadowy cellar. Lamps flashed overhead, flooding the room with a rose-coloured gloom. She soon realised why Aunt Mag didn't want her to touch anything, remembering what she'd said when Metty had first arrived at Winter's Knock: *You'll be glad to know that the real monstrosities are locked downstairs in the vault . . .*

Cursed antiques were shut up in dozens of glass cabinets. Metty kept away from them, sticking to the middle of the vault, and gulped as she spotted an eerie skull with a long snout and glaring eye sockets. Who knew what something that monstrous was designed to do? No doubt it was illegal like the spirit phone.

'This way,' Aunt Mag said, and led her further into the cellar. It twisted away from the staircase, winding like the streets of New London.

Before long, they'd reached the back of the vault and Aunt Mag stopped.

'This is what I wanted to show you,' she said.

Metty came to stand beside her and stared at the ground in fascination. Built into the stone floor was a black-and-white mosaic showing the Jones family tree. There weren't any portraits, only names, and no spouses either. Every person on the tree had been born a Jones, from Majestic right at the top to Meticulous at the bottom.

Metty counted five generations altogether, following her own direct line (herself, Moral, Miraculous, Morose and Majestic). There were candles scattered across the mosaic, placed beneath certain names.

'What are these for?' she asked, squatting to look at the blue one resting on her own square. It was stumpy, with a pale flame.

'They're life candles,' Aunt Mag replied, surveying the family tree herself. 'Magical, of course. Only the living have them.'

'Oh,' Metty said, standing up. A feeling of dread scuttled through her insides as she glanced around at the candles again.

There was a large pink one near the top of the tree by

Melancholy Jones (Metty's great-great-aunt, who lived in New London, according to Aunt Mag, but was off travelling the world), then a tall green one under Monotonous Jones (Rupert), and an even taller purple candle for Aunt Mag. There was only one candle shorter than Metty's, and it was the red one placed by her father's name: Moral Jones. His was barely a puddle of wax with a sputtering flame.

'Glad to see Aunt Colly's doing well,' Aunt Mag said cheerfully, pointing at the pink candle near the back. 'Look at the size of it – you'd never think she was older than New London.'

Metty struggled to swallow, nerves clogging her throat. 'Do these candles – do they show how long you've got left to live?'

Aunt Mag barked a laugh. 'No, no, no, don't be silly. Bless your heart – yours must've given you a fright. No. They only show whether a person's life is imperilled. See, when you're fit and healthy and keeping out of trouble – mostly – you end up with a nice tall candle.'

'But when you're in danger . . .' Metty said, looking at her feeble blue one.

'It shrinks down, yes,' said Aunt Mag with a frown. 'But it can sprout back up again. I've seen it happen many times.'

Together, they gazed at the captain's candle, or what was left of it.

'So . . . my dad's still alive,' Metty murmured. She wanted to coax the candle up, to treat it like a wilting flower and nurse it back to health with sun and water. 'But he's in danger, wherever they've put him.'

'It does seem that way,' said Aunt Mag, the lines on her forehead deepening like cracks in clay. 'But I want to reassure you that I'm doing my very best to track him down.'

'This is all my fault,' Metty said in a clenched voice. She tore her eyes from the candles, looking up at her aunt. 'They took him because of me, because of my stupid fate. But why? What do they think it means? Maybe if I could just change it . . .'

'No,' said Aunt Mag firmly. 'I told you already, that's not the answer.'

'Then what is?' Metty demanded, watching her father's candle flicker. She couldn't afford to let it get any shorter. She had to act now.

'Listen to me. Rupert and I have powerful friends, and we're all looking for your father. We will find him, I swear.'

'But what if you're too late?'

Aunt Mag gave Metty a kind look. 'I doubt the Black Moths will hurt him. Obviously, they need him for something, but you can come down here as often as you like and check on the candles. At least this way we'll know if anything happens.'

Metty looked at the captain's stubby candle with a pulsing sense of dread. If it shrank any more, it would vanish altogether.

She couldn't get to sleep that night. Nothing would distract her, not even her music box that kept popping open and belting out: *'What shall we do with a drunken sailor . . . EARLY in the MORNING!'* Pumpkin was some comfort, at least, nestled in her arms (though he was cold and heavy).

In the end, Metty got out of bed and put on her dressing gown and slippers. Her walls were a stormy blue with moody grey patches when she slipped into the hallway.

Morning must have been approaching, for the light had a misty quality, the kind you only see at dawn and dusk. She walked to Sundar's room and knocked quietly on the door. She'd never been inside before; they usually hung out in the playroom upstairs.

'Come in,' he called, so she pushed her way inside.

Sundar's bedroom was not what she expected. For one thing, it was an absolute tip, every surface taken up by clothes, books and toys.

His bed was spectacular, however, and filled Metty with envy. It was boat-shaped and suspended from the ceiling on ropes. Sundar was rocking it by gently kicking the wall. It swung back and forth as he stretched his legs, lying on his back with his arms folded beneath his head.

'You're awake too,' Metty said, picking her way through all the rubbish on the floor.

'Couldn't sleep.'

'Me neither.'

'Want to come up?' Sundar said and tossed a climbing rope over the side of his bed.

He helped Metty once she was near the top, and they lay side by side on the squishy mattress. She found herself relaxing at once, soothed by the rocking motion of the bed as she and Sundar pressed their feet to the wall and sent it flying.

'*Reasons for being "The One",*' the boy said suddenly, to Metty's confusion. He was holding something tucked under one arm. '*Too secretive. Annoyingly stubborn.*'

'Oi!' Metty cried, realising what he was reading. She lunged across Sundar and tried to grab her dictionary. He giggled, holding it out of reach.

'*Stupidly bossy. Doesn't like Pumpkin.*'

'Sundar—'

'*Frowns too much?*'

'Give that back,' Metty snapped and wrenched the book off him. 'Where did you even find it?'

'You left it on the stairs. I don't think you can murder someone just for being grumpy,' Sundar said, grinning at her.

'You'd better hope Mag doesn't read this.'

'It's supposed to be private.'

She'd updated her list of reasons under Aunt Mag the other night and added Faith O'Connell to her dictionary. The girl's fate was a little complicated.

DIAMOND RINGS: *associated with jewellers, or extravagant proposals*, it said, but underneath the main meaning was a second one:

DIAMOND RINGS WITH A HAND: *associated with thieving, or a hideous lack of morals*

'I hope you didn't read the whole book,' Metty said, scowling at Sundar.

The boy looked sheepish. 'I didn't realise it was, like, your diary. You don't really . . . *want* to be a murderer, do you?'

'Of course not! But if I don't keep track of everyone I could end up hurting, then I'm worried my fate'll creep up on me, especially now I've got a tether. This way I can figure out who I'm most likely to . . .' Metty swallowed and shook her head, holding the book shut. 'Obviously, I'd never murder anyone on purpose.'

'Good,' Sundar said. 'Not that I thought you would. You're much too nice.'

Metty blushed. No one had ever said that to her before.

Once they'd settled down again, kicking the wall to rock the bed, she told Sundar about her conversation with Aunt Mag.

'She won't even talk about getting my fate rewritten. She seems to think it's a stupid idea, but really it's not. I mean, if it actually worked, it could solve all our problems. The main one being that I wouldn't, you know, end up murdering someone. And it would mean that I could use magic without worrying all the time.'

Metty held up her tattooed hand. 'If this stupid thing *is* the reason the Black Moths keep coming after us, then, once I change it, they might let the captain go. And the theatre was the last place we know he was for sure. I bet there'll be clues there about where the Moths took him.'

'Maybe Mag has a point about your fate though,' Sundar said, drawing a fierce look. 'What? She's pretty smart. And if it was that easy to get fates rewritten then wouldn't loads of people do it?'

'I don't care what Aunt Mag thinks,' Metty said with determination. 'I can't just stay inside and do nothing and wait for the next awful thing to happen. They've got the captain – I have to do something. I'm going to see Madame LeBeau whatever she says. It's not like she can stop me.'

Sundar looked alarmed. 'You have met Mag?'

'Then I'll make sure she doesn't find out. The poster I

found said there were more shows at the theatre this week. There's no way I can sneak past Aunt Mag right now – she'll be watching me like a hawk – but if I wait for the last show in a few days, I bet she'll think I've given up. The city should've calmed down too by then, so it'll be safer to travel. You could come with me, you know.'

'Me?' Sundar said, rubbing the back of his head. 'I don't know what use I'd be.'

'What about *your* fate?' Metty said eagerly. 'Don't you want it rewritten?'

'No.' Sundar laughed. 'Why would I?'

She was taken aback. 'Well, I . . . it's just you're always so secretive about it – you never let me see your hands. I just assumed you were ill-fated like me.'

'Well, I'm not.'

There was an electric pause.

'So what is your fate then?' Metty said at last. She couldn't believe she might finally find out Sundar's secret.

The boy didn't answer right away, gnawing on his bottom lip. He slowly brought his left hand out from behind his head and pulled the right from his pocket, showing them both to Metty. She stared at his bare skin in disbelief. 'But where is it?'

Sundar shrugged. 'Don't have one.'

'How can you . . . How old are you?'

'Same age as you.'

Metty blinked in surprise. 'But everyone gets fated when they turn ten. It's the law.'

'It's a stupid law. Being fated hasn't made you happy, has it?'

'No, but I got unlucky. What happened? Were you late to your fating or something?'

Sundar wasn't looking at her any more, focusing on the ceiling instead. 'Got really sick, so I couldn't go.'

'That's awful,' Metty said in a sympathetic voice. Even though she hated her tattoo, it was surely better than being fateless. She sat up and flashed a brilliant look at Sundar. 'That settles it. Now you've *got* to come with me.'

'Because . . .?'

'Because then we can both see Madame LeBeau. We'll corner her backstage and question her about the captain, see if she knows anything. After all, the Black Moths were keeping him inside her theatre. And then we can get her to change my fate and give you yours!'

'I don't think it'll work,' Sundar said. 'You only get one chance, don't you, on your tenth birthday? I've never heard of anyone getting one later on.'

'Well, yes, but that's really unfair, and I bet they make exceptions sometimes. Anyway, Aunt Mag said the governor wants to raise the age of fatings, so it *must* be possible. We'll just explain things, say you missed getting your fate, but that it wasn't your fault. I'm sure we can talk her round.'

'I dunno . . .'

'Look, you don't really want to be fateless for the rest of your life? It's not normal. People won't trust you, and you'll never be able to use a tether. Say you'll come with me, please.'

Sundar was silent again. The only sound in the room was the solemn creak-creak of the swing-bed. 'You're bananas,' he finally muttered, frowning at the ceiling.

But he didn't say no.

CHAPTER TWENTY-FOUR

A Night at the Theatre

M etty kept quiet about her plan to get back to the theatre over the next few days. She hoped Aunt Mag would think she'd forgotten all about it while she and Sundar tiptoed around, plotting in the dead of night. It hadn't taken long to persuade him. He seemed excited by the prospect of getting a fate and enjoyed speculating with Metty about what it might be.

'A lion, or some kind of hunting bird like a falcon, or – no, I know, a dagger!' he said one day when they were strategising in the playroom. 'I'm pretty sure that means I'll become an assassin.'

'You want to go around killing people?' Metty said with heavy disapproval.

'Well, no, not really,' Sundar said. 'It would be cool, that's all.'

'Trust me, it wouldn't.'

They knew it was a long way to the theatre and walking wasn't the safest option. Metty decided they would flag down a gondola and fly there instead, although that required money. She was surprised when Sundar appeared from his room with a fistful of banknotes and a few coins. There was fifty-two pounds altogether.

'Why d'you have all this if you're never allowed out?' Metty asked, counting the money.

'It's what I've saved up over the years. Birthdays and stuff.'

Metty gasped, staring at one of the banknotes. She knew New London had its own currency, based on British sterling, but she'd never looked closely at the money before.

'Look at this,' she said, holding up a ten-pound note. Printed on it was a man with fair hair and a long, clever face. Metty thought she recognised him from a portrait she'd seen in the drawing room. *MAJESTIC JONES* read the name under his picture. 'I think . . . isn't he my great-grandfather – no, hang on, my great-*great*-grandfather? What's he doing on here?'

Sundar didn't seem surprised. 'Well, he *was* a founder.'

'A founder?'

'Yeah. You know, the people who built New London. They're on all the banknotes – look.'

He showed her the twenty-pound note dedicated to a man called *TOSHIRO SHIMA*.

'Oh,' Metty said, staring at the money in fascination. She knew the Joneses were important in New London, but the captain had never explained quite how much. For some reason, he hadn't bothered to mention that their ancestor was an actual founder, someone who'd been instrumental in the creation of the city itself. Metty couldn't think why her father would have kept something like that from her.

'Didn't you know about Majestic?' Sundar asked as she tidied away the cash.

'My dad never told me.'

'Oh. That's weird.'

Metty shrugged, trying not to show that she was hurt. What else had the captain kept secret over the years? And why did he never talk about growing up in Winter's Knock with Aunt Mag and Rupert, or why he'd left New London behind? She wished he was there to answer her questions.

'I guess that sorts out transport,' she said, forcing herself to concentrate on the plan. This was hardly the time to start digging up mysteries from the past. 'Now all we have to worry about is getting past Aunt Mag.'

Soon five days had passed since Halloween, and Madame LeBeau only had one show left in New London. Metty fidgeted with impatience as she waited for the sun to go down. This was her last chance to get to the theatre and track down the prophetess before Madame LeBeau left the city.

She and Sundar distracted themselves in the playroom, finding outfits for the theatre and changing their hair with the magical comb. Metty became a redhead like Faith O'Connell, although it didn't suit her much.

Despite her hopes, Aunt Mag clearly expected her and Sundar to try and escape Winter's Knock. She'd barricaded the front door with a pile of cursed objects, arranging them like a minefield on the floor. The back door in the kitchen was just the same.

'Great,' Metty grumbled. 'What are we supposed to do now?'

Sundar was confusingly chipper. 'It's all right – there's another way out. Mag thinks I don't know about it, but I've used it a couple of times before. It's like an emergency exit. Come on! I'll show you.'

He brought Metty to the library, tiptoeing past Aunt Mag's study. They could see the cobalt sky through the round glass ceiling, sprinkled with stars. Metty assumed there would be some special book in the library that would tilt like a lever and operate a sliding bookcase. Winter's Knock was just the sort of house to have secret passageways.

Instead, Sundar led her up two spiralling staircases until they reached the highest balcony.

'Not this one,' he said, pushing one of the armchairs. It moved with a loud scrape. He tried the next. 'Can't remember which . . .'

The chairs on the lower balconies were plump and pillowy with pink and green cushions, but the ones at the top of the library were heavy old-fashioned things made of stiff brown leather.

'Aha,' Sundar said when he reached the third one along and gave it a good shove. The armchair refused to budge. 'This is it. Come and sit down – we'll both have to squash on.'

'What does it do?' Metty asked, ignoring a tingle of nerves.

'Gets us out of here,' Sundar replied and plonked down in the chair, squeezing up to make room for Metty. Once she was sitting too, he reached for a handle on the side of the chair. 'Hold on.'

Grinning, Sundar pulled it and the armchair shuddered. Metty hardly had a chance to grab on, digging her fingertips into the leather, before the chair gave a violent lurch and rocketed towards the ceiling, rising on a metal pole. She glanced up with a rush of panic. Any second now, they would crash into the glass.

Fortunately, a panel on the ceiling slid sideways, creating an open window. The leather armchair thrust Metty and Sundar up into the bitter night, then stopped with a sudden jolt.

They were still for a moment, admiring the sublime view they had from the rooftop. The night was a rich tapestry of blue, threaded with silvery clouds, and the city below was dazzlingly alive, lit by the birds of New London and their shining hearts. All the Halloween decorations had been taken down, and now a thin frost dusted some of the rooftops. The ink river had turned white as pearl, as though to reflect the starlight.

'We'd better go,' Metty said. She slid off the armchair, stepping onto the domed roof, then turned to look at Sundar. 'Uh, how do we get down from here?'

'Can't you just . . .?' He wiggled his fingers.

'Of course not. Aunt Mag'll know if I use magic. She might not notice if I only use a tiny bit, but it's too dangerous anyway.'

'No magic, got it.'

'Not unless I absolutely have to. If you've snuck out this way before, then how did you get down last time?'

Sundar shrugged. 'Climbed.'

Metty didn't find that option very appealing.

'I've got a better idea,' she said, then whistled for one

of the gondolas gliding above their heads.

The ride cost more than she expected and only left them with twenty-nine pounds. Metty realised with a squirmy feeling that they wouldn't have enough to pay for theatre tickets *and* a return journey, not unless they jumped out early and walked some of the way back. The same thought seemed to cross Sundar's mind.

'At least we made it here in one piece,' he said with a nervous smile. 'No run-ins with anyone dodgy.'

'Let's get inside the theatre,' Metty replied, glancing up and down the street.

A few people were ice-skating in Winter Park, and the boarded-up toyshop further along had replaced its giant nutcracker soldiers with a new pair in green coats. A large shadow of a moth stained the pavement in front of the shop, chasing away anyone who walked near it. Metty felt sorry for the owners. The shadow couldn't have been good for business.

A crowd was gathered on the steps of the theatre and heading slowly inside; ladies in faux fur and satin gowns and gentlemen in expensive tuxedos. Security guards flanked the theatre doors, and Metty spotted several police officers prowling up and down the streets. Clearly, they were worried about another attack. Still, there was a lot of excited chatter and a feeling that something extraordinary was about to begin.

Metty and Sundar joined the queue, standing behind a couple with a child. Maybe it would be impossible to buy tickets without an adult. They would have to come up with something if that was the case and find another way in.

'. . . can't wait to tell everyone at school about this,' the boy in front of them said in a carrying drawl. There was something familiar about his voice. Where had Metty heard it before? 'Half my classmates are so uncultured, you wouldn't even believe it. Their parents never bring them to anything like this.'

It hit her suddenly, like a finger jabbing her right between the eyes.

'Benedict Finch,' she muttered.

The boy turned round with a startled expression and peered down at her. He was just like she remembered, only taller, with his neat dark hair and shoes so polished they looked like shiny black mirrors.

'Oh, it's you,' he said, eyes widening at Metty. 'I remember – we were fated together, weren't we? Fancy running into you. Although your hair wasn't always that colour, was it?' He turned back to his parents before Metty could answer, a handsome couple having their own hushed conversation. 'Mum, Dad, this is the girl I was fated with!'

'How nice, dear,' Benedict's mother replied, giving him a brief smile. She was elegant and dark-haired, eye-catching in a sequinned navy dress.

'What was your name – Megan or something?' Benedict asked, spinning on the steps again.

'Metty.'

'Motty, that's right. Short for Margaret, I guess. Or is it one of those stupid made-up names some people have, like Moonbeam or Tinsel? There's a boy at my school called Feather, really there is. Anyway, it's so weird bumping into you – I thought we'd never see each other again. But then I guess we do have something in common.'

Benedict nodded at a picture of Madame LeBeau stuck to the theatre wall.

'Truth be told, I don't believe in ghosts and all that. Dad says it's just trickery, but at least Madame LeBeau knows how to put on a great show. Is this the first you've come to? We're given free tickets to all sorts of events because of Mum. She's the new governor, you see. At first, we were worried she'd get some backlash because she actually wants to change things around here, but luckily everyone loves her and—'

Benedict's mother touched his shoulder. 'No politics tonight, darling,' she said in a warm but firm way.

Finch. Of course. Metty eyed the lady with interest. So

this was Nadiya Finch, the woman who wanted to bring strict magic laws to New London. Apparently, she'd been listening to their conversation.

'Anyway,' Benedict continued, lowering his voice a fraction, 'we're all very proud, of course. And my father, well, *he* runs the biggest bank in New London. What do your parents do?'

'Er, my dad was in the navy,' Metty said, distracted. They were progressing up the steps, getting nearer the foyer.

'And your mother?' asked Benedict.

'She . . .'

Metty wasn't sure what to say. What *did* Daphne do apart from send postcards?

'What about you?' Benedict said to Sundar when she failed to answer.

'Dunno,' Sundar replied, hands in his pockets. He was standing close to Metty and radiating discomfort.

Benedict's lip curled. 'What do you mean you don't know?'

'Don't live with them any more. But my guardian collects dangerous curses.'

'Oh. Isn't that quite disreputable? Although obviously one can make a *lot* of money doing that sort of thing. Anyway, that reminds me of something my father said about . . .'

Metty zoned out while Benedict waffled on. She was relieved when they reached the foyer and the boy's beautiful, rich and highly accomplished parents steered him away.

'Good to see you, Motty!' he called back to her, waving a hand – the one with his fate tattoo. She still thought it looked more like a meteor than a sack of gold. 'Enjoy the show, and perhaps I'll come and find you at the interval.'

'God, I hope not,' Metty whispered to Sundar once they were alone.

Sundar giggled, but then the joy ebbed from his face. He'd spotted the ticket prices written on a board above the front desk. There were only a few seats left, some of the most expensive in the theatre.

Metty gasped. 'Eighty pounds!'

'Each,' said Sundar.

They exchanged a worried look.

'But we can't afford it,' Metty said.

'What are we going to do? We can't give up now,' Sundar replied, looking around anxiously. People were already leaving the foyer. The show was starting soon.

'No, we can't.' Metty rubbed her forehead. 'Just let me think for a second.'

She was running through scenarios in her mind – most ended in catastrophe with Aunt Mag storming into the theatre, eyes ablaze like a vengeful angel – when something grabbed her attention. A tinkling laugh that travelled across the foyer. A laugh she knew achingly well. A laugh she'd missed terribly.

Metty turned slowly, feeling disorientated. She could hardly believe her eyes. It was like stumbling into a dream.

Standing on the other side of the room, wearing a pink silk dress and a strawberry diamond on a choker, looking the very picture of glamour, was her mother, Daphne.

CHAPTER TWENTY-FIVE

Daphne

But that was impossible. Daphne was in New Paris, according to the last postcard she'd sent, although she changed cities so often that Metty could barely keep track. When had she even arrived in New London?

'Daphne!' Metty blurted out. The name shot from her mouth like a bullet. There was no drawing it back.

Daphne was still laughing as she turned round, entertained by something her companion had said. She was standing next to a tall, dark-haired man, her fingers resting on his elbow. Her sapphire eyes moved round the foyer, searching for whoever had called her name, then sharpened with surprise when they landed on Metty. Daphne's lips parted, becoming a perfect circle.

'Oh my goodness!' she cried, then flew across the room.

Her perfume poured over Metty, filling her nose with a sweet scent: apricot and vanilla. Daphne pulled her into a tight hug, and Metty found her cheek pressed to the cold silk of her mother's dress.

'Sweetheart, you're *here*!' Daphne said, pushing her back and holding her at arm's length. 'My God, I can't believe it! How long has it been? And look at you! Such a beautiful young woman! You must stop growing up – you make me feel so old! But what have you done to your hair? Oh, honey, that's not a flattering look. You don't have the right complexion for red.'

'Daphne . . .' Metty breathed. She could hardly believe it. She'd been longing for her mother all week. 'I don't understand. What are you doing in New London?'

'What am *I* doing here?' Daphne said with another silvery laugh. 'Darling, don't you know I travel everywhere? I arrived days ago. Surely the captain gave you my latest postcard?'

Metty shook her head, tears pricking her eyes. 'He's missing.'

Saying the words out loud to Daphne made them feel even more real.

'Missing?'

'Since my birthday. We don't know where he is, but—'

'Your father. Isn't he the worst?' Daphne sighed, wafting a hand. Her tether was a pale satin glove with a panel cut out to display her rose tattoo. 'Always making everyone worry about him. I'm sure he'll turn up soon enough. Now you have to come and meet Charles – he's just going to love you. Charlie, sweetheart?'

Before Metty could get out another word, Daphne grabbed her shoulders and steered her over to the tall man she'd been standing with before. He turned to face them with a polite smile, his wavy hair slicked back and shining in the lamplight. The man reminded Metty of the captain. He was in his early forties with similar dark eyes, though his were glassy where her father's were warm, and his skin was bone-white.

'Metty, this is Charles Tanner, only one of the smartest men I know.'

The gentleman breathed a laugh. 'High praise indeed.'

His gaze flicked down to Metty, coldly curious, pinning her to the spot. He wore a dark suede tether that revealed his fate, like Daphne's, and held a cane topped with a snarling wolf's head. Metty tried not to show her instinctive disgust as she looked at the man's tattoo: a fist clenching a black, rotting heart. She had no idea what such a fate meant, though probably something foul.

'And who's this?' Tanner asked.

'*This*,' Daphne said, beaming with pride, 'is my little girl, Metty. I know, I know, you'd never believe I was old enough to be her mother. But look, Charlie, can't you see the resemblance? She has my eyes, lucky thing. Oh, Metty, I have so much to tell you.' Daphne held out her left hand, showing off a diamond ring. 'Isn't it gorgeous? You know what it means, right? Mr Tanner's asked me to marry him, and obviously I said yes!'

'You're getting married?' Metty said in a stilted voice. This whole conversation was too much, her mother's words raining down on her like hail.

Daphne's excitement faltered, but then she pasted on a smile. 'Aren't you happy for me, darling? Anyway, what are *you* doing here? Surely you're not by yourself.'

'Uh, no, I'm with . . .' Metty glanced around for Sundar. He was hovering awkwardly across the foyer. She waved him over. 'This is Sundar, my friend. We're here to see Madame LeBeau, in case she knows something about the captain. He's missing, like I said, and—'

'But isn't someone with you?' Daphne interrupted, frowning in concern.

'No, but listen, I'm trying to find—'

'Baby, you can't be here on your own,' she said, squeezing Metty's arm. 'Don't you know how dangerous the city is at night? Anything could happen. We need to get you somewhere safe.'

'But what about Madame—'

'Never mind the show. We've got you to worry about now, and Charles doesn't mind, do you, sweetheart?'

Tanner didn't answer, though his smile looked forced.

'I know where we'll go,' Daphne said, taking Metty's hand and leading her to the theatre doors. 'I can take you back to my hotel and show you all the wonderful things I've bought since I arrived. I have so many presents for you – I know you'll adore them all. And we'll fix your hair. Red's *really* not your colour.'

'Wait, what about the plan?' Sundar whispered in Metty's ear, jogging to keep up as Daphne swept her through the foyer and down the steps outside.

'Daphne, we really do need to see Madame LeBeau,' Metty said, digging in her heels.

Her mother only flicked a hand. 'Don't worry about that, sugar. You know Fayola's an old friend. I can introduce you any time. In fact, if you come along now, I'll phone the theatre from the hotel and see if she'll agree to drop by after the show, how's that? Charlie, would you get Mr Flint to bring round the gondola? I cannot walk a mile in these heels.'

Metty pinned her hands between her thighs and glanced over the side of the gondola. The pavement seemed awfully far away as they soared through the liquid night, casting a shadow on the cobblestones below. She was squashed onto a bench with Sundar, opposite Daphne and Tanner and the gondolier at the end of the boat.

Guilt and curiosity battled inside her. What would Aunt Mag do when she realised they'd snuck out of Winter's Knock and flown off with Daphne?

Then again, Metty was with her mother, not some dangerous stranger. Daphne could take her wherever she liked. And meeting Madame LeBeau in a hotel was probably safer than talking to her at the theatre. Plus, once she and Daphne were alone, Metty could explain about the captain and the Black Moths. Surely her mother would help them look for him once she realised how dire the situation was.

'I've really missed you,' Metty said, trying to ignore Tanner, whose looming silhouette unnerved her. The man was incredibly tall, his eyes like black beads of glass. He'd removed his bow tie as they left the theatre and dropped it in his pocket.

Daphne leaned forward, patting Metty's knee.

'I know, honey. I've missed you too. Honestly, if I'd had it my way, you would've come to live with me years ago, but here we are now! I'm so glad we ran into each other. And who knows? Maybe we can finally arrange something.'

'I've been staying at Winter's Knock with Aunt Mag.'

Daphne made an appalled face, rolling her eyes. 'Urgh, not that place. Don't you find the house cold? And so old-fashioned. I've never liked it. You'll be much more comfortable with me at the hotel.'

'Where is your hotel?' Metty asked, frowning as they flew out of Inkshimmer. Surely all the fanciest places were at the very top of the city?

'Not too far,' Tanner replied. His voice was smooth, dripping with confidence. He struck Metty as somebody who lived in an exquisite house and kept a lot of staff, the kind of man who was used to being obeyed and having everything just so. She shot him a steely look from the corner of her eye.

Sundar kept poking her in the ribs.

'What?' she muttered, glaring at him.

To her alarm, the boy's face looked stricken, and he was staring wide-eyed at Tanner. Metty turned her head, following Sundar's gaze. There was something pinned to the man's collar, just visible in the shadows.

A jet-black moth spreading its wings.

Fear made the air crackle in Metty's lungs. She almost gasped but stopped herself, sucking in her lips. Tanner seemed to notice her attention, his mouth twisting into a sly smile as he tugged his collar, concealing the pin. Metty looked at Daphne, who was watching the moon with a serene expression. Did her mother have any idea that Tanner was a Black Moth?

Sundar poked Metty again, hard enough to make her wince. She shook her head, encouraging him to stay quiet. She needed to think, to plan. Then her attention snagged on the gondolier at the back of the boat. The man Daphne had called Flint.

She knew that face, knew those sharp teeth, that wolfy smile.

The man from the alleyway . . .

She and Sundar were trapped, like stupid birds that had flown thoughtlessly into a cage. One question kept repeating itself inside Metty's head, hammering into her brain: did her mother know?

'Oh good, we're here,' Daphne said, rubbing her hands excitedly as the gondola swooped down to the pavement. It had brought them to the chasm that split the city, the one with the rotating bridges named after engineers and inventors who'd used ink in their creations. But why on earth were they *here*?

'Not long to wait now,' Daphne added, climbing gracefully from the gondola with Tanner's assistance.

Metty hopped over the side before he could help her. The pavement felt unsteady beneath her, like the cobbles were made of jelly. Sundar came and stood close by, his breath warming her ear. They would have to make a run for it, try and race back to Winter's Knock, but how were they supposed to get away? That awful man, Flint, had planted himself behind them like a brick wall.

'We'll take Nobel, I think,' Tanner said. He approached the lip of the chasm, twirling his cane absent-mindedly. A white bridge was floating towards them and would arrive any minute. They had no opportunity to escape.

'Come hold my hand!' Daphne called back to Metty, smiling. She held out her satiny palm. Metty took it reluctantly, clutching Sundar's arm with her other hand. Nobel Bridge slowed as it made its way along the bank. They all stepped onto it, led by Tanner, with Flint at the rear.

'You know, it's so lucky that I ran into you tonight,' Daphne said, pressing Metty's stiff fingers. 'Some friends of mine are just dying to meet you. I've told everyone what a special girl you are, and they'll all be so thrilled when I bring you home.'

'Special?' Metty squeaked, the word almost sticking in her throat.

'Of course! You're quite a treasure.'

'A rare jewel,' Tanner said.

Metty's dread thickened. She had to stay calm, had to try and think clearly.

'You mean because of my fate?' she said, looking up at her mother.

Daphne seemed surprised, tilting her head. 'You know? Did Moral finally tell you?'

'Tell me what?'

'Metty,' Sundar hissed, prodding her side again.

He was watching Tanner, who'd taken out his magic meter. The man placed his tethered hand on the wall of the bridge and concentrated hard. The stone shivered under their feet, and they all wobbled as the bridge rocked. It seemed to resist Tanner's will, trying to continue along its normal route, but he was forcing it to drift away from both banks.

Metty tore her hand from Daphne's. She and Sundar stumbled back and dodged round Flint who was struggling to stay upright. The three adults were standing between them and the way back to the upper half of New London as Nobel Bridge twisted slowly in mid-air.

'It's just a short flight. No need to be afraid,' Tanner said calmly.

Daphne put out her hand again, still hanging on to the wall of the bridge. 'Come forward a bit, sugar. Don't want you falling off the edge.'

Metty shook her head, backing up further. She and Sundar could still reach the lower bank if they hurried, but the others would surely come thundering after them. Flint seemed ready to grab them if they moved another inch.

'Trust me, sweetheart,' Daphne said, a note of desperation entering her voice. 'Don't you want to come and meet my friends? I've told them so much about you.'

Suddenly Metty knew the truth. It slid into her heart like a cold blade. Her mother wasn't just with the Black Moths: she was *one* of them.

'This is bad,' Sundar whispered, pulling Metty's arm. 'This is very bad. I think you should do something.'

The bridge was turning faster now. In a few seconds, they wouldn't be able to reach the bank. Drawing a shaky breath, Metty uncurled her right hand and pointed at the bridge. She didn't know what to do. Her imagination was in a tangle, but she had to try something. Magic coursed through her fingers. It felt wild, like something impossible to rein in, but Aunt Mag's voice rang in her head: *You just have to take control.*

'Metty,' Daphne said without blinking. Tears polished her dark blue eyes. Her hand was still outstretched, but wavering. 'I've waited so long to see—'

A deafening crunch silenced her as a crack appeared in the middle of the bridge. Metty stared at it, concentrating. The gap widened, dropping fragments of stone that plunged thousands of feet towards the dark ocean. White dust swirled in the air, swept up by the wind. Metty's palm was burning, though the sensation quickly faded. She couldn't believe she'd actually torn apart a bridge.

'Come on,' Sundar said, dragging her away.

The adults were in chaos on the other side of the divide. Tanner looked outraged, his eyes shining like black ice. Flint was getting ready to leap across the gap. Daphne stared silently at Metty, her gaze full of hurt, her hand still extended.

'Metty, we need to go!' Sundar yelled.

Glancing away from her mother, Metty turned and sprinted. She didn't slow down, taking a running jump, and closed her eyes as her feet left the bridge. She flew through the air for a nauseating heartbeat, too afraid to look down at the deep blue ocean glimmering far below.

And then she landed on the edge of the bank. Sundar touched down a second later, wobbling dangerously until Metty grabbed his shoulder. They rushed forward together, stepping onto firmer ground. Behind them, the bridge was crumbling into pieces.

For an awful second, Metty thought that this was the moment, that her fate was finally coming true: that her own mother might be 'the one'. She whirled round, terrified of what she might see. But Tanner and Daphne were clinging to a piece of the broken bridge, Tanner using magic to guide it towards the bank. They were coming after them.

'Don't look back,' Sundar said, clasping Metty's hand. 'Just run!'

CHAPTER TWENTY-SIX

The Long Way Home

'We're going the wrong way!' Metty gasped as she and Sundar raced round another corner. Most of the shops in New London were closed for the night, leaving the streets quiet. The slap of their footsteps echoed around them, bouncing off the walls and the shadowy cobblestones.

'Doesn't matter!' Sundar shouted back. He was faster than Metty and running a few feet ahead of her. 'Just keep going!'

She hardly dared stop, though she was already getting out of breath, her eyes streaming in the cold.

'Wait,' Metty panted, doubling over. 'I just need . . .'

Sundar's hand clapped onto her shoulder. He pointed at something behind her, a silhouette at the end of the street. Flint's sharp teeth flashed in the light of a lamppost, bared in a hungry smile.

'Metty, come on,' Sundar said, grabbing her hand again, 'we have to go!'

They ran for what felt like hours, hurrying through the maze-like streets, getting further away from Winter's Knock with every step. Metty skidded to a halt when she spotted one of the New London stations. It was still lit up and open to the public.

'Quick, over there,' she said, tugging Sundar's arm.

The warmth of the station washed over them as they tumbled through the front doors and came to a breathless stop, heels squeaking on the floor. Some heads turned in their direction, but the place was mostly empty. Only a few gondolas were loading passengers, then exiting through an archway at the back of the hall.

Metty turned to the station doors. Nobody had entered since them, so maybe they'd managed to lose Flint. It seemed foolish to just stand around, so she grabbed Sundar's hand and pulled him into a quiet corner of the station.

'What now?' he whispered once they were away from any eavesdroppers. 'How are we meant to get home without running into *them*? And did you see that guy's fate?'

'You mean Tanner's?'

Metty grimaced, remembering the rotting black heart tattooed on his hand.

'It was horrible,' Sundar said. 'What d'you think it means?'

'I don't know.' Metty was struggling to make sense of anything, her thoughts rattling in her head like a bunch of loose coins. Tanner had been trying to take them somewhere, using the bridge to soar off into the night – but where? She took a deep breath, forcing herself to concentrate. 'Maybe . . . maybe Aunt Mag'll come and find us. I mean, she must know I used magic back there.'

'A lot of magic,' Sundar agreed.

'Grade four, at least. Which means there won't be much ink left in the meter, by the way, so we need to be careful. Look, there's the stationmaster over there. I bet she could—'

'No!' Sundar said, panic brightening his eyes.

'What's the matter? Why can't we ask—'

'Look, we can't speak to anyone official, okay? Just . . . please, Metty.'

'Hey, it's all right. Don't get upset.' Metty sighed through her nose, biting her lip. Not being able to trust the authorities made things a lot trickier. 'But I'm not sure how else we're meant to . . .'

Something twinkled in the corner of her eye: a vending machine full of silver bells.

'I've got it,' she said with a surge of excitement. 'We've still got some money, right? Hand it over. Oh, and keep an eye on the doors. We don't want that creep sneaking up on us while we're distracted.'

Metty snatched a twenty-pound banknote from Sundar and fed it into the vending machine. The money disappeared, and a moment later one of those funny direction bells clunked into the drawer at the bottom. She crouched and took it out. The bell was about the size of an apple, and it made no sound when Metty shook it.

'Do you think it's broken?' Sundar asked, frowning over her shoulder.

'No, I saw one do this to somebody else. I'm not really sure how it works.'

'Try saying where you want to go.'

'Okay,' Metty muttered, thinking for a moment. 'Winter's Knock,' she said in a clear voice, then shook the bell again. Still nothing.

'Let's have a look,' Sundar said.

But as she moved to pass him the bell it gave a soft tinkle.

'Hang on a minute,' Metty said, then spun slowly in a circle. The ringing got louder as she turned until the noise was piercing, then it softened and faded to silence when she kept on spinning. 'I think I get it,' she said, turning until the bell clanged again. 'They're *direction* bells. They ring when you're heading in the right direction and go quiet when you're not, don't you see? It rings when I'm facing the station doors because that's the way to Winter's Knock!'

'Great,' Sundar replied, scratching his brow. 'Except we already know where Winter's Knock is. Finding our way home's not the problem – it's getting past the Black Moths.'

'But maybe we can use this to find someone who can help us. Someone not official,' Metty added at the boy's fraught expression. 'Hang on, let me try . . . Kiki Darego!'

But the bell wouldn't ring. It didn't matter what direction Metty faced, twirling around until she felt sick.

'She might not be in New London right now,' Sundar suggested.

Metty frowned, worry settling in her stomach like a rock. She wasn't sure who else to try. There was no point asking the bell to find Aunt Mag or Rupert. They would surely be at Winter's Knock, way up in Highfate, and impossible to get to while the Black Moths were after them. Metty didn't really know anyone else in New London. An idea flashed through her mind, taking the shape of a foxy face with hazel eyes and a mass of ginger hair.

'I think I know someone who might be able to help,' she told Sundar. 'At the very least, she knows this city better than anyone I've met so far.'

'Try it then,' Sundar said.

Metty nodded, concentrating on the bell. 'Faith O'Connell.' But the bell wouldn't sing for Faith either.

'This is ridiculous,' Metty snapped, shaking it in frustration.

'There's no way they've both left the city. Maybe the stupid thing is broken.'

'Or it doesn't lead you to people, just places.'

'Right. That would make sense.'

Metty heaved a sigh. She had no clue where to find Faith. Except . . . hadn't that police officer mentioned somewhere, the one who'd treated Faith like vermin? Metty groaned, tapping her forehead.

'Oh, what did he say? Something beginning with "S" . . . Wait! Sundar, where did we go on Halloween, that place with the tree? The district for ill-fated people?'

'Sinner's Oak?'

'Sinner's Oak, that's it!' Metty cried, beaming at him. She repeated the name to the direction bell, then spun round giddily. It tinkled as she turned to face the station doors. 'Sundar, you're a genius!'

'Thanks. I mean, I've been told before, but—'

'Let's go!' Metty said, dragging him along by the hand. 'And keep your eyes peeled for Flint. I bet we haven't lost him.'

WELCOME TO SINNER'S OAK.

The bottom of New London was a world apart from the clean and colourful roads above, especially without all the Halloween decorations to mask the grimness. Metty had walked through some of these streets six days ago, but they seemed more frightening at night, without Rupert and the crowds of trick-or-treaters. She and Sundar stayed close together as they hurried through Sinner's Oak, wincing at the signposts: CROOKED COURT, BLACK-KNUCKLES ALLEY, JINXED LANE. Metty refused to walk through a place called the Blood Quarter, not that Sundar was keen either.

She couldn't help feeling sorry for Faith, being stuck somewhere so dreadful just because of her tattoo. Though Metty wondered again if she belonged down there as well, with all the other ill-fated people.

The deeper they travelled into Sinner's Oak, the worse it became, full of wonky houses and alleyways overrun by weeds. Mangy cats slunk along the pavements, their eyes flashing in the dimness. Laundry lines crisscrossed overhead, strung from every windowsill, and there was a stubborn smell of soot and overflowing bins.

'It's so shadowy down here. You'd think we were in the Darkness,' Sundar said as the bell led them through the gloomy streets. They hadn't stopped moving since they'd left the station. There was no sign of Flint, at least.

'The Darkness?'

'It's what they call the lowest bit, you know, right at the bottom of the city – where they drop your house if you can't pay the rent.'

'*Drop* you?' Metty said, paling at the thought. She imagined a building sinking through the air like a damaged ship. 'What happens if you already live down there and you run out of money?'

Sundar mimed a house falling with his right fist. His left became the ocean.

'Splash!' he said. 'Or smash, I guess, at that velocity. But they always evict the residents first. Although I've heard some people refuse to go.'

'That's awful,' Metty said. She couldn't bear to think of Winter's Knock plunging into the ocean and finding a watery grave on the seafloor.

'That's life. Don't worry though. We'd have to drop a long way before we even reached the Darkness.'

'That's not the point, Sundar. Ouch, watch where you're going. You keep stepping on my foot.'

'Sorry, can't see a thing. Hey, why don't you call down one of the birds? You know, the lamppost ones?'

Metty frowned, struggling to make out anything in the dimness. 'Can you do that? Summon the birds?'

'Can *I* do it? Doubt it, but you should be able to. You're a Jones.'

'So?'

'One of your lot enchanted them all. Didn't Mag tell you? Think it was Magnetic or Munchable, somethinglike that.'

'There's never been a Munchable Jones,' Metty said crossly. At least she hoped not.

'Give it a go,' Sundar said, knocking her with his elbow. 'Go on – we're practically blind down here.'

'I'm not sure how,' Metty said and looked around for the nearest solar bird.

The lampposts were spaced far apart in Sinner's Oak and didn't seem to attract many of the lovely creatures. No doubt they preferred the clean air of the districts above. There was one that looked like a pigeon further up the street. Threads of golden light glimmered on its feathers.

'You just whistle, I think,' Sundar said. 'I saw Mag do it once.'

Lowering the direction bell, Metty brought her tongue to her teeth and whistled. The bird immediately spread its wings and swooped towards them, yellow light streaking along the pavement beneath it. Metty started to back up, suddenly nervous, then stopped as the bird landed on her shoulder. Its talons were heavy, digging into her skin. The light radiating from its chest warmed the side of her face.

'Hello,' she said, stroking the bird's head. It gave a disgruntled coo.

'That's better. Now we can actually see,' Sundar said, reaching out to pet the bird as well. To Metty's surprise, it responded better to him, fluffing its neck feathers and clicking its beak.

'Come on then,' she said, shaking the direction bell again.

About five minutes later, Metty spotted a plaque that said CUTPURSE CORNER.

'Wait!' she cried, grabbing Sundar's wrist. 'Cutpurse – isn't that another word for thief? I bet this is where Faith lives. Come on!'

Cutpurse Corner turned out to be a cul-de-sac with shabby houses and rooftops like mushroom caps. Metty knew at once that they'd found the right place. Playing outside a house with a lopsided green door, and a letterbox shaped like a sleeping dragon, were a bunch of ginger children. Several pairs of hazel eyes turned to look their way.

'This is it,' Metty said quietly to Sundar.

'What are you all doing out here?' Faith demanded as she stormed through the front door. Her sleeves were rolled up, and her arms were pink like she'd just been scrubbing dishes in hot water. 'Ma told you lot to get to bed!'

'She told you too,' a younger girl snapped while the others tramped obediently inside.

'Yeah, well, that's only cos she got me muddled up with Kate. I go to bed whenever I want, which happens to be never. Unlike some lazybones, I've got work to do. Now get in the house before I—'

Faith never finished her threat, noticing Metty and Sundar.

'Jones,' she said, then waved them over with a crooked smile.

'O'Connell,' Metty replied, trying to keep a straight face.

'Surprised you remember my name. Rich folks ain't usually good at recalling us little people.'

'Funnily enough, you were quite memorable.'

'Suppose I was. Nice trick with the bird, by the way.' Faith's eyes narrowed in suspicion. 'What you doing all the way down here? Sinner's Oak ain't safe at night – or in the day for that matter, not for fancy sorts. And who's your friend?'

'This is Sundar,' Metty said, pressing the boy's shoulder. 'And I hope you don't mind, but we've come to ask for your help.'

'My help? I'd love to know what you think I can do for someone like you.'

'You know this city well, don't you?'

'Like the back of my hand,' Faith said, still wary.

'Well, Sundar and me, we need to get up to Highfate, but these people are chasing us and—'

'What sort of people?'

'Bad ones,' Sundar said.

'And why they after you?' said Faith.

'It's complicated,' Metty replied in a serious voice. 'And private. It's probably better for you if we don't explain. Anyway, we really need to get home, but we can't travel out in the open and I was hoping you might—'

'Find a way that's more discreet,' Faith said, dusting her knuckles on her jacket.

Metty nodded.

The girl considered, chewing the side of her mouth.

'All right,' she said after a tense silence. 'You was pretty good to me the other week, and us ill-fated should look out for each other, right?' She raised a bony finger, pointing it right at Metty's nose. 'But this means you owe me, got it? Owe me big.'

'Absolutely,' Metty said, a relieved sigh expanding her chest.

'All right,' Faith said again, then turned round, marching back to the house. She called over her shoulder, 'Know a few routes that might work, but the thing we'll want most is speed. Are these "bad people" chasing you on foot?'

Metty and Sundar both nodded.

'That works for us,' Faith said. She threw open the front door and bellowed: 'Griff! C'mere!'

Half a minute later, a teenage boy emerged from the house. He looked like an older, lankier version of Faith with the same freckled skin and rumpled red hair. His fate was a magpie with something shiny in its beak.

'This is Griff, my brother,' Faith said, punching his arm. 'Griff, these are mates of mine. Metty and . . . sorry, I forget your name.'

'Sundar.'

'Sundar, right. Anyway, I said I'd do 'em a favour and guide them back to Highfate. There's fellas after 'em, bad sorts, so we'll need to be quick.'

She stopped talking, staring at her brother with a pleading expression. Griff rolled his eyes and smoothed down his messy hair.

'I hope you ain't asking what I think you are,' he said wearily.

'You know we won't all fit on mine.'

The boy expelled a long sigh. Faith seemed to take this as a sign of compliance and turned to Sundar and Metty with a toothy grin.

'Right,' she said, bringing her hands together. 'Something tells me you two ain't got much experience with wind bikes.'

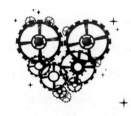

CHAPTER TWENTY-SEVEN

Ride Like the Wind

Metty had a nasty feeling she was doing something stupid and probably very dangerous as she pulled herself onto the handlebars of Faith's wind bike. At least she could hang on to the leather grips. Griff held the bike steady for them while Metty climbed up and Faith settled on the seat.

Wind bikes were much larger than ordinary bicycles, so they weren't too cramped. Faith's had an umbrella with olive green and yellow stripes, whereas the umbrella curving over Griff's bike was pink and advertised cherry-scented shampoo. Metty wondered fleetingly if the wind bikes were stolen, then decided she didn't care.

Once she and Faith were ready, pedalling round the cul-de-sac to build some momentum, Griff returned to his own bike and held it so Sundar could lift himself onto the handlebars. Soon they were all set to go.

'Right,' Faith said, twisting a dial that looked a bit like a gear changer. Suddenly the umbrella on the back of her bike puffed up like a stripy jellyfish, and they soared forward with a great gust of air.

Metty shrieked, clutching the handlebars so tightly that her fingernails hurt. She'd seen wind bikes whizzing through the streets of New London, but it was quite another thing to be riding on one with the air blowing against her face, making her eyes sting and her cheeks flap.

Faith whooped behind her, apparently having fun, as they flew away from Cutpurse Corner and started rocketing through Sinner's Oak. She turned the dial a few more times to build some real speed. The umbrella behind them swelled and swelled like somebody taking an enormous breath. They were riding uphill, towards the chasm with the bridges and the top half of New London. Griff and Sundar kept drawing alongside them, but Faith was determined to stay ahead, urging on her bike.

'*Sloooow down!*' Metty wailed, wobbling on the handlebars.

'No way!' cackled Faith and pedalled harder.

'Isn't this great!' Sundar yelled from the front of Griff's bike.

Metty stared at him in outrage. 'No!'

It felt like she'd left her stomach behind in Cutpurse

Corner, along with her courage and any hope of reaching home in one piece.

Before long, they were whooshing out of Sinner's Oak. Metty was relieved to rise above the sooty darkness and find herself in a brighter, more familiar part of the city. Faith and Griff seemed to know where they were going, racing intuitively through alleyways and cobbled squares that were eerily empty.

Metty shut her eyes and winced as they hurtled towards a solid wall, but the bricks parted round them like mist and delivered them to another quiet street. They couldn't have been far from the split in the city, where the floating bridges were. Metty cautiously began to think that they might make it back safely.

And then Faith pointed at a knot of clouds above their heads.

'Reckon your mates have caught up,' she said, prompting Metty to look skyward.

Sure enough, a gondola was cutting through the clouds like a black blade. It turned whenever they turned, following their route. Somebody leaned over the side – she couldn't see who – and made an ominous fist.

Faith swore as the pavement in front of them curled suddenly, ripping up like a strip of carpet. She and Griff had to turn abruptly, swerving in different directions. Faith hurtled down a narrow passage on the right while her brother screeched around and disappeared the way they'd come.

'Wait!' Metty cried, almost flying off the handlebars. 'What about the others? I can't leave Sundar.'

'He'll be all right,' Faith panted, pedalling as hard as she could. 'Griff knows what he's doing. Worry about us – we're the ones being chased.'

She was right. The gondola had changed direction too and was knifing after them again.

'What do we do?' Metty said.

Faith gritted her teeth. 'Go faster.'

She gave the gear shift a violent twist. The umbrella stretched even wider behind them, propelling the bike along at a stupendous pace. It rattled as they dodged round corners, flying through false walls, powering up sloped alleyways, staying just ahead of the gondola in the sky.

And then there was a loud tearing sound.

'What was that?' Faith asked, having to shout over the roaring wind.

Metty turned on the handlebars to look. Her heart plummeted. There was a hole in the fabric of the umbrella, and the rest of it was flapping wildly. The bike was already slowing down.

'It's broken!' Metty cried, throwing a panicked look at Faith. 'It's ripped!'

What on earth were they going to do now, stranded in the middle of New London with that gondola streaking after them and no way to outrun it?

'Hang on. We're nearly there,' Faith said, then took a sharp left down an alleyway. She was having to pedal extra hard. Sweat glistened on her forehead, trickling down her rosy cheeks.

Metty kept her eyes on the gondola. It was descending now, spilling its shadow over them as it sank towards the pavement. Was Daphne inside it with that cold-blooded man Tanner?

'Hold on tight,' Faith barked when they erupted from the alleyway into a wider street.

Metty wasn't sure she could squeeze the handlebars any tighter. There was a strange tunnel in the ground up ahead, like a monstrous mouth, and Faith was cycling towards it with furious determination. The gondola was only five or six feet above their heads when they rolled into the tunnel and began speeding downhill.

The darkness was impenetrable – Metty couldn't see a thing, which made the downward journey so much more frightening. A scream tore from her throat but, to her relief, they slowed a little as the tunnel levelled out.

A ring of bulbs suddenly flashed around them, flooding the space with vivid blue light. Their speed picked up again.

A flash of green, of glaring yellow, of fiery orange . . .

Each belt of light accompanied a powerful wind blast that launched them through the tunnel faster and faster until Metty couldn't stay upright any longer, tipping backwards into Faith who, fortunately, didn't lose control of the bike. Finally, they passed through a bright violet archway that shot them forcefully out of the tunnel and up onto the pavement again.

The tunnel catapulted them through several streets, and soon they were near the chasm separating the two halves of New London. If the gondola was still following them, it had fallen some way behind.

They only began to slow as they approached the edge of the pavement. Faith pressed the brakes, but they were going too fast, and the bike skidded with an ear-splitting screech.

A crowd of pedestrians and police officers were gathered on the bank up ahead. Most turned to look as Faith and Metty careened towards them. They would collide any moment or ride straight off the side of New London.

Faith tried to swerve, but that only resulted in her and Metty flying off the bike at breakneck speed. For a second, Metty twirled in mid-air, vaguely conscious of the ground rising to greet her, and then she impacted with a painful thud, sliding along on her front.

She frowned as she came to a stop, not far from the chasm's

edge, lying face down on the cobblestones. That should have hurt a lot more than it did.

The texture of the street had changed, becoming light and squishy like a feather bed. Metty stood up and glanced gratefully at the crowd, not certain who'd used magic to soften her fall. Some people were glaring at her and Faith and muttering in disapproval. Others had returned their attention to the broken shards of Nobel Bridge, floating up and down in the middle of the chasm. The other five bridges had stopped turning like a carousel and were fixed in place for once, connecting the two banks.

'Oi, c'mere you,' said a husky voice behind Metty, and a hand seized her arm. It belonged to a police officer. The woman's partner had restrained Faith, who was putting up a good fight, squirming and scratching like an alley cat.

'Let go,' Metty said, trying to free herself from the officer's grip.

'What d'you think you're doing, going at that speed along here? You idiots could've killed somebody, never mind yourselves. What business you got in the top half, eh?'

'I live there,' Metty replied indignantly.

The woman laughed. 'Yeah, right. Look at the state of you.'

Metty's clothes were filthy, covered in smears of soot. Her tatty hair was losing its redness and darkening in patches, turning stripy like a tiger's fur. Glowering at the officer, she opened her mouth to protest, but was silenced by a furious shout: 'Get your hands off my sister!'

Faith's brother was shoving his way through the crowd, his face so red that it was hard to see his freckles. He barrelled into the other officer and tried to wedge himself between the man and Faith. Metty glimpsed Sundar hiding nearby among a group of strangers.

'We got as much right to be here as anyone else!' Faith shrieked while Griff wrestled with the flustered officer. The woman holding Metty snatched up her whistle. She blew into it sharply, and two more police officers came weaving towards them. This was turning into a complete disaster.

'Excuse me, officer, those children are with me!' somebody called out, and a hand waved above the crowd; a hand tattooed with a golden mask. Metty exhaled in relief as Rupert pushed his way over, looking pink-faced and out of breath.

'Is that so?' said the police officer.

Rupert straightened up. 'Yes, it is, and I suggest you unhand them at once,' he said with icy calmness, then reached into his jacket for something. 'These are my papers,' he added, pressing them into the officer's hand. 'You can see quite clearly that I'm a resident of Highfate.'

The officer pursed her lips, but then her expression changed as she studied Rupert's ID.

'I see, Mr Jones,' she said with a new tone of deference.

'And do all these children belong to you?'

Metty threw her uncle a beseeching look.

He returned a tight smile. '*All* of them.'

'I'll see that you two get back to Sinner's Oak without any more trouble. And of course we'll cover the cost of any repairs to your wind bikes or purchase new ones if necessary,' Rupert reassured Faith and her brother as they were approaching Winter's Knock.

Metty had explained the night's events after they'd grabbed Sundar from the crowd and crossed Edison Bridge, although she hadn't named the Black Moths. She'd also neglected to mention that Faith was a pickpocket, although Rupert could probably tell that from her fate. He seemed grateful to the O'Connells, who were still bristling from their encounter with the police.

'First, I need to get these two runaways home,' he added, nodding at Metty and Sundar. 'Mag is *not* happy, by the way, although she'll be glad to know you're safe and sound.'

Metty could no longer ignore the dread worming around in her stomach, especially as they came within sight of the house. She'd been trying not to think about Aunt Mag all night.

'Thanks for everything. You really saved our skin,' she whispered to Faith when they were about to part ways. She pulled the girl into a stiff hug. Faith didn't seem sure what to do, holding her arms out awkwardly, though she was hiding a smile when Metty let go.

'Remember,' she said, 'you owe me big.'

'Definitely. If there's ever anything I can do . . .' Metty hooked her thumb at Winter's Knock. 'Well, obviously, you'll know where to find me.'

'Oh, trust me, I'll be in touch,' Faith said, then grinned and bumped Metty's shoulder. 'Tonight was fun. I mean, not the being arrested part, but—'

'The part where we crashed and nearly died?'

'More racing through the city. Oh, and the wind tunnel – that was awesome. Anyway, don't forget: you owe me, Jones.'

Rupert unlocked the door to Winter's Knock, then left with the O'Connells. Metty watched them go from the front steps, waving goodbye to Faith, then she followed Sundar into the entrance hall. It was chilly and unwelcoming, the cabinets painting shadows on the floor.

'Are you all right?' Metty asked Sundar, who seemed shaken.

Before he could reply, there was a rush of frantic footsteps and Aunt Mag appeared from a room down the corridor. She looked frazzled and tired and quite unlike her usual self.

'Oh, thank God,' she groaned, bounding over to them. She grabbed Sundar's face and attacked the boy with fierce kisses.

A moment later, she did the same to Metty, then stood back, eyes blazing. 'You bloody idiots. I could strangle you both.'

'I'm so sorry, Mag,' Sundar said. He sounded tearful, though his eyes were dry, his hands trembling at his sides. 'I don't know what I was thinking. It was so stupid. I just—'

'It's all right,' Aunt Mag said, recovering her temper. She gave Sundar a meaningful look. 'Did anyone recognise you?'

He shook his head.

'Good. That's something.'

'I just wanted . . .' he murmured. 'I just thought if . . .'

'It's all right,' Aunt Mag repeated and grazed his cheek with her knuckles. 'It wasn't your fault.'

Her frosty gaze shifted to Metty. Suddenly it was quite clear whose fault it was.

'You and I are going to talk,' Aunt Mag said. 'Now.'

'I told you I needed to go back to the theatre,' Metty said, pacing round Aunt Mag's study. The room had never felt so claustrophobic.

'Sit down,' her aunt requested coldly.

Metty ignored her, storming back and forth. It felt like her blood was boiling, like she was full of hot water and if she stayed still she'd drown. 'It's the last place I saw the captain, and I know you don't believe someone can rewrite their fate, but how do you know if you haven't tried, and it's not like I—'

'*Sit* down,' Aunt Mag snapped and Metty reluctantly threw herself into a chair.

'You're angry with me,' she said to her aunt.

'Yes, dear, that's stating the obvious.'

'Because I didn't listen to you. Because I made my own decisions. Because I won't just sit around doing nothing and wait for everything to magically get better.'

Aunt Mag leaned forward. 'Because you don't understand the full situation.'

'And why's that? Because you won't tell me anything!' Metty cried, flattening her hands on the desk. 'Did you know Daphne was a Black Moth?'

'Your mother's a complicated woman. She's doing what she believes is right, which seems to be precisely what *you* did tonight, endangering yourself and Sundar for the sake of some ridiculous, half-baked—'

'Sundar wanted to come,' Metty said. 'He wants to find out his fate, and I don't see why he shouldn't just because he missed his stupid fating. Otherwise, he'll never get to use magic. And *you* won't let him go outside. You're keeping him locked up in this house like a prisoner. Is it any wonder he wants to escape?'

Aunt Mag's mouth was so small it was almost invisible. 'It's for his own good.'

'How can you think that?' Metty cried. 'Being shut up and

treated like a criminal isn't good for anyone! Do you have any idea how it feels?'

'Metty, Sundar is not an ordinary boy.'

'I don't care. He deserves to live like anyone else, and if he wants to get his fate—'

Aunt Mag was shaking her head in frustration. 'You *don't* understand. That sort of magic won't work on him.'

'Why not?'

'Because he isn't alive!'

Aunt Mag breathed out and sank slowly back in her chair. It was as if all the energy was leaving her body, draining out of her like water. She steepled her fingers before her mouth, staring at Metty over their tips, her eyes afraid. There was a moment of stunned silence.

'What do you mean?' Metty said.

'I mean,' her aunt replied, hardly moving her lips, 'precisely what I said. That he isn't alive. Or, at least, he hasn't always been.'

'I-I don't understand . . .'

'Of course you don't,' Aunt Mag said, then closed her eyes, thinking hard. When she opened them again, they were shining with tears. 'Metty, I'm going to tell you something and you must never breathe a word of it to anyone, do you understand? Not if you care about Sundar. His safety depends on it.'

Metty gave a tremulous nod. 'I understand.'

Aunt Mag seemed satisfied. 'All right,' she said in a firmer voice. 'The fact is that Sundar . . . the truth is that he was brought to life. With magic. Five years ago.'

'Brought to life? How? By who?'

Metty needn't have asked. The answer was written all over Aunt Mag's guilty face.

CHAPTER TWENTY-EIGHT

The Twin

Aunt Mag picked up a framed photo on her desk and passed it to Metty, who frowned at the picture. She'd seen it before, the photo of Sundar and his mother, eating ice cream and wearing a familiar sunny smile. Only there was something off about the boy's appearance that Metty hadn't noticed last time. His eyes held an expression she didn't recognise, and his nose wasn't quite straight, nor his teeth. He looked altogether messier, from his windswept hair to the ungraceful slant of his feet.

'This is Sundar?' Metty said, glancing at her aunt.

'That's Arjun.'

'Oh.' Metty remembered the label she'd seen in Sundar's jacket. 'His twin.'

'My best friend's son.' Aunt Mag sighed. She took back

the photo, gazed at it for a moment, then tore her eyes away as though she couldn't bear to look any longer. 'He became very sick and passed away, years ago now. His parents were obviously devastated – their only child taken from them . . .'

Aunt Mag paused. Talking about the past seemed to sap her energy.

She continued in a dull voice. 'His mother, Geeta, was my oldest friend. She came to me a few months after the funeral with a doll she'd had commissioned: a life-sized doll with a clockwork heart. It resembled Arjun in every way, down to the very last detail, and she wanted me to bring it to life. Of course, I thought it a terrible idea – not to mention spectacularly illegal. But I couldn't turn her away, not when she was so desperate.'

'So you did it?' Metty said incredulously. 'You made the doll come to life?'

To do such a thing must have taken seriously powerful magic, and a *lot* of ink.

'I did, Metty. I broke the Pinocchio Law. And at first things seemed better. Geeta found the child a comfort, for a time anyway. But then it all went wrong, just as I feared. You see, the more Sundar learned about the world, the more he grew into himself, and the less like Arjun he became – until eventually Geeta couldn't stand to be near him. It felt cruel to her, a stranger wearing her son's face. So she brought Sundar back to me, insisting we'd made a terrible mistake, and she begged me to disenchant him, said she was afraid of being found out.'

'She wanted you to *kill* him?'

'She was heartbroken, Metty. That sort of grief, it warps a person. She wasn't acting like herself, and of course I couldn't do it. I lied to Geeta, told her I'd disenchanted Sundar just to put her mind at ease. She moved away shortly after that, and we haven't spoken much since. I think it's all too painful for her. But Sundar's been here with me these last five years, living in Winter's Knock. We have no choice but to hide him away. After all, he doesn't eat or sleep, he never ages, and if anyone recognised him . . . if the police ever discovered his existence . . .'

'What would happen to you if they found out the truth? You'd go to jail, right?'

A humourless smile crawled across Aunt Mag's face. 'For a very, very long time.'

'I can't believe it,' Metty said, leaning back in her seat. 'I can't believe I didn't notice. He's just like Pumpkin.'

'No,' her aunt snapped, and she raised a finger. 'You need to understand that Sundar isn't some pet. He's intelligent and funny, brilliantly alive, as real as you or I.'

'Sorry, I didn't mean . . .'

'I know,' Aunt Mag said in a gentler voice, massaging her

eyelids. 'Forgive me. It's been a difficult night, and I haven't explained this to anyone in a long time.'

'Does my father know?'

'Yes, and Rupert, obviously. And now you. We Joneses seem to collect secrets, don't we? This whole house is full of them.'

'Like the captain,' Metty muttered, staring at her knees. She tried to ignore the hurt growing stubbornly inside her like a thistle. 'He never told me about living here, or about our ancestor being one of the New London founders. He never told me I had a connection to this place.'

'Being a Jones isn't always easy, Metty,' Aunt Mag said kindly. 'I suspect your father wanted you to have a normal childhood, without the scrutiny and expectation that comes from being who we are. He probably wants you to be yourself, not the great-great-granddaughter of Majestic Jones. You're so precious to him, just like Sundar is precious to me.'

'I wouldn't have brought him with me tonight if I'd known. I'd never want anything bad to happen to—'

'I know.' Aunt Mag sighed. 'It's my fault. I should have told you sooner. I was afraid, that's all, and I didn't want to make you complicit. You remember what I said about disenchantment?'

Metty nodded slowly. 'It's like death.'

'Yes. And I can never let that happen to Sundar. It's my job to protect him, and to protect you – which is rather tricky when you keep flinging yourself in the path of danger.'

'Sorry,' Metty said in a small voice.

'It's all right. Listen, I know this is a lot to take in. Why don't you go to bed and we can talk some more in the morning? I need to speak to Sundar anyway.'

There was a soft scrape as Metty got to her feet, pushing back her chair. She walked over to the door, then stopped. 'Is his heart . . . is it really clockwork?'

It seemed impossible that a person as vivid as Sundar, so full of joy and excitement and mad ideas, could secretly be made from cold, hard parts.

Aunt Mag gave a small shrug. 'He's a remarkable creation. But then aren't we all?'

Metty's bedroom walls were a melancholy blue when she woke late the following morning. Everything that had happened the night before felt like a peculiar dream: discovering her mother was a Black Moth, realising how Daphne had betrayed her – and the captain. Her mother must have known where he was all this time, where the Moths were hiding him. She was keeping him from Metty, from her own daughter. It seemed so cruel.

And then there was the truth about Sundar. The wildness of it all made Metty's head spin.

Sundar had been the same age for the last five years, and

he would never grow up, never change while the rest of them became old and grey. What would happen to him after Aunt Mag died? Who would look after the boy then?

Metty got dressed, then whistled for Pumpkin, who flew to her shoulder and wrapped his arms round her head. It felt like being hugged by a stone koala. She headed down to the kitchen, intending to make breakfast, and found Sundar waiting for her at the round table.

'Morning,' she said, feeling shy.

'Only just. It's nearly noon,' the boy replied with a broad smile. He seemed almost like his normal self, only a fraction too cheerful. Maybe he was trying to convince Metty that nothing had changed.

She used the snack pocket to make a tower of pancakes, then grabbed some cutlery and dug in. Her eyes kept flicking back to Sundar as she chomped her way through breakfast. How had she never noticed that he didn't eat? She supposed they didn't really have meals together at Winter's Knock. Aunt Mag and Rupert were always too busy.

'Mag's out, by the way,' Sundar said as though he'd read her mind. 'Apparently, she's got some important business and she doesn't know when she'll be back, but Rupert's here so we'd better not try anything crazy. I told her no promises.'

'There's not really much we *can* do,' Metty said glumly.

She'd been so distracted by last night's chaos that she'd

forgotten all about her scuppered plans. A knot of fear tightened in her chest when she remembered her father. It was unbearable, feeling so close to finding him and so far away at the same time.

Sundar's eyebrows twitched together. 'You're not giving up? What about the captain?'

'Madame LeBeau was only performing for one more night, and we missed the show. It's over. Oh, Pumpkin, stop chewing the table! It's bad for your teeth.'

'Okay, so she hasn't got any more shows, but that doesn't mean she's left New London. She might still be here.'

'Even if she is' – Metty sighed, putting down her knife and fork – 'we can't exactly go out looking for her. It's too dangerous.'

Sundar grew stormy. 'You mean because of me?'

'Of course not.'

'I'm not made of glass, you know. You don't have to treat me like I'll break.'

'What *are* you made of?' Metty asked. The words slipped out before she could catch them. Sundar looked shocked, as though she'd leaned across the table and slapped him. 'Sorry if that was . . .' she said quickly, warmth creeping down her neck. 'I didn't mean to be insensitive. Obviously, you're made of normal things, like skin and stuff.'

Sundar gave a tiny snort. 'As opposed to cogs and screws?'

'I'm really sorry. That was a stupid thing to say. I know you're not like . . . I mean, you're just you. You're my friend.'

'I am?'

'Well, yeah,' Metty said. It was her turn to look surprised. 'Unless you don't want to be.'

'It's not like you've got competition. I don't get out much.'

'Me neither. I've spent the last year stuck in a farmhouse in Wales.'

'It's a good job we get along then, isn't it?' Sundar grinned. But then his smile faded, and a thoughtful expression clouded his eyes. 'Do you want to hear it?'

'Hear what?'

'This.' He spread his hand over his heart.

'Do you mind?' Metty asked, full of buzzing curiosity.

Sundar didn't answer, but he got up and came to stand next to her. Metty leaned closer and placed her ear to his narrow chest, listening.

For a moment, there was nothing at all. And then *ti-tick, ti-tick* . . . It was a faint mechanical noise, mimicking the *ba-boom, ba-boom* of a real beating heart. Metty was so surprised she jerked back her head, then glanced up at Sundar, a chuckle fluttering in her throat. He seemed hesitant, as though afraid of what she might say.

'That's incredible,' Metty said softly. 'Really, it is. Will it go on ticking forever?'

'Think so,' Sundar said, returning to his seat. 'It doesn't creep you out?'

'Of course not. Do I creep you out?'

'All the time.'

Metty rolled her eyes. 'I meant because of my fate. You know what I'm destined to do to someone.'

'Only if we don't sort you out,' Sundar said with sudden determination. 'I say we try and contact Madame LeBeau. What if we find the phone number for the theatre, then they might tell us where she's staying? Rupert could help.'

'Wait,' Metty said as an idea flowered in her mind. Why hadn't she thought of it before? It seemed so obvious.

'What is it?' Sundar frowned, sensing her excitement.

'We don't need to ring the theatre. I know how to get in touch with Madame LeBeau. We could have spoken to her this whole time.'

'What do you mean?'

Metty jumped to her feet and ran.

She half expected Aunt Mag's study to be locked, but the door creaked open and admitted her and Sundar into the room. Pumpkin waddled in after them and started clambering over the furniture.

'Look,' Metty said, gesturing at the copper telephone on the desk. A ghostly purple mist oozed from the mouthpiece.

'The spirit phone?' Sundar said, looking uncertain. 'You didn't tell me the woman was dead.'

'She's not, silly. Don't you remember the poster I told you about? *Madame Fayola LeBeau in Conversation with the Spirits.* She's got one of these phones too. I know she does. I saw it when I was being fated down in Darkwell, and it was on the poster for her show at the theatre, which means—'

'We can use one of the ghosts to get a message to her.'

Metty beamed, her chest swelling with pride. 'Exactly.'

'That's brilliant,' Sundar said.

'Thanks. Should I try it now?'

'Might as well before Mag comes back. I'm not sure she'll approve.'

'Probably not,' Metty agreed, reaching for the phone. Its metal was cool and slippery beneath her fingertips. She could already make out the hiss of voices. Exchanging a nervous glance with Sundar, she picked up the receiver and brought it to her ear. It crackled just like it had before, filling her head with staticky noise.

'Is somebody . . .' Metty had to clear her throat. 'Um, is anybody there?'

There was a spell of silence. Then came a drawn-out rattle like a dying breath.

Is that you, boy . . .? rasped an old man's voice. *Have they come for you yet . . . the men with sticks and chains . . . they know what you are, oh yes, they do . . . and they'll come for you in the night, they will . . .*

'Wait,' Metty muttered, glancing at Sundar. He'd gone stiff beside her, his face scrunched up like he'd stubbed his toe. All this time, she'd thought the vicious old man had been talking to her, warning her about the Black Moths. But he must've mistaken Metty for Sundar the first time she'd used the spirit phone.

They know what you are . . .

'The men with sticks and chains,' she said aloud, ignoring the ghost who was still chanting spitefully.

'He means the police,' Sundar whispered.

You think people won't be able to tell what you are . . . You're not real, boy, and they'll come for you, oh yes . . .

'Right,' Metty said, bristling with anger. She clenched the spirit phone so tightly that purple fog slimed from the mouthpiece and puddled on the desk. 'Terry, isn't it? You can stop that nonsense right now. You're not speaking to Sundar – you're speaking to Meticulous Jones. How dare you try and frighten him like that, you disgusting old dead . . . thing. Neither of us wants to hear from you ever again, so you can put someone else on the phone. Go on! I'm not talking to *you!*'

There was a sullen silence.

Who d'you want? said the gravelly voice at last.

Metty was taken aback. She hadn't even considered that she might have to pick somebody. She racked her brain, trying to put together a list of the dead. Fortunately, everyone she loved was still alive.

'What about one of the Joneses?' Sundar suggested.

It wasn't a bad idea. There were certainly enough of them, though it wasn't easy to choose one. A muddle of names swam around Metty's head, half of them made up by her panicking imagination. She was pretty sure there'd never been a Moronic Jones, and Mechanical seemed unlikely too. What was her father's father called? Her grandparents had died not long after Rupert was born, when the captain and Aunt Mag were still children, so Metty had never met them.

'Majestic,' she finally said, blurting out the first real name she could think of. 'I'd like to speak to Majestic Jones.'

CHAPTER TWENTY-NINE

Conversations with the Dead

Minutes passed before a new voice broke through the white noise.

'Yes, what do you want?' said Majestic Jones. He didn't sound unkind, but his voice was crisp with impatience. It was also very Welsh. 'I have an obscene amount of work to get through, and it appears that I've misplaced my glasses. I don't suppose you've seen them? Cannot think where I last . . . Who is this, by the way? Who am I talking to?'

Metty was stumped for a moment. Conversing on the phone with her dead great-great-grandfather was a pretty unusual experience. She wasn't sure how to respond.

'Uh . . .' was all she said, which wasn't very helpful.

'Come along, speak up. You might have all the time in the world, but I happen to be extraordinarily busy. For heaven's sake, don't you read the papers? The city takes flight in less than a week, and the core still isn't fit for purpose. Damn. What *have* I done with my glasses? This isn't Maud, is it, playing some sort of trick?'

'I'm not Maud,' Metty said, throwing a flustered look at Sundar. The boy only grinned at her and stuck up both his thumbs.

'Who the blazes is this then? And I warn you, if you don't provide a satisfactory answer in the next five seconds, I shall terminate this conversation . . . Very well, good day.'

'Wait, wait, I'm – my name is Metty.'

'Metty?' Majestic said, then hummed thoughtfully. 'I don't believe I know a Metty. Rather an unusual name. Short for something, I suppose, unless . . .' He gave a musical chuckle and sounded much friendlier when he spoke again. 'Splendid! I do believe I'm talking to a fellow Jones. I am, aren't I?'

'Uh, yes,' Metty said, feeling a little stunned.

'Metty, *Metty* . . . Now what could that be? No, don't tell me. I shall guess it, you'll see. I'm excellent at this game. Methodical Jones, isn't it? I'm certain there's a Cousin Methodical somewhere.'

'Listen, um, Majestic, I could really use your—'

'Incorrect, eh? Well, that was only my first try. Is it Mettlesome, perhaps? No? Am I at least getting close?'

'I need a favour and—'

'Surely not Meteoric? That would be too silly for words.'

'Mr Jones!' Metty snapped. 'I know you're busy, but I really need your help.'

'Do you indeed?' said her great-great-grandfather in a withering way. Metty got the feeling he was used to barking orders, not receiving them from mysterious strangers on the telephone. She would have to stand her ground.

'Yes,' she replied. 'And if you refuse, I . . . I won't tell you where to find your glasses.'

There was an outraged pause.

'What a mean-spirited trick!' Majestic suddenly boomed in her ear, making her pull back the handset. 'This *is* Maud, isn't it? How many times have I told you not to play childish—'

'No!' Metty groaned, kneading her forehead. 'I'm not Maud. Look, I need you to get a message to someone. I'm trying to reach a lady called Madame Fayola LeBeau, and it's urgent I speak to her, a life-and-death situation, you understand?'

'Your impertinent tone implies that you think me a simpleton.'

'No, no, I don't. Please.' Metty sighed. 'This is important.'

'And what message should you like me to deliver to this Madame LeBeau, if I do find her? Although I don't see why I should go to the bother for a rather rude *minor* cousin.'

'I'm not a minor . . . Never mind. Just tell her that Metty Jones wants to speak to her. She'll know who I am.'

'Very well,' said Majestic in a tone of great exasperation. There was a loud click, and the line went dead.

Metty lowered the handset with a sigh. Sundar was waiting, wide-eyed.

'Well? Is he helping?'

'I'm not sure,' Metty said. 'He thinks I'm someone called Maud, and he doesn't seem to know he's dead.'

'No, they hardly ever do. Best not to tell him. Might be a bit of a shock. I know, you wait here and see if he calls back and I'll stand guard at the door.'

Fifteen minutes crawled by while Metty waited for the spirit phone to ring, spinning around in Aunt Mag's chair to distract herself. Sunlight filtered through the gaps in the blinds and painted golden bars on the wall, lighting up some of Aunt Mag's framed certificates. It seemed she'd studied curse mythology at Harvard, magical engineering at the University of New Tokyo, and was a member of several prestigious societies including the League of Shadows, whatever that might be.

An idea occurred to Metty suddenly, and she took out her dictionary. She hadn't thought to look for Tanner's horrid fate in there, not that she expected to find one so specific.

HEARTS, she read in the dictionary.

Associated with surgical ambitions, or a charitable nature.

Metty pursed her lips. Tanner hadn't struck her as charitable in the least, although the book didn't mention anything about a rotten heart being crushed by a fist. She put it away with a sigh.

She was watching Pumpkin gnaw his way through the spine of an ancient book (definitely valuable and probably cursed) when the phone came to life with a shrill *bringggg*. Metty lurched out of the chair, whacking her knee on the desk, and grabbed the handset.

'Are you there?' Majestic barked before she could say anything. 'Dear me, I haven't got all day. If you won't even bother answering—'

'I'm here,' she spluttered.

'Oh yes. So you are.'

'Did you get through to Madame LeBeau?'

'I did, as a matter of fact. I gave the lady your message and I have one for you in return. It sounded rather odd, so you should pay close attention. I don't intend to repeat myself.'

'What did she say?' Metty asked, heart thumping.

'If I remember rightly, the warning came first. Something about having to be careful what you say. Apparently, you're being watched.'

'Watched? By who?'

'No idea. The lady didn't care to specify, but whoever it

is can hear every word you say and it seems they're always listening. Rather disconcerting, if you ask me.'

Madame LeBeau must have been talking about the Black Moths. Who else could she mean?

'What else was in the message?' Metty pressed.

'Let's see. There was an awful lot . . . I believe the lady wishes to meet you face to face, and she wanted me to pass on some instructions. You're to wait until sundown, then find her in the Astronomy Quarter. You're to come alone. She'll be at the Starlight Café, and apparently you must turn the moon three times counterclockwise.'

'Turn the moon? What does that—'

'I hope you don't expect *me* to understand. Of course, I am merely the messenger, and this friend of yours sounds rather dubious. I wouldn't go at all if I were you.'

'Was that it?' Metty said, trying to smooth out the impatience in her voice.

'One more thing. These spies she mentioned – apparently, they still have your father, and if you breathe a word of this to *anyone* they shall do something very unpleasant to him.'

Fear coiled round Metty like an icy snake. 'Did she say where they're keeping him?'

'Afraid not. It sounds like you're in quite a pickle. If I were you—'

'I have to go,' she mumbled, dropping the handset.

'Wait!' cried Majestic with fiery indignation. 'You haven't told me where to find my—'

Metty slammed down the telephone. She could feel the rhythm of her heartbeat in her throat. What would the Black Moths do to her father if she told Sundar or Aunt Mag about her plans to meet the prophetess?

'What happened?' Sundar said, jolting her back to reality as he bounced through the study door. 'Did he find Madame LeBeau? What's the matter? You look all weird.'

'She's gone,' Metty said in a hoarse voice, forcing herself to meet Sundar's eye.

The boy frowned. 'What do you mean she's gone?'

Metty had to lie. Telling the truth, and taking him with her, would put the captain at risk. And even if it didn't she couldn't endanger Sundar again, not after everything Aunt Mag had said last night. She would have to find the prophetess on her own. She couldn't trust Madame LeBeau – after all, she was friends with Daphne – but maybe they could strike a deal, or Metty might at least find out why the Moths were after her. If anyone understood her fate, it was surely the woman who'd given it to her.

'Madame LeBeau's not in New London any more,' she said in a firmer voice. 'She left first thing this morning.'

'Okay,' Sundar said slowly. His eyes flicked round the room as he tried to come up with a new plan. He gave Metty an encouraging smile, misinterpreting her dull expression. 'Hey, don't give up, all right? We'll think of something. Trust me.'

'I know we will,' Metty replied.

Dread had hollowed out her stomach, creating a hole for all her fears to pour into like freezing water. Aunt Mag was gone, and she couldn't confide in Sundar or Rupert.

She was on her own.

Metty was pretty sure the Astronomy Quarter was between the districts of Highfate and Inkshimmer at the top of the city. They'd passed it on Halloween, an area made up of academic buildings and observatories for stargazing, plus the University of New London. At least it wouldn't be a long walk from Winter's Knock.

Aunt Mag still hadn't arrived back by the time the sun sank towards the ocean, washing the city in deep pink light. Metty was almost disappointed. If Aunt Mag was home, she would've been tempted to communicate the truth to her somehow. But she didn't have time to wait.

Ignoring a twist of guilt, she gave Sundar the slip and crept downstairs to the back door. Fortunately, the streets were still busy and she didn't feel too exposed as she made her way along the pavements, sticking close to other pedestrians. Were the Black Moths watching her at that very moment, scuttling between alleyways, or soaring through the clouds in a gondola? The thought made a shiver run down her spine.

Twenty minutes later, she reached a polished archway welcoming her to the Astronomy Quarter. Metty hurried through it into a square, looking around for the Starlight Café. She spotted a teashop covered in flowers, and a pub full of students and professors bearing impressive fates like scrolls and stars – tattoos associated with ambitious thinkers. It was a few minutes before she thought she might have found the right place.

The café was opposite a giant statue of a telescope in the heart of the district. It was easy to overlook, a tiny building squashed between two normal-sized shops. Metty frowned, peeking through the window in the door. The glass was dark and dusty, impossible to see beyond.

She glanced around, checking that no one was watching, then tried the door. It opened, to her relief, and let her into a dim corridor. Metty crept inside with a growing sense of dread. What was this place? There was no sign of any customers, no tables and chairs, no waiter to greet her, just a hallway without any doors. It took her a moment to notice something glinting on the far wall.

Metty approached it cautiously and discovered a crescent moon fixed to the wallpaper, a bit like the key in a music box. She stared at it in confusion, then looked around again, convinced that someone must be watching. Majestic's words repeated in her mind: *Turn the moon three times counterclockwise.* Was this what he'd meant?

Taking a deep breath, Metty gripped the crescent moon and twisted it hard to the left. It was stiff, but slowly turned with a loud *click-click-click.* The third time she spun it, there was a tremor in the walls and a rumbling sound as the floor shifted. Startled, Metty tried to jump back, but it was too late. The wall was spinning, taking some of the floorboards with it, and suddenly she was standing on the other side, cut off from the exit back to the square.

Now she was in a new corridor, the same length, but with a different door at the end. Blue light rippled over Metty in watery shimmers. She gripped the crescent moon on the wall, unsure what to do. She could twist it again, take herself back to the first corridor. Heading into the unknown felt ridiculously stupid.

But no, she couldn't turn back now. She'd come to find Madame LeBeau – and to rescue the captain. Her father needed her to be brave. Who knew how long the Black Moths would keep him alive?

Light-headed with nerves, Metty walked down the corridor, opened the new door and stepped into a large, round room. Jazz music came from hidden speakers, rolling around what appeared to be a restaurant full of tables and cushiony armchairs.

Her jaw dropped as she glanced at the ceiling. It had been painted to look like a night sky, with stars twinkling on a midnight blue background and a full moon gleaming behind wispy clouds that drifted like ripples of silk. Every few seconds, one of the stars would tumble from the ceiling, shooting down the walls with a streak of light, then disappear into the blue-tiled floor.

Above the bar was a silver sign that read: THE STARLIGHT CAFÉ.

There were only a handful of customers being served by waiters in pale suits. One person caught Metty's eye, raising a hand to get her attention: a woman in a dark scarlet dress. She wore a matching tether on her left hand and a feather in her deep brown curls that rolled all the way to her hips.

Madame LeBeau's fiery eyes locked onto Metty, and a smile teased the corner of her lips. They were painted the same moody red as her dress, complementing the eye tattooed on the back of her hand. The lady curled a finger, inviting Metty to join her at the table.

CHAPTER THIRTY

The Starlight Café

Metty was so distracted by the ceiling that she only noticed the rotating floor when she tried to cross it. The tables were shifting very slowly, orbiting in different directions like planets in a solar system. She nearly lost her footing as she made her way to Madame LeBeau, having to steady herself on a waiter who was strolling along quite easily with a platter of food balanced on his hand.

She stumbled over to Madame LeBeau's table and dropped, panting, into the empty chair opposite her.

'So you got my message. I take it you've come for my help,' Madame LeBeau said.

Metty had forgotten how pleasant her voice was, deep and silky, almost hypnotic. She was observing Metty over the rim of a black teacup. Steam wafted from the drink and filled the air with a tangy smell of citrus and honey.

'You said *they've* got the captain,' Metty whispered, struggling to sit up in the squishy armchair. 'You meant the Moths, right?'

Madame LeBeau's long eyelashes fluttered as she brought a finger to her lips. 'I'd be careful what you say in here. You never know who might be listening.'

Metty stiffened and glanced around at the other diners, hardly daring to take her eyes off the prophetess. 'You don't expect me to trust you? I know you're friends with Daphne.'

'I'm sure you're far too sensible for that. But you came here because you need something, and clearly you believe I might be able to assist you.'

'I need to find my father. They took him,' Metty said in a furious whisper. 'Dragged him out of your theatre. Do you know where he is?'

'I know all sorts of things courtesy of my friends on the other side. You look pale, child. Let me order you a drink.' The lady clicked her fingers before Metty could decline, and one of the waiters glided over. His suit was silvery like moonlight. 'Be a dear and bring my friend something to drink. Make it hot and sweet – she's a little distressed.'

The waiter nodded and danced away again. If Metty wasn't so tense, she might have enjoyed gently spinning round the room. It was like taking a ride on the world's slowest fairground waltzer. The moon gleamed right above their heads.

'Beautiful, isn't it?' Madame LeBeau said, watching Metty. One of her eyebrows flicked upwards. 'It changes, you know, to match the real moon.'

'Why did you want me to come here?' Metty asked suspiciously.

'I thought we should meet somewhere private, where we were less likely to be overheard. Ah, here he comes.'

The waiter returned to their table with a tall glass that he placed in front of Metty. Her mouth salivated as she breathed in the smell of a rich and creamy hot cocoa. There was a spoon next to the glass made entirely of chocolate.

'Drink up,' Madame LeBeau suggested with a smile that was almost girlish. 'It'll make you feel better.'

'No, thank you,' Metty muttered as ribbons of steam curled up her nose. 'Do you know what they want with my dad?'

'Child, isn't that obvious?' Madame LeBeau said, sipping her own mysterious drink.

'You mean they're trying to get to me?'

'Some of us are rare jewels. We find ourselves coveted.'

Metty glanced at her right hand, curled in a loose fist on the table. 'It's because of my fate, isn't it?'

Madame LeBeau's eyes were unblinking. 'Naturally.'

'Do you know what it means, the skull and the glove?

It definitely suggests I'm a murderer, right?'

'Interpreting fates isn't part of the service.'

'But you painted it,' Metty said, desperation creeping into her voice. 'You chose it, didn't you? That's the whole point of elite fatings. But why? Do you know how it feels to be stuck inside like a prisoner all the time, for everyone to be afraid of you? Why did you do it? Why not choose something – anything – else?'

'I didn't *choose* your fate, dear,' Madame LeBeau said. 'It was always in your future. Every child has many possible fates, not just one, and they're all true in their way. Your life is like a jigsaw, made up of a thousand pieces, all the things you'll do, your work, your passions, the traits that make you up. Prophetesses like myself simply choose one piece of that jigsaw and bring it to the fore.'

'But you could have picked something else then, if there're always lots of options. You wanted me to have this fate in particular. Why?'

Madame LeBeau only smirked. Metty was tempted to throw her drink at her. How could she sit there, sneering, when she'd caused so much grief, when she was partly responsible for what was happening now?

'If I'm right and my fate *is* why the Black Moths want me, then it doesn't even matter what it means, not unless . . . If I could change it, then they'd stop coming after me. They'd leave my family alone, wouldn't they?'

Madame LeBeau gave a lazy shrug. 'Perhaps.'

'Then is it possible?' Metty said. 'Do you think you could do it? I'd find some way to pay you. I'd do anything.'

'A person's fate is inkbound. Nothing can change it,' Madame LeBeau said, her calm words sliding into Metty's heart like pins. 'You could travel the whole world looking for a miracle – many have – but the truth is we are what we are, and we must do what we can with the gifts that are ours.'

'But my fate isn't a gift!' Metty cried, forgetting to lower her voice. 'It's a curse!'

Madame LeBeau was quiet a moment, her orange-brown eyes strangely cold.

'I'm sorry you feel that way,' she said at length. 'Maybe one day you'll change your mind.'

Metty sank back in her chair, disappointment smouldering inside her. She knew she would never, ever change her mind. Why did Madame LeBeau even want to meet if she wasn't willing to rewrite Metty's fate? Of course, this could all be a trap, but surely the prophetess wouldn't try and kidnap her in a room full of strangers.

Metty cupped the hot cocoa on the table, and a warm tingle spread through her palms.

'Drink,' Madame LeBeau said with a sympathetic smile. 'I promise it won't kill you.'

'I'd rather not risk it, thanks,' Metty replied, removing her hands from the glass. Steam was still wafting from the top, filling her nose with a delicious, almost spicy smell.

'I'd like to help, you know,' Madame LeBeau said. Her voice sounded oddly far away, like an echo over water. 'I could tell there was something special about you from the off. I thought at first that you were one of my kind. A prophetess. That's why I asked if you were left-handed. We always are, you see. But no, your talents are quite different from mine.'

'What talents?' Metty mumbled.

She blinked, feeling groggy. The walls were blurring around her, the stars becoming a white smear. Was it her imagination or was the floor getting faster, sweeping them round the room in hastening circles? Metty glanced at the glass on the table, at the steam drifting out of the cocoa – the steam she'd been carelessly breathing in. Madame LeBeau's gaze was heavy on her face.

'I'm sure you'll find out soon enough.'

The prophetess's features began to twist, turning into a frightening portrait. A few seconds later, she was just a shadow. And then darkness closed round Metty like the folds of a black curtain.

The stars were still there when she opened her eyes, sparkling on the ceiling of the Starlight Café. Only now there was a powerful draught in the room, chilling Metty's hands and face. She wrinkled her nose in confusion as she breathed in sharp, cold air. There was something hard underneath her. She was lying on freezing stone, and there was somebody standing by her feet, facing away from her. She could only just make out the lines of their back and shoulders.

Moaning, Metty tried to raise her head. It was like dragging up a boulder, and pain stabbed through her neck. Had she fallen on the spinning floor?

The truth washed over her like a torrent of icy rain. She wasn't lying on the floor of the Starlight Café, but flying through the real starry night on a grey stone bridge – a bridge she recognised with a start.

'*Edison*,' she whispered, the word almost catching in her throat. It seemed impossible, like she'd tumbled into a vivid dream, only the wind was too fierce to be imaginary and the moon dizzyingly bright.

Fear pulsed through her, leaving an ashy taste on her tongue. There were people silhouetted all around her, men and women guarding her like stone angels, at least eight of them. Black Moths.

Lying a little way from Metty was another sleeping figure. She couldn't tell who, though it was clearly a child.

And approaching in the distance was a shadow staining a canvas of clouds. An island floated in the moonlight, too small to be New London and far too dark. Metty recognised it with a start: those stately glass pillars, pointed rooftop and the royal blue moat of ink surrounding the building.

The Ink Museum.

She'd seen it once before on Halloween, bobbing in the distant clouds. And now they were swooping towards it, using Edison Bridge like a gondola. Metty tried to twist her head, tried to glance back and search the sky. The museum normally flew around the city, but she couldn't see New London anywhere.

'Oh dear, I see we've woken a little early,' said a familiar voice. The man at her feet turned round. A pair of black eyes glistened at Metty, sunken in a long white face that widened with a sly smile.

'Someone put her back to sleep,' Tanner said. 'Wouldn't want to tire her out too soon.'

Metty tried to squirm away as a hand came towards her, but it was as though her limbs were weighted with rocks. Warm fingers tapped her brow, and drowsiness gathered behind her eyes. Her head was already sinking, bumping against stone. The darkness was curling round her again. She snuck another desperate look at the child sleeping on the bridge, but it was still impossible to make them out. Metty prayed it wasn't Sundar.

Straining her eyes, she caught a final glimpse of the museum swelling against the clouds. Its glass columns twinkled in the starlight, full of glorious ink that was seeping into them from the moat. The liquid flowed up the pillars, making them glow, then disappeared into the building, as though the museum was drinking it up. Metty remembered her uncle telling her something about the island's core, the first one ever built, but her thoughts were stumbling inside her head as her eyelids grew heavy.

'Go to sleep, Miss Jones,' Tanner sang, triumphant. 'I need you nice and rested before the real work begins. Your mother will be so glad to see you again.'

CHAPTER THIRTY-ONE

The Ink Museum

Metty was no longer outside when she woke with a fuzzy head and a sense of time having passed. Groaning, she opened her eyes and found herself lying on a cushioned bench pressed against the wall of a draughty hall. She sat up in alarm and glanced around.

The space was cavernous with a high ceiling and lots of doorways leading off it, each of them labelled: NEW BERLIN, NEW OTTAWA, NEW NEW DELHI. A front desk stood across the room, and there was a board nailed to the wall behind it, showing ticket prices. This must be the entrance to the Ink Museum, Metty realised.

Nearby was a set of grand double doors and above them an archway that read: NEW LONDON. There was no one else around, no quiet tread of footsteps or whispering voices. It seemed she was all alone.

Metty knelt on the bench, peering through a long window. All she could see was one of those ink-filled columns, and beyond that nothing but a dark ocean of sky.

Dry-mouthed, she got up from the bench, then glanced down in alarm as the floor began to shine. Metty stared at it, realising for the first time that the entire floor was made of glass. A glittering, swirling pool of ink flowed beneath it, the same royal blue as the moat outside. The magical liquid seemed to respond to her, creating golden halos of light round her feet. When she walked forward, her glowing footsteps stained the floor behind her, then faded a few seconds later.

Metty might have been entranced if she wasn't so anxious. But then she noticed something else – her bare right hand. Somebody must have stolen her tether while she slept. But where were the Black Moths now? And why had they brought her *here*?

She scanned the room again to make sure no one was watching, then ran over to the main entrance. The doors were locked. Of course she was trapped in the museum, and she couldn't even use magic to blast her way out. Metty thought for a moment, then tried the doors leading to the New London chamber.

They eased open with a low creak and revealed an even

grander hall with archways leading off it to smaller rooms. Floating in the middle of the space, as though suspended on an invisible wire, was a model version of New London.

Metty crept forward and circled it slowly, leaving a trail of golden footprints behind her. She stared in awe at all the tiny buildings and the little ink river twirling through the city like a purple string. Some places were old-fashioned and probably long gone, but others she recognised, like the bank, and the university, certain shops, and theatres – buildings that were eerily familiar, only shrunken, like dolls' houses. She even spotted a miniature Winter's Knock that looked identical to the real house. Her heart ached to see it, and she wished more than anything that Aunt Mag was with her.

Leaving the model city, Metty turned her attention to the five archways scattered round the room. Each had a different name printed on a plaque above it.

The third name gave her a funny chill. He'd been dead for more than half a century, yet she'd spoken to him on the telephone that very day.

MAJESTIC JONES.

She walked over to her ancestor's archway, curiosity pulling her along like a string. The chamber beyond it was full of machines, and there were dozens of photographs and newspaper clippings in frames on the walls.

A MAJESTIC INVENTION! SOLAR BIRDS TO LIGHT THE DISTRICT OF HIGHFATE.

JONES VOWS TO TACKLE TURBULENCE BEFORE NEW LONDON'S FIRST ANNIVERSARY.

MAJESTIC JONES: THE MAN WHO MADE A CITY FLY.

It seemed that, in his day, Majestic had been a celebrated inventor, as skilled with ink as all the magical engineers that Metty had learned about in school. She couldn't think why the captain hadn't told her any of this. Wasn't he proud of their family history?

She approached one of the glass cases. It was full of coins shining under a naked bulb. Metty pulled a lever on the front of the case, then flinched as the bulb turned blue and crackled with tendrils of electricity. A second later, the coins quivered, then rose into the air where they floated like corks in water.

The light flickered again when Metty thrust down the lever, and all the coins slapped back to the bottom of the case. According to the information board, the machine was an early antigravity pocket designed by Majestic Jones himself.

Metty looked around at the other inventions. She found one case that had a metal heart inside it made of gold and glass with tubes poking through it like real arteries. She pressed a button and the case lit up with a funny noise, but nothing else happened. There was something dark and powdery inside the heart's glass tubes, like old blood that had long dried up.

Frowning, Metty left the case to look at something else. The front page of a newspaper caught her eye, enlarged on the wall. The article was an obituary written for her great-great-grandfather. There was a grainy photo of Majestic standing with his family in front of the Ink Museum. The island on which it was built, she noted, was floating in the ocean, and hadn't yet taken flight.

Above pictured Majestic Jones, read the caption under the image, **his wife, Sarah, and their eccentrically named children, Maudlin, Morose and Melancholy.**

Majestic looked just like his portrait in the drawing room at Winter's Knock, tall and gangly with fair hair and a distracted smile. His fate seemed to be a light bulb. Metty searched for her dictionary, relieved to find it in her pocket still. At least the Moths hadn't taken that away.

LIGHT BULBS: *associated with bright minds, or inventors*

The youngest child in the picture – Metty's great-great-aunt Melancholy – was only a baby in her mother's arms, but the other two were dressed in smart white clothes and grinning at the camera: a girl of about seven, who must have been Maudlin (*So that's Maud!* realised Metty) and a boy a little younger. This, she thought in wonder, was her great-grandfather: Morose Jones.

Underneath the newspaper clipping were some leather binoculars attached to a chain. Frowning, Metty picked them up and brought them to her eyes. It was like one of those toys where you click a button and it shows different images, only the pictures weren't frozen inside the binoculars. Instead, they moved like a black-and-white film.

A small boy cradled a bird-shaped ornament in his hands and kept glancing uncertainly at someone behind the camera.

'Go on,' said a familiar voice, making Metty jump. It was as if Majestic Jones had spoken right in her ear. '*Show them, Ross. It's all right.*'

The blond boy chewed his lip, then looked down at the bird, concentrating hard. Metty recognised Morose from the photograph.

There was astonished laughter and a smattering of applause as the ornament in his hands transformed. Its stone skin cracked, revealing feathers underneath and a beak. Within seconds, the ornament had become a real living bird that flew to Morose's shoulder, puffed out its chest and trilled.

'*It isn't an enchantment?*' said an American voice Metty hadn't heard before.

'No, no,' Majestic replied, '*it's quite alive, I assure you. I've seen him do it many times. I tell you, Dr Tanner, the boy's a marvel!*'

Dr Tanner . . .

Metty was so startled, she almost dropped the binoculars. The film had finished and gone back to the start, playing in a constant loop. Now the bird was stone again, lying cold and still in Morose's hands.

'*Go on,*' said Majestic Jones.

Metty put down the binoculars. It felt like a dozen thoughts were rampaging in her mind, so many it was hard to single one out. She kept thinking of the stone cracking around the bird, of its shivering feathers and sharp little beak emerging from a cold, hard shell. Sundar had told her that one of the Joneses had enchanted all the solar birds in New London. Could that have been her great-grandfather, Morose Jones?

And how had he done it, really brought the bird to life? It was just like Aunt Mag pouring life into Sundar. From the way Majestic and Dr Tanner had responded in the film, it didn't seem like a common talent that anyone could do. Metty knew from the swirling feeling in her stomach that she'd just seen something important.

Unsettled, she returned to the New London hall. Metty walked past the other four archways, checking the plaques above them. ARTHUR HAZELWOOD. TOSHIRO SHIMA. ELIAS WOLFF. She stopped opposite the last chamber with an unpleasant tingle of surprise. DR ELIZABETH TANNER.

Metty knew the lady was related to Charles Tanner the moment she saw her portrait inside the chamber. Dr Tanner had the same chilly black eyes, shrewd with intelligence.

Her room wasn't circular like Majestic's, but twisted like a maze and it curved downwards. Metty followed the corridor, passing cases with more models inside them, like a miniature Winter Park and six tiny floating bridges. It seemed Elizabeth Tanner had been an architect, who'd designed many parts of New London.

Metty's mouth fell open when she reached the end of the sloping corridor and came to a glass wall, separating her from a vast, shadowy room. Filling up the space was an enormous gold and glass heart, just like the one from the case in Majestic's chamber, only a thousand times bigger. She'd never seen anything so spectacular, like a giant piece of art. Rich blue ink poured along the glass tubes that wove in and out of the heart, pumping round and round like blood.

Was this the core of the museum – what kept the island floating through the clouds? If so, she could only imagine the size of the heart at the centre of New London.

Metty's stomach lurched as she noticed something in one corner: a steel table in the shadow of the core. Somebody was lying on it, their arms and legs fastened to the table with straps. They looked dead, their limbs stiff and unmoving, eyes closed and face slack. A crumpled trilby lay on the floor by the table, as if it had fallen off and been trodden on.

Metty forgot to breathe for a heartbeat, fear making her vision blur.

'Dad!' she shouted, pounding on the glass. A scream was trying to worm up her throat, but she forced it down, begging herself to stay calm. There was no door, no way for her to break through the wall and reach him. 'Dad, wake up! Wake up, it's me!'

Metty was thumping the glass so hard, her knuckles began to crack, but she didn't care. She had to know that her father was alive, willing his chest to rise. He seemed impossibly still. Maybe he couldn't hear her.

'Metty?' said a quiet voice, and she spun round in alarm.

Daphne was standing in the corridor behind her, eyes wide with worry.

'It's all right, sweetheart. It's all right,' she soothed, rushing over to Metty and drawing her away from the glass. Daphne's fingers were warm on her face, wiping the tears from her cheeks. Metty hadn't even noticed she was crying.

'Is he . . .?' she gasped, looking back at the captain. 'Is he . . .?'

'He's not dead, just sleeping. He didn't really give us much choice. You know how stubborn your father can be. Oh my love, come here,' Daphne said, pulling her into a hug. Her hands smoothed Metty's windswept hair. She felt so warm, so solid and steady, that Metty almost forgot to be furious. When anger did surge inside her, it was like breathing in pepper.

'Let go!' she snapped, wriggling away from Daphne.

Her mother looked hurt. 'Honey, what's wrong? You don't think I'd let them harm the captain?'

'You're with them, aren't you? The Black Moths!'

Daphne's face relaxed, and she gave one of her tinkling laughs. 'Well, of course I am. So's half the city.'

'But you're hurting people!'

'Not if we can help it. Look, if history's taught us anything, it's that nobody really listens when you ask nicely. Sometimes good people have no choice but to use a little force, otherwise things just don't change. You're so young. I know it might be hard for you to understand, but—'

'They're using you,' Metty spat, glaring at her mother. Daphne seemed confused. 'The Black Moths, Tanner – they're just using you to get to me.'

'Oh, honey.' Daphne sighed. Bending down, she placed a hand on Metty's shoulder. 'Bringing you here was *my* idea. I wanted to give you an opportunity to shine! To show the world your talents, to make sure nobody ever forgets your name. You're special, Metty, *so* special.'

'How?' Metty snapped, shaking off Daphne's hand. 'Because of my stupid fate, something I can't even control? How am I special?'

'You have a gift.'

'*What* gift?'

Daphne's blue eyes were round as marbles. Reaching out again, she grazed Metty's cheek.

'Darling, you give life.'

CHAPTER THIRTY-TWO

The Gift

Anger flared Metty's nostrils, making her breaths come out hot and shallow.

'What are you talking about, Daphne?'

'I should have realised sooner, but you appeared after your fating with that hideous skull on your hand and I just thought . . . Well, how was I to know? I was so furious with Fayola about the whole thing, I refused to speak to her afterwards, so it was months before I found out what your fate really means.

'Moral already knew, of course. He'd seen it before, and then he whisked you off before I could even . . .' Daphne's lips tightened in frustration. She shook her head. 'Locking you up like a common criminal, keeping you shut away from the world. He knew I would never approve.'

'He did that to protect everyone,' Metty said, her eyes flicking to the captain.

'No, Metty, it was his misguided attempt at protecting you. See, people with talents like yours are rare, especially these days, and he knew that some of us would rather put your gift to good use than let it go to waste.'

'But . . . what do you mean I give life? Loads of people—'

'Oh sure, we can all enchant things,' Daphne said. 'But to create a real spark of life, something that lives and breathes and *thinks*, something that feels . . . Not many can do that, not many at all.'

'But I haven't . . .' Metty stammered, feeling light-headed. 'I've never . . .'

'It doesn't matter if you haven't done it yet.' Daphne smiled, catching Metty's hands. She was wearing a tether to match her cornflower-blue dress. 'Obviously, we know you will. It's your fate! And apparently it runs in the family – something Moral conveniently forgot to mention. That's how he knew what it was, of course.'

'But I'm ill-fated. I'm a-a murderer!'

'No, that was my mistake,' Daphne said, sobering again. Her fingers tightened round Metty's. 'And I'm sorry for that, truly I am.'

'The – the skull – it means death . . .'

'And the glove means magic. Don't you see? Don't you

understand what an extraordinary person you are? Metty, you have *the ability to defy death with magic.* That's your gift. And we cannot waste it. I know I haven't been the best mother, but I swear to you now, I will never let anyone underestimate you again. You will have respect and power, and *everyone* will listen to what you say. And all you have to do is let me guide you. We can help you use your talents. I don't want to lock you away in a cage,' Daphne said, brushing a strand of hair behind Metty's ear. Tears were shining in her eyes. 'Darling, I want to set you free.'

Metty swallowed. It felt like her throat was stuffed with sand.

'I'm not going to hurt anyone,' she said slowly.

Daphne smiled, a tear slipping down her cheek. 'No, baby.'

'I'm not a bad person?'

'Of course you're not. And' – Daphne fixed her with a brilliant smile – 'you're going to do something incredible. Trust me.'

Metty wet her lips. It seemed miraculous, the idea that she wasn't bad, wasn't black and rotting at the core, that she might even be *incredible.*

'What about the captain?' she asked, glancing at her father.

'I'll always protect him, you know that, but if you come and work with us then I can ask Charles to let him go.'

'They won't hurt him?'

'No, honey. I'd never allow it.'

Doubt flickered in Metty's heart like a dying ember, stubbornly burning. She couldn't trust the Black Moths: they'd terrorised the city for years. But if she refused to help them then they might never release the captain and they would both be trapped on the island.

What the Moths wanted wasn't *so* terrible, was it? No more restrictions on magic; equal access to ink for everyone . . .

Metty sighed and met her mother's eye.

'What would I have to do?'

Daphne gave Metty her tether, then led her to a set of doors at the back of the museum. Cold air blasted Metty in the face as they stepped outside, finding themselves at the top of a stone staircase. Blue ink oozed round the museum, giving off a faint but spicy aroma of magic.

'This way,' Daphne said, beginning to climb down the steps. 'The others are waiting for us in the garden. Don't look so afraid, honey. I'll be with you the whole time.'

She paused and held out her hand. Metty took it, looking around uneasily. The sun was rising, bubbling on the horizon and turning the ocean to liquid gold, though most of the sky was still grey. She noticed something shining in the distance: New London, lighting up the clouds like a chandelier. The museum must have drifted close enough to see it at last.

The sight of the city filled her chest with joy, and she felt courage gathering inside her. Home wasn't so very far away.

There was a garden at the bottom of the island, surrounded by a tall iron fence. A crowd of Black Moths waited for Metty there. They looked solemn and still, just like the five statues decorating the lawn: the founders of New London. Metty recognised Majestic Jones, although his iron face was sterner than in his pictures.

Tanner was standing by the statue of his own ancestor, Elizabeth. How similar they were, tall and thin with knife-like faces. He smiled as he turned to Metty, his dark eyes glittering with anticipation. Daphne let go of her hand and went to stand by Tanner, who was holding a cane with a snarling wolf's head – the same one Metty had seen at the theatre.

'Wonderful, you're here. How's your head? I've heard being put to sleep is not the most pleasant experience.' Tanner's jaw tightened when Metty didn't answer, clenching her hands to stop them shaking. 'I apologise for the travel conditions, but we weren't sure how compliant you'd be. I take it your mother has impressed upon you the importance of our work?'

'She's willing to help,' Daphne said, beaming proudly at Metty.

Tanner's face expressed some doubt, but he kept up a smile. 'That's good to hear. In that case, I suppose we can finally get to work.' He swept a hand around the garden. 'Please, Miss Jones, take your pick.'

Metty blinked. 'I'm sorry?'

'Didn't you explain, my love?' Tanner asked, addressing Daphne, who blushed slightly. He waved his hand again. 'No matter, it's quite simple. We require a little proof, that's all, that you are what you say you are.'

Frustration left a hot flush in Metty's face. She'd never claimed to be anything, and now all these strangers were staring at her like she was an attraction at a fairground. What did they expect her to do?

'One statue should be sufficient for now,' Tanner said.

Daphne flashed Metty an encouraging smile. 'Remember what we talked about before? Your gift.'

Metty looked round at all the Black Moths. There must have been twenty of them, at least. 'You want me to bring something to life?'

'As soon as you like,' Tanner said crisply.

'But I don't know how. I've never—'

'Just try, sweetheart,' Daphne said.

Taking a deep breath, Metty approached one of the statues. She chose Majestic. Reaching out with her tethered hand, she placed it on his chest. She had no idea what to do, but closed her eyes and willed something to happen. She tried to imagine life flowing into the statue like blood. A familiar tingle spread through her palm, and her hand began to burn.

'Not quite what I had in mind,' said Tanner behind her.

Metty opened her eyes. The statue of Majestic had started to melt, dripping strings of steaming metal into the grass. She gasped and took her hand away, then looked at her mother.

Daphne seemed anxious and disappointed, although she spoke in a cheery voice, touching Tanner's shoulder: 'Give her a little time, Charlie. She's only just woken up.'

Tanner patted her hand, his gaze locked onto Metty. 'It's all right. We assumed something like this might happen. I'm sure she only needs an incentive.' He turned to one of the Black Moths and, with a jolt, she recognised the wolfish Flint. 'Bring them down, would you?'

Metty's heart hammered in her chest. Her palm was sweaty under her tether.

'Is that necessary at this stage?' Daphne asked softly. 'I'm sure if we're patient—'

'Trust me,' Tanner replied.

A few minutes later, another group of Black Moths appeared from the museum, making their way down to the garden. A wave of nausea rolled through Metty. Her skin felt tight, like she was wearing clothes a size too small. Two of the Moths were supporting the captain, whose arms drooped round their shoulders. He was still asleep, his head bumping his chest. Behind them was another pair escorting a smaller figure: a child with flaming hair.

'Faith,' Metty whispered, staring at the girl in dismay. Faith was slow and sluggish, but seemed half awake.

'Jones?' she mumbled as they reached the garden.

'I thought you might benefit from some motivation.' Tanner smiled, flexing his fingers. He was wearing a dark purple tether with a smoky black pattern. 'So we borrowed your friend. I doubt she'll be missed. There were a depressing number of children in that squalid house.'

'What's going on?' Faith said in a groggy voice.

Metty couldn't answer, watching in horrified silence as the Black Moths laid her father on the grass. Flint knelt and took him roughly by the chin, trying to shake him awake. The captain let out a quiet groan, but didn't open his eyes.

'Stop it!' Metty cried.

'Charles,' Daphne said sharply.

Tanner raised his hand. 'Be gentle for now. Anyway, I think we'll start with the child.'

Metty's blood ran cold. What did he mean?

'Charlie,' Daphne murmured, massaging his arm. 'You're not serious. She's just a kid.'

'It's fine, Daphne. If your daughter's as brilliant as you insist, then you've nothing to fear. Well, Miss Jones,' Tanner said, bringing his thumb and middle finger together. Excitement

336

shone in his black eyes. 'Time to prove your worth.'

He snapped his fingers.

Faith made a terrible noise and clutched her chest. Her eyes bulged from her head, seeking Metty across the garden. Her legs wobbled as her face turned pink then reddish-purple, and her lips paled to blue.

'Stop!' Metty screamed, glancing at Tanner. He was watching with fascination. 'You're killing her!'

But the man did nothing, only lowering his hand.

Metty ran over to Faith, but the girl collapsed before she could reach her and dropped to the ground like a stone, eyes rolling back in her head. Gasping, Metty fell to her knees and tried to pull Faith upright. She was limp and heavy in Metty's arms, her cheeks still a mottled purple. She wasn't breathing. Metty brought her head to Faith's chest, listening for a heartbeat, but there was silence. She was dead.

'Undo it,' Metty said, looking desperately at Tanner. Daphne was pale beside him, covering her lips with a hand. 'I said undo it! Bring her back!'

'I'm afraid I can't,' Tanner said calmly. He turned his wrist, showing her his awful fate, the rotting black heart clenched in a fist. Metty realised what it meant with a wave of disgust. 'My gift isn't like yours. I can stop a heart with a snap of my fingers, but I can't start it again. There's only one person here with that talent.'

'I don't know how!'

'What a pity. Perhaps I chose the wrong heart. Should I try your father next?'

Fear tightened round Metty's lungs like a chain.

'Daphne!' she cried, turning to her mother. 'Make him stop, please!'

'Charles, this is cruel,' Daphne said in Tanner's ear.

'No, it's necessary. I need to know what the girl can do. Time's a-wasting, Metty,' he said, tapping his wristwatch. 'The longer your little friend stays dead, the harder it will be to bring her back.'

Breathless, Metty glanced down at Faith. Her skin looked waxy and unnatural in the weak light. She might have been a porcelain doll.

'Focus,' Metty told herself, shutting out all the others, their eager eyes and whispering mouths. She placed her hand on Faith's chest where she thought her heart would be and pressed into it with all her strength. She could do this. She *had* to do this . . .

'Start,' she said, murmuring the word through her teeth. Metty pushed down harder, encouraged by the heat building in her palm, crackling like electricity. 'Start, start . . .'

And then she felt it. Energy radiated from her own heart, turning it into a fiery ball. Light spilled from her hand, a blinding beam that tunnelled into Faith's chest and seeped through her skin, making it shine like a star. Even her hair lit up with threads of gold as though sunshine was pouring over her.

And as the warmth drained from Metty, leaving her cold and shivery, she felt a pulse flutter under her palm. Colour washed back into Faith, spreading a healthy glow in her cheeks. The girl's eyes flickered open and found Metty. They looked panicked.

'It's all right,' Metty stammered, holding Faith's shoulders.

'Very good,' said Tanner, clapping his hands. The other Moths joined in with the applause. Metty resented them with every fibre of her being. 'You're quite right, Daphne – the girl's remarkable. We'll have the whole garden up and moving in no time.'

'Don't you think that's enough for one day?' Daphne said in an uncertain voice.

Tanner only laughed. 'Enough? We've barely got started.'

CHAPTER THIRTY-THREE

Life

Metty had never felt such exhaustion. Her body ached as she dragged herself back to her feet. The air seemed to resist her. Moving was like wading through water.

Faith was sitting up on the grass, trembling all over. She appeared to be in shock.

'Right then,' Tanner said eagerly, rubbing his hands together, 'I think we'll try one of the statues again, test your limits before the real work starts. Go ahead, Miss Jones.'

Metty hardly had the strength to argue. She stumbled over to the nearest figure – Elias Wollf, according to the name plaque. Even in her tiredness, she felt a spark of recognition. Elias Wollf was her ancestor too, related to Daphne. Breathing heavily through her nose, Metty gripped the statue's arm and wished it to life like she had with Faith.

Nothing happened. Her hand was numb, her eyelids drooping.

'I can't,' she said, glancing at Tanner over her shoulder.

Impatience gave him a prickly aura. 'Somehow I find that hard to believe. Bringing a statue to life is surely easier than performing a resurrection. You might apply yourself.'

'I can't!' Metty groaned.

The man's lips thinned, and his eyes slid over to the captain. 'I wonder,' he said in a quiet, slippery way, 'how many times a heart can stop before it refuses to beat again.'

'Charles, you promised not to—'

'Quiet, Daphne,' Tanner snapped, his voice cracking like a whip. 'You devised this entire plan – don't undermine it now.'

'She's a child – you're exhausting her!'

'You're underestimating her,' Tanner said, returning his blistering gaze to Metty. He nodded sharply. 'Go on. Show us what you can do.'

Metty didn't have a choice. She had to protect the captain and Faith. She concentrated on the statue of Elias Wollf with a blunt anger, summoning the light that had burst from her once already. It took every scrap of energy she had. Her knees buckled as life flowed from her hand into the statue.

The light wasn't as strong as it had been the first time, but Elias Wollf began to move with a screech of metal limbs. His head shifted. His eyes stared down at Metty, chillingly blank, and then he raised his stiff legs one after the other and stepped down from the plinth.

'Bravo!' Tanner laughed, clapping once more. Cheers rang out round the garden as the iron statue walked slowly through the grass, looming over all the Black Moths. 'Well done, Miss Jones, well done!'

For a moment, Metty's vision went dark, and then the world came back to her in blurry fragments like a painting left out in the rain. She was kneeling on the ground, steadying herself on the empty plinth where Elias Wollf had just stood. She could hear the slow pulse of her heart and the *swoosh-swoosh* of blood in her ears. Metty frowned down at her hand. The skin of her wrist looked strange where her tether stopped, thin and wrinkled like it belonged to an old woman.

Her gaze wandered over to Daphne who was standing silently across the garden, holding Tanner's cane. Its silver head was glowing in her fist.

'Get the girl back on her feet,' Tanner called out. 'Never mind statues. Now it's time for the real test. Let's take her to the core.'

The core? Metty stared at Tanner in bewilderment. Why would he want to show her that?

He grinned cruelly when he sensed her watching him. 'I take it your mother didn't tell you any of this, why we require your particular talent. We need you to start a heart, Miss Jones. A very large heart.'

'You mean the core?' Metty said weakly.

But it was already working. She'd seen the ink pumping round it like blood, and the museum was still gliding smoothly through the clouds.

Tanner's smile broadened. 'We need you to take part in our little experiment. You know how a core works, I assume? The New Capitals need ink to fly and a heart that keeps it constantly churning, but if that heart were to stop for some reason . . .' He twisted his hand again, drawing attention to his ugly fate. 'Well, that would cause quite a panic, wouldn't it? And I suspect Governor Finch will take our demands seriously once we have control of New London.'

Crouching before Metty, he tapped the tattoo on the back of her hand.

'But what's the point of hijacking a city that'll crash into the ocean a few hours later? Stopping a heart's *my* area of expertise, but starting it again . . . that's another talent. Your ancestor had it. Little Morose. He's the reason New London even exists, the boy who brought his father's city to life. And now it seems, after all this time, there's another Jones with the same gift. You and I are going to work together, Metty. I'll stop the heart and, once we have what we need from Finch, you'll be there to start it again. You're going to be part of something very special, a moment in history no one will ever forget.'

Tanner's words cut through the fog of confusion in Metty's head. He was talking about New London, planning to stop the core, even though that meant endangering thousands of people, even though the whole city could plummet.

'You can't do that! What if it doesn't work? What if I can't—'

'Then the city falls,' Tanner said coolly, his eyes flatter than ever. 'Maybe it should. New London was never meant to be *this*. It's supposed to represent freedom. If the politicians have their way, it'll end up no different to any city on the ground. The Black Moths want to make a better world, Metty, and you have a chance to be part of it.'

Metty shook her head. Tanner couldn't do it without her. He needed her to restart the heart once he'd got whatever he wanted from the governor, a promise for fewer magic restrictions, control of the city . . . His plan didn't work without her.

But how could she refuse? Metty glanced desperately at the captain and poor Faith, still shaking on the ground.

'The plan was always to start with the museum,' Tanner said, his voice echoing round the garden as he strode away from her. 'It won't be so easy to get at the core of New London – we'll only have one shot when the time comes, so first we'd better make sure you're up to the task. But I have high hopes. So far, you've more than exceeded my expectations. You and I should make a formidable pair.'

Metty stopped listening, Tanner's awful words drowned out by the roar of blood in her ears. Her gaze drifted to the statue of her ancestor. Elias Wollf had paused in the middle of the garden, raising his head to admire the sky.

Look at me, Metty said in her mind.

To her amazement, the statue seemed to listen, slowly turning his head. He stared vacantly into her face. Tanner was so busy congratulating himself that he hadn't even noticed. Voices rolled around Metty, interrupted by peals of birdsong. The dawn was coming on fast.

Can you hear me? she asked the statue, communicating with her eyes. It felt like they were on fire.

His face was so still, she was sure he couldn't. But then he slowly tilted his chin. A tingle of hope spread in Metty's chest.

I need to get away from here. Will you help me?

The statue considered for a long moment while Metty held her breath. Then he nodded again, more firmly this time. She swallowed, drawing a shallow breath through her nose.

Then create a distraction. Stop the Black Moths.

For a second, Elias Wollf only gazed at her, his face inscrutable. But then he began to move, stomping towards the nearest Black Moth – which happened to be Flint.

A gasp rang out as he swung down his metal fist and struck Flint on the head, knocking him out cold with a single blow. Metty laughed in shock, bringing a hand to her lips. The other

Moths started to panic. Some came forward to try and restrain the statue; more backed off or rushed towards the stairs.

Metty glanced at Tanner, expecting him to be outraged, but he was grinning in amused fascination.

'Go for Tanner!' she yelled out loud as Elias Wolff grabbed one of the Moths and tossed him over the iron fence like a rag doll. He paused, already reaching for another victim, then spun round and marched in Tanner's direction.

Now the man's smile slipped. He looked at Metty, his eyes coldly furious and fearful at the same time.

'Call it off,' he hissed, then raised his tethered hand when Metty shook her head. He brought his fingers together, getting ready to snap them, to use his dark gift and stop her heart. But he never got the chance. Elias Wolff seized Tanner by the throat and raised him several feet off the ground.

'Metty!' somebody shouted, and she turned her head.

It was Daphne, calling to her across the garden. She held up Tanner's cane, then threw it as far as she could. It didn't quite reach Metty, smacking onto the ground, its wolf's head shining, sending silver beams of light through the grass.

Metty scrambled over to the cane and snatched it up, then glanced at her mother in confusion. Daphne was pointing at the clouds.

'It's ready!' she cried.

Metty knew what to do in a heartbeat. She ran across

the garden, using all the energy she had left, ignoring the panicked screams, and only stopped when she reached Faith and her father.

'Faith,' she said, shaking the girl. 'Help me – I need you to grab the captain. Faith, please, grab his arm!'

Faith seemed to snap out of her trance. She bent down and seized one of the captain's arms. Metty grabbed the other, then thrust the cane up into the air. The clouds immediately darkened overhead, turning a deep, stormy grey. The wolf's head shone even brighter, stretching apart its snarling jaws.

'Whatever you do, don't let go!' Metty bellowed at Faith who grasped the cane with her free hand, still hanging on to the captain with the other. The girl nodded, eyes wide with fear.

Thunder rang through the blackening skies. The lightning was getting fiercer.

Metty threw a final glance across the garden, searching for Tanner. He'd got away from Elias Wollf, who had picked up two Black Moths and was smashing their heads together with vicious satisfaction. His eyes hardened as he spotted Metty with the cane, and he started towards her, hand outstretched.

The last thing she saw was his murderous face, white as snow and shot through with veins, and then a blue dagger of lightning broke from the clouds and pierced the wolf on the cane.

And the whole world imploded.

CHAPTER THIRTY-FOUR

Moral and Mag

It felt as if Metty was folding in on herself, like she was being crushed into a new boneless shape. Thunder boomed in her ears. Everything became a dizzying blur, and then, just as her fingers began to slide from the cane, it was over.

Clean morning air breathed upon her face. She opened her eyes to a vista of marbled pink-and-white clouds drenched in sunlight. But she only had a second to enjoy the view. Then they were falling, hurtling towards the ocean – her, Faith and the captain, arms flailing, clothes billowing.

Metty gasped as they came to a stop, bouncing into an invisible soft wall. It was just like the first time she'd travelled by lightning. One of the New London stations must have locked onto their position and was reeling them in towards a lightning chamber, like three fish hooked on a line.

Exhaustion made Metty's thoughts swim. She looked over at Faith, who seemed more alert now they were away from the Ink Museum, her hazel eyes sharper, searching the horizon for any sign of the Black Moths. She and Metty were still holding on to the captain, each gripping one of his arms. He floated between them like a dead body in water.

'Are you all right?' Metty asked hoarsely.

Faith's gaze snapped back to her. 'Not really, no. Are you?'

Metty slowly shook her head. Her eyelids were getting heavier by the second, and there was a painful pressure inside her skull. She glanced at the city rising beneath them. Daylight was climbing up the sides, transforming New London into a golden bell. The ink river rolled through it like a silk ribbon, deep pink with flashes of gold to match the dawn clouds. The view was spectacular.

'Jones,' Faith said, grabbing her attention. 'Are you all right? You look a bit . . .'

'Hmm,' Metty mumbled, rubbing her brow. An intense pulsing filled her head. Darkness was swallowing up her vision like a swarm of insects, blotting out the light.

'No, no, don't pass out,' Faith said, swimming towards her through the air. She seized the front of Metty's shirt. 'D'you hear me, Jones? Stay awake! We're almost there, see!'

Metty didn't see anything apart from Faith's wavering face, dotted with ginger freckles, getting fainter every moment.

And then the darkness returned for her and, closing her burning eyes, she sank into a deep, dreamless sleep.

Waking up was like rising to the surface of a black ocean, having to fight her way back to the light.

Metty took a sharp breath as she came to, opening her eyes. The brightness softened after a few seconds, morphing into a sunlit ceiling. She was lying in a strange bed. Frowning down at her chest, Metty realised she was wearing a hospital gown.

She pushed herself up on the mattress, aching all over, and looked around the room. It was small but airy, with three long windows, and the walls had been painted to resemble a forest. Rows of thin trees swayed in a non-existent wind, their branches home to sparrows and red squirrels. The effect was quite soothing.

Metty's ears pricked as she caught the rumble of familiar voices. The door to the room was ajar, and through the crack she could see a sunny corridor. Swinging her legs out of bed, she padded over to the door and brought her eye to the gap.

Her heart swelled with delight as she glimpsed the captain and Aunt Mag some way down the corridor, talking to a man in a white coat. Her father was in a wheelchair and had his back to Metty. Aunt Mag wore a pinstriped grey-and-black dress with broad shoulders that made her seem even taller than usual.

Metty's legs carried her forward before she even had time to think. The captain wheeled round at the sound of her footsteps, then choked out a laugh when Metty launched herself into his arms, squeezing him as hard as she could. She never wanted to let go.

Her father's eyes were misty when she forced herself to pull away.

'You're awake,' he said, taking her face in his warm hands. 'My God, it's good to see—'

'Where have you been?' Metty asked furiously, legs wobbling. She was too weak to stand for long.

Her father's smile faded, guilt shining in his dark eyes. 'Metty, I . . .'

'Why don't you two go and talk while I finish speaking to the doctor?' Aunt Mag suggested, placing a steadying hand on Metty's shoulder. 'I think this conversation deserves some privacy, don't you?'

Metty was tempted to argue. She wanted to speak now, to finally get answers. But her father looked almost as exhausted as she felt, and her legs were threatening to buckle any second. It was even worse than when she'd first travelled by lightning.

She and the captain made their way slowly down the corridor. Metty sat down on the bed as soon as they were back in her room, relieved to get off her feet. Her father stopped his wheelchair beside her.

'I was so worried about you,' she said accusingly.

'I know. I'm so sorry, Met. I never meant for any of this to happen,' the captain said with a helpless expression. 'It seems I've made a real pig's ear of things.'

'Will you be – will you need that forever?' Metty asked, nodding at the wheelchair.

'No, no. Only while I get my strength back. Perhaps they'll give you one too. How are you feeling, by the way?'

'Tired,' Metty said.

'Well, that's understandable. You've had quite a—'

'Why didn't you tell me?'

The captain's smile wilted again. 'Tell you what?' he asked gently.

Metty rolled her eyes. 'What do you think? About my fate, about Majestic being a founder, about any of it? You kept everything a secret. Why?'

'Because . . .' His shoulders sagged. 'Because I wanted you to make your own choices, to decide who *you* wanted to be. I thought if I didn't tell you about your . . . gift, then perhaps you wouldn't use it, not until you were older. What you can do, bringing things to life – it's dangerous, Met. You could seriously hurt yourself. Or worse.'

He looked at her right hand. Metty glanced at it herself, remembering the way her skin had aged after she'd brought the statue to life in the museum garden. To her relief, her hand and wrist had gone back to normal, the wrinkled skin smoothed out again.

The captain heaved a sigh. 'I hoped if you didn't find out then you might live an ordinary life away from all this chaos. That's all I ever wanted. It's hard enough being descended from a founder, but people like you and . . . people with rare abilities, with fates you won't find in your dictionary, they're often sought after and misused by others.'

'You mean by people like the Black Moths?'

Like Daphne, whispered a bitter voice in Metty's head.

'That's right,' the captain said, looking grave. 'And nobody's life should be decided for them, especially before they've had a chance to grow up and experience the world themselves. I wanted you to choose your own future, to be who you truly are, your own brilliant self.'

'But you let me think I was a murderer,' Metty said with a stab of hurt.

The captain gazed at her sadly. 'Darling, that's exactly my point. I tried to tell you otherwise many times, but you wouldn't have it, not once the seed had been planted in your mind. Whatever I said, you were determined to believe the worst of yourself. I shouldn't have let you get fated in the first place, but, I'll admit, curiosity got the better of me. I wanted to know if you could . . . Well, as you now know, it runs in the family.'

'You make it sound like a bad thing,' Metty said, glancing

at her fate. Somehow the skull seemed less menacing than before, its hollow eyes no longer brimming with malice.

'I suppose it doesn't have to be,' the captain said. He tried to smile, though it fell rather flat. 'Although it will cause you a lot of bother, I'm afraid.'

'Everyone keeps calling it a gift,' Metty said quietly, tracing the tattoo. It was coarse under her fingertips like a scar.

The captain reached out and spread his hand over hers, his eyes earnest and full of love. 'You are a gift, and nothing could ever change that. And it sounds like I owe you my life. Your friend explained everything when we landed in the city. Quite an interesting character, young Faith, and rather feisty. She's fine, by the way. Apparently, if it wasn't for you, I'd still be stuck in that awful museum, dead to the world.'

'You're welcome,' Metty said, inspiring a loud laugh.

'Yes, I'm obviously very grateful,' the captain said. He sobered a bit, and his eyes looked serious. 'But I'd appreciate it if you would never do *anything* like that ever again.'

'And just leave you to die?'

'Yes, please, if you don't mind,' her father said with a slight chuckle. He pressed Metty's hand again, then returned his own to his lap.

Metty pursed her lips. 'No promises.'

Somebody knocked on the door before the captain could reply. Frowning, he turned in his wheelchair to see who it was.

Aunt Mag leaned into the room.

'Moral, the doctor wants to speak to you outside.'

'Oh, all right,' the captain grumbled, spinning himself about. He rolled his eyes at Metty. 'Soon it'll be your turn to be poked and prodded and told what to do. It's all very tiresome.'

'Do stop being such a child about it,' Aunt Mag said with a sigh as her brother wheeled himself through the door.

The captain grinned up at her. 'No promises.'

'Honestly,' Aunt Mag said, crossing the room to sit on the end of Metty's bed, 'you'd think an ex-captain in the Royal Navy would have learned how to take orders. Anyway, how are you feeling? You gave us all a dreadful fright.'

'Sorry,' Metty said, observing her aunt carefully. Aunt Mag was wearing her favourite tether, the black satin one with the bones.

'What is it?' she asked, noting Metty's attention.

Metty took a deep breath. 'You're like me, aren't you? When you talked about bringing Sundar to life . . . you made it seem like something everyone could do. Not like it was a special gift.'

'Yes,' said Aunt Mag, looking slightly guilty. 'I didn't want to draw too much attention to it. I'd promised your father not to say anything.'

She considered for a second, then removed her tether

finger by finger and extended her hand on the bed. Metty leaned forward to see. Tattooed on her aunt's skin was a skull held by a gloved hand, only hers was black rather than purple, with a bony pattern on the knuckles. Had Aunt Mag picked out that tether on purpose, to match her fate?

'When did you find out what it meant?' Metty asked.

'Oh, when I was about your age. The family tried to hide it from me too, but I kept bringing things to life without realising, rather like you and Pumpkin, and made myself quite ill in the process.'

'Wait, what do you mean like Pumpkin? I just found him. I didn't bring him to life.'

Aunt Mag smiled warmly at her. 'Of course you did. You didn't notice, that's all.'

'But I-I didn't even have a tether at the time.'

'You don't need one, not for that. Listen, there are some forms of magic that are innate. That means they exist deep inside us. Those of us who are naturally gifted can do certain things without a tether and ink.' Aunt Mag's expression shifted, becoming more sombre. 'Which makes those gifts very dangerous. If you're not careful, you could drain yourself of life while you're giving it to others. People die, Metty. This kind of magic, it has to be used sparingly. What's wrong? You look upset.'

'I'm not,' Metty said, drawing a circle on the blanket with

her finger. 'It's just . . .' She raised her head suddenly, fear zapping through her like lightning. 'The Moths! Did Faith tell you? They're planning an attack!'

Aunt Mag seemed unconcerned. 'They're always planning something.'

'No, you don't understand. They want to break the core – New London's core – by stopping its heart. Tanner can do it; he's gifted like us. They're trying to take the city hostage so the governor will do whatever they want, but they need someone to get the heart started again once they've—'

Aunt Mag silenced Metty, grabbing her hand. 'Then it sounds like they'll have great trouble managing it without you.'

Metty exhaled, sinking back against her pillows. Aunt Mag was right. The Moths couldn't do anything now, not without her. She glanced up as a thought occurred to her.

'But why didn't they come after you? If we've got the same gift, then why bother kidnapping me? You were right under their noses all this time, and I bet you're way more powerful than I am.'

Aunt Mag shrugged. 'Not many people have seen my fate. The family's always kept it secret. As have I, with a few exceptions – Kiki, of course, and my old friend Geeta. So perhaps they don't know about mine. Even if they do, I suspect capturing me would prove rather challenging.'

Metty silently agreed. It was hard to imagine Aunt Mag falling victim to the Black Moths, or to anyone for that matter.

'D'you think it would've worked, Tanner's plan? He said Morose Jones brought New London to life all those years ago, that he started its heart, but surely that's not possible. Wouldn't that mean the city was sort of . . . alive?'

'It is,' Aunt Mag said with a strange smile. She leaned forward and dropped her voice to a whisper. 'Between you and me, I've started a few New Capitals myself.'

Metty's eyes widened. 'You have? But that's . . . Wait, I thought no one knew about your fate?'

'I said there were a few exceptions. These things are always done quietly, and most people have no idea what it takes to make a city fly. Though I must say, the pay is rather spectacular. Didn't you wonder where all the Jones money comes from?'

Metty was quiet a moment, absorbing her aunt's words. Her mind was full of soaring cities, each with a golden heart pumping ink at its core, buried under buildings and cobbled streets like a piece of hidden treasure.

'Were they all started by Joneses?' she asked after a pause. 'The flying cities?'

Aunt Mag shook her head. 'We're not the only family gifted like that. It's rare, that's all. Maybe one day you'll launch a few yourself.'

Metty's own heart took flight at the prospect, excitement spreading a buzz all the way to her fingertips.

Suddenly her aunt transformed, looking like her old stern self. 'But for now let's focus on getting you better, and we'll deal with the Black Moths another day. Agreed?'

'They won't stop coming after me, will they?' Metty said, biting her lip.

'No, I expect not. But we'll protect you, all of us, so try to put it from your mind.' Aunt Mag's dark eyes twinkled again. 'Anyway, I know someone who's been missing you terribly. Let's see about taking you home, shall we?'

CHAPTER THIRTY-FIVE

The One

The door to the conservatory was a bit short. Metty had to duck to avoid bumping the frame, although at least she didn't have to stoop constantly, like poor Rupert, whose head grazed the ceiling. He was over in the kitchen while Sundar was making his way towards the cellar, aided by Pumpkin who was rolling the dice on the boy's behalf.

'Right,' Metty said once she was inside the conservatory.

She could just see the playroom through the glass walls and her own ghostly reflection, dressed in striking blue. Her clothes had changed the moment she'd decided to play as Mrs Peacock, her denim dungarees and shirt becoming a stylish ballgown and pearl necklace. Metty threw her gaze around the room, taking in the cartoonish furniture, then she cleared her throat.

'Let's see. *I* think it was Colonel Mustard in the conservatory with the candlestick.'

There were two loud pops as a candlestick arrived in Metty's hand and Rupert appeared in the middle of the room, surrounded by a cloud of pink smoke. Her uncle wafted it away, looking slightly peaky, then tossed Metty an irritable glance.

'I wish you'd stop doing that. You know perfectly well it wasn't me,' he said. He was dressed in a yellow military uniform and had grown an impressive walrus moustache.

Metty gave a villainous chuckle, then checked her notepad.

'Anything to show, Sundar?' she called out. They were standing inside a large doll's house, its wooden floors divided into squares like a board game.

'Nope!' the boy shouted back gleefully.

Metty raised her eyebrows at Rupert. 'And you?'

Grumbling under his breath, Rupert wrote on his own pad and a second later a picture appeared on Metty's card. She grinned and made a note of it. So her uncle had the candlestick . . . Unfortunately, she still had a lot more clues to gather before she could win the game. Sundar seemed confident already and was rolling to try and get to the cellar.

'Your turn now,' Metty said to Rupert, who used his tether to summon the dice. He was about to roll when Aunt Mag called for Metty up the stairs.

'Better go,' she said, climbing through the conservatory window. Disappointingly, her ballgown fell away in blue ribbons and turned back into boring dungarees.

'No, you can't!' Sundar moaned. He was playing as Professor Plum and wearing a purple suit with a bow tie and owlish glasses. Pumpkin rode on his shoulders and seemed to be having a marvellous time chomping on all the murder weapons whenever Sundar made a guess.

Metty kept trying to cheat by sending Pumpkin messages in her mind, just like she had with the statue of Elias Wollf, asking him to tell her the answers on Sundar's card. She couldn't believe she'd never noticed that she could communicate with him that way. Unfortunately, the only response she heard in her head was a very confused: *Eat?*

'Sorry.' Metty shrugged, already backing towards the playroom door.

'But I'm only three squares away! I'm about to win the game!'

'Stop whingeing, Sundar,' Rupert said from the conservatory. 'We'll hold our positions and wait for you to come back, Metty.'

'Thanks!'

'You're only saying that because you've already lost,' she heard Sundar reply as she ran downstairs. Metty laughed. She'd never known him to be so competitive.

She found Aunt Mag and the captain waiting for her in the study. Aunt Mag welcomed her inside, holding open the door. It was a chilly day but surprisingly bright, and sunshine washed the walls of the study. The captain was sitting on the desk at the back of the room. After a week's rest, he didn't need a wheelchair anymore, though his legs were still stiff.

'What is it?' Metty said, looking from her aunt to her father. Neither of them seemed especially cheerful, although they weren't cross either. The captain was holding a present wrapped in starry paper.

Before Metty could ask about it, Aunt Mag grabbed a newspaper from the desk and showed her the front page. Metty stiffened in shock as she stared down at the picture on the cover. It was of Daphne and Tanner photographed together at some swanky event, holding glasses of champagne. Daphne was performing for the camera whereas Tanner was rigid and unsmiling, his dark eyes stony with boredom.

'What is this?' Metty said, glancing up at Aunt Mag.

'Read the headline,' her aunt said and tapped it with her thumb.

BLACK MOTHS ON THE RISE. LARGE REWARD FOR THE CAPTURE OF RINGLEADERS, NOW IDENTIFIED AS DAPHNE WOLLF AND CHARLES TANNER.

Swallowing, Metty skimmed through the article underneath. It talked about her mother and Tanner, 'descendants of two of the New London founders', stirring up trouble and putting their beloved ancestors to shame. No one had so much as glimpsed the Ink Museum since the night the Moths had kidnapped Metty, and it didn't seem like the police would recover the island any time soon.

There was a strange knot in Metty's chest. She should have been satisfied. Daphne and Tanner had been outed as Black Moths, and now it seemed the police were after them. Surely that meant they could do less harm.

And yet a needle of sadness slid into her heart. Daphne was her mother, and she'd helped Metty escape the island with Faith and the captain. Maybe they would never see each other again. Metty didn't doubt that her mother loved her, that she'd meant everything she'd said that night, about her being special and destined to do something incredible.

'The Black Moths might be interested in you,' Aunt Mag said. The newspaper rustled as she folded it away. 'But Daphne and Tanner being identified will make it a hell of a lot harder for them to approach you in public. They'll have to be more careful in future.'

'Does that mean I can go outside?' Metty said with a burst of hope. She glanced at the captain who was smiling. There was just a hint of sorrow in his eyes.

'I don't think we need to be quite so worried now. Anyway,' he said and held out the mysterious package, 'I've got something for you, a belated birthday present. Come and get it.'

'What is it?' Metty said, taking the gift from his hand.

The captain nodded encouragingly. 'Open it and see.'

Metty tore off the paper and discovered a small black box. Inside it, nestled on a velvet cushion, was a silver magic meter shaped like a pocket watch.

For a heartbeat, a familiar sense of fear sank into Metty. After so many months believing that she and magic were a deadly combination, it was hard to shake the habit. But then a grin stretched across her face as she took out the meter and held it in her palm. It fitted snugly, like it belonged there.

'Turn it over,' her father said.

On the back was a crystal raven, its wings spread in flight. It matched the one hidden on Metty's tether.

'I love it,' she said, throwing her arms round the captain. 'Thank you.'

'I thought it was about time you had your own.'

'It only allows up to grade four magic,' Aunt Mag said, crossing her arms.

'And you'll have a strict ink allowance, so you won't want to do anything too wild,' the captain added. He winked at Metty. 'I heard about the jungle in the entrance hall. Although that's not half as bad as some of the things Mag got up to at your age.'

'Yes, well,' Aunt Mag said, briskly changing the subject, 'look at the time. We'd better hurry if you still want to meet your friend.'

'All right,' Metty said, running back to the door. 'But let us finish our game upstairs. I promised Sundar we could – he's about to win.'

Aunt Mag sighed. 'Wonderful. So I can expect him to be charmingly obnoxious for the rest of the afternoon. You know, I'm not sure I approve of these games. They seem to bring out Sundar's worst side. And Rupert's for that matter.'

The captain gave an incredulous snort. 'I think you're forgetting the last time you and I played chess.'

'That chandelier came down on its own! It was an unfortunate coincidence.'

'Hmm. Very unfortunate. For me.'

Metty left them to bicker, racing back up to the playroom. That afternoon Aunt Mag was taking her to a district called Sweet Paradise where they would meet Faith and her brother Griff and visit a famous café that sold ice creams of a thousand flavours. She could hardly wait, but first she would show Sundar her brand-new magic meter.

Metty turned it over in her hand as she ran up the stairs and traced the crystal raven. Joy fizzed inside her like a firework about to explode and flash bright colours everywhere. Her mind reeled with possibilities, all the things she could do now she had her very own meter – now she could use magic safely.

She'd spent a whole year dreading her fate, worrying that she would hurt somebody, so certain she was destined to be bad. But 'the one' didn't even exist. Or if they did, it had been Pumpkin all this time. And Faith O'Connell. And the statue of Elias Wollf, wherever he might be now. Everyone and everything she'd brought to life with magic.

And she didn't need to be afraid any more.

Metty bounded up the last few stairs, her new magic meter warm in her hand.

For the first time in her life, she felt entirely free.

AN INDEX
OF
COMMON FATES

BANDAGES: *associated with nursing, or clumsiness*

BEES: *associated with beekeeping, or a hard-working nature*

BOOKS: *associated with teachers, librarians, or being a dreadful know-it-all*

BRIEFCASES: *associated with careers in business, secretiveness, or a great success*

CATS: *associated with veterinary work, aloofness, or witchcraft*

CHAINS: *associated with policing, or a life of crime*

CLOCKS: *associated with watchmaking, or an unusually long life*

CROWNS: *associated with royalty, or bossiness*

CUTLERY: *associated with chefs, or enthusiastic eaters*

DICE: *associated with gamblers, or taking dangerous risks*

DOGS: *associated with dog-walking, or overexcited personalities*

FLAMES: *associated with firefighting, arson, or explosive tempers*

GLOBES: *associated with newsreaders, or travelling*

HAMMERS: *associated with builders, or antisocial behaviour*

HOUSES: *associated with estate agents, homemaking, or agoraphobia*

LIGHTNING: *associated with electricians, lightning travel, or quick and dramatic deaths*

LIONS: *associated with zookeeping, bravery, or glorious hair*

MIRRORS: *associated with beauty, or excessive vanity*

QUILLS: *associated with writers, or extreme ticklishness*

SCORPIONS: *associated with danger*

SCROLLS: *associated with scholars, or studious personalities*

STARS: *associated with astronomers, space travel, or a tendency to daydream*

SUNS: *associated with meteorologists, or overbearing positivity*

TELESCOPES: *associated with explorers, or a tendency to get lost*

TOMBSTONES: *associated with gravediggers, early deaths, or macabre personalities*

WRENCHES: *associated with mechanics, or excellent practical skills*

ACKNOWLEDGEMENTS

Becoming a published author has been the most wonderful experience of my life so far, and there are many people I have to thank.

First, my spectacular agent, Hannah Sheppard, who has been a constant source of patience, reassurance, encouragement and brilliant advice. I was desperate to work with you from our first conversation, and I'm forever grateful that you took a risk on me and Metty. Amy Cloud and Natalie Doherty, thank you for choosing my book and transforming it with your passion, creativity and incredible insight. I'm hugely grateful to Megan Reid for taking on *Inkbound* halfway through the publishing process and for being so fantastic. I feel really lucky to have worked with not just one brilliant editor, but three!

A massive thank you to everyone at HarperCollins *Children's Books* and Clarion Books for supporting *Inkbound* with so much enthusiasm. Thank you to Charlotte Winstone, Jess Williams, Jane Baldock, Charlotte Crawford, Hannah Marshall, Elorine Grant, Sandy Officer, Nick Lake, Cally Poplak and everyone who has worked so hard on the book. Thank you to Jane Tait and Tracy Roe for your brilliant copyedits, to Sam Lacey for proofreading, and to Brie Schmida, Devin Elle Kurtz and Nicolette Caven for bringing this world to life so beautifully.

I'm so grateful to the international agents that have helped Metty travel across the world, and to all the amazing editors that have shown such passion for *Inkbound*.

I've had so much support from my amazing family and friends that I can never express my gratitude in words. Mum, this book is for you. You are my inspiration, my constant cheerleader, my best friend, and the bravest person I know. Sharing this journey with you has been so special, even through the darkest of times. I hope I can write you many more stories.

Dad, thank you for believing my books were great before you'd read a single word. Thank you to my brothers Rob and Chris for brainstorming ideas with me and being so excited for every piece of news. Elizabeth and Phillippa – I love you both so much. I hope that your amazing children will enjoy my stories one day, and thank you delightful Iris and Nancy for providing me with plenty of inspiration.

My enormous gratitude to the Bells, especially to Hatti, my own magnificent aunt. Also, to my wonderful godparents Sue, Rod and Michelle, to the Leathleys, to Katie, Alyssa, Louise, Jack, Fiona, Martin, Becky, Adhel, Anthony, Helen, Jeremy, Cath, Adrian, the staff at Hull Libraries and the Hull School Library Service, especially Amy and Claire, and to everyone who has been so kind and supportive of my writing and my family for the last few years. Also, to my grandparents and Auntie Jackie who left us too soon, but who I know are cheering me on from afar.

Thank you to the booksellers, librarians, bloggers, reviewers and the many awesome authors who have been so welcoming and supportive. And last of all, thank you to every reader who has picked up a copy of *Inkbound*. I hope you've enjoyed it!